Dedication

To Helen Curl, Jeffrie Story, and my Brian—you are the wind
beneath my wings.

Chapter 1

Maggie Martin snapped her laptop shut and set it on the coffee table. She'd been reviewing spreadsheets for hours. The formidable financial problems facing Westbury would still be there tomorrow. It was New Year's Day, after all, and Westbury's hard-working mayor deserved some time off. She'd worked every day since she'd taken office last spring. She stretched and slid over on the sofa to snuggle her fiancé of almost twenty-four hours, John Allen.

John put his arm around her and hugged her, his eyes glued to the college bowl game on television. "Only two minutes left," he mumbled. "Then we can …"

Maggie interrupted him. "And there's another game right after this one. Enjoy. I know you're reliving your glory days on the gridiron. I'm going to let the dogs out and call Susan and Mike. I have big news, you know."

John smiled and patted her arm.

Maggie summoned Eve and Roman, tucked her chestnut bob into the collar of her down jacket, and wound a scarf around her neck. She picked up her cell phone and headed to the back garden. The dogs raced ahead of her as she sought protection from the icy wind under a pine tree on the lawn and tightened the scarf around her neck. She'd lived in Southern California most of her adult life, and these Midwestern winters were not easy to get used to.

1

She turned to study the edifice of Rosemont. The warm tones of its stone walls and the symmetry of the mullioned windows elicited the same visceral response in her as the first time she saw it. Rosemont embodied stability, order, and security—exactly what she was looking for when she moved here to restart her life after her husband Paul's sudden death. And not at all what she'd found. Never in a million years would she have imagined she'd be elected to public office as a write-in candidate.

Just yesterday, she'd been prepared to hand in her resignation as mayor. The constant criticism of the local press and a vocal segment of the community were demoralizing, and a lucrative assignment offered by her once trusted colleague, Professor Lyndon Upton, seemed too good to turn down. Uncovering collusion between Upton and local town councilman Frank Haynes had changed everything. They weren't going to get rid of her that easily. She would stand her ground and do everything in her power to restore the town's financial footing. She'd make sure those responsible for the fraud and embezzlement that left the general fund and the town workers' pension plan on the brink of bankruptcy were brought to justice. So much had changed in the last day. She pulled her phone out of her jacket pocket and dialed Susan's number.

"Hey, Mom, Happy New Year!" Susan sounded cheery, as she almost always did these days now that Aaron Scanlon had come into her life.

"Same to you. How did you two ring in the New Year?"

"We went to dinner at this swanky hotel that had a ten-piece orchestra, and dancing afterward, like out of an old movie—so glamorous."

Maggie smiled. "What did you wear?"

"That long, slinky midnight-blue dress with the slit. Remember? We found it on clearance, and you insisted I buy it. You promised I'd have a chance to wear it. You were right, Mom."

"What was that again? You're breaking up—I can't quite hear you."

"You heard me, Mom. But if you want to hear it again—you were *so* right."

Maggie laughed. "The words every mother loves to hear."

"How about you? Did you and John do anything special?"

"It was quite a day."

"Did you turn in your resignation?"

"Turned it in and went back and tore it up."

Maggie heard Susan take a sharp breath.

"So you're not going to take the expert witness gig that Professor Upton offered you? You won't be traveling to California all the time and coming to visit us?" Maggie could hear the disappointment in her daughter's voice.

"No, honey, I'm sorry. It's a long story. I suspect Frank Haynes and Don Upton have been working together to convince me to resign."

"Why do you think that?"

"I saw a text message from Don on Frank's phone—congratulating him on my resignation."

"How?"

"I ran into Frank—literally—on the steps of Town Hall after I turned in my resignation yesterday. I slipped on the ice, and my purse went flying down the steps. When Frank helped me pick everything up, I grabbed his phone by mistake."

"When did you see the text?"

"Later that afternoon—when John and I were sitting in a movie. The phone started beeping. I scrambled through my purse to find it, and that's when I saw the message."

"Why would Councilman Haynes and Professor Upton conspire against you? It doesn't make sense."

"I agree. I don't know, but there's something more between the two of them."

"So what did you do?"

"John and I sat in the lobby of the movie theater and talked it out. The more we talked, the madder I got. One thing is certain: I am not going to let them orchestrate my resignation."

"What does John think about all this?"

"He's in total agreement. He drove me to Town Hall, so I could take back my resignation letter. We burned it in the fireplace at Rosemont."

Susan was silent.

"What are you thinking, honey?"

"You did the only thing you could do, Mom. It all sounds very fishy. I'm disappointed you won't be here on a regular basis, but I'm behind you one hundred percent, and Mike will be as well."

"Thank you, honey. I'm really sorry I won't be seeing you guys more often. Plus the money would have been nice."

"You've got enough money, Mom. Sounds like your New Year's Eve sucked. I'm sorry."

"It wasn't all bad …" Maggie paused, unsure how her daughter would take the news of her engagement. Both of her children got along famously with John, but changing status from boyfriend to husband might be another matter entirely. "John proposed. And I accepted."

Susan squealed. "Mom! That's fantastic news! Mike and I were both hoping the two of you would get married. I was devastated when you broke up last year. You belong together."

"Thank you, honey. Your blessing means the world to us."

"Mike will be thrilled." Susan drew a deep breath. "We need to get going on the wedding."

"We haven't made any firm plans yet. It'll be a small affair, here at Rosemont. I'd like to get married in the garden," Maggie said, looking over the now empty flowerbeds. "Maybe June? We wanted to check with you and Mike to see when it would be convenient for you."

"I've got a trial that ends in April, so June is fine with me. The whole town will want to be there, with you being mayor and John a hometown boy and the local vet."

"That's why we're going to keep this really quiet. We don't want a massive affair."

"It would be lovely ..."

"You can have a big wedding at Rosemont or anywhere you choose. John and I don't want that."

"Come on, Mom. You love to throw a party. You and Dad got married at the courthouse, and you didn't even have a new dress. This has to be a grand affair. The back garden would be lovely, but outdoor weddings can be tricky. Why not get married inside Rosemont? The place looks like a movie set from an English period drama. A gorgeous stone manor home—it's a perfect wedding venue. You could be in front of the fireplace in the library, or in the living room. We could all sweep down that staircase." Susan sighed. "And you have to wear a wedding gown."

"Honey, I'm too old for a wedding gown, don't you think? Won't I look ridiculous? I was thinking of getting a really nice evening suit. Then I could wear it again."

Susan snorted. "Get yourself an evening suit if you want one, but you're not getting married in it.

"I'm logging into Pinterest right now. I'll create boards for your dress, the food, and the flowers. What does your ring look like?"

"He didn't give me a ring."

"What? You've got to have a ring, Mom. You love jewelry. I'm starting a board for your ring, too."

Maggie laughed. "Slow down, princess. All in good time."

"Check my Pinterest page tonight—I'll have gobs of pins by then."

"I will. And I'm grateful for your enthusiasm. You get busy with Pinterest. I'm standing outside and am frozen stiff. I need to round up the dogs and head inside."

"Give John a big hug from me. Love you both."

Maggie opened the back door, and Eve darted inside to her warm basket in the corner of the kitchen.

"Where's Roman?" Maggie asked as her beloved terrier mix nestled into her blanket. Maggie leaned out the back door and whistled, pausing to listen for the familiar sound of Roman's tags jingling on his collar as he ran up the hill. The only sound was the wind rustling through the branches.

Roman must have found a dead bird or some other treasure at the bottom of the vast lawn; she'd have to go back into the blustery afternoon and bring him inside. She trudged down the hill, alternatively whistling and calling Roman's name, becoming more concerned with each step. She'd never known John's Golden Retriever to disobey a command. By the time she reached the thin strip of woods at the bottom of the hill, Maggie knew he was gone. She raced up the hill and burst into the library of Rosemont.

She bent over, thoroughly winded, and gulped air. "Roman got out. He's not in the garden."

John leapt to his feet. "It's not like him to run away," he said, rushing past her to the back door, not stopping for his coat. Maggie followed in his wake.

Chapter 2

Maggie and John stepped over the stone wall together and began searching the shallow stretch of woods along the fence, calling to Roman, hoping against hope that he was there distracted by something—or maybe even hurt. John found Roman's empty collar snagged on a post near a small break in the fence.

John turned to Maggie, silently holding the collar up for her to see. Fear settled on them both like a thick fog. Roman was, indeed, gone.

"Oh, God," Maggie said. "We're right next to the road."

John nodded, looking at the road nearby. "He's a smart dog, and he's street savvy. He'll be all right."

They hurried back to the house. He couldn't fool her. She knew John was trying to put a brave face on it, but he was as worried as she was. "Let's take separate cars to search."

He nodded. "I'll turn north out of the driveway and go back to my house. He may be headed home."

"We'll find him," Maggie said, but John was already in his car, starting the engine.

———

Maggie pulled into the berm along the road below Rosemont. She grabbed the flashlight from her glove box to boost the thin late afternoon sunshine. She picked her way through the thick brush to the spot at the edge of the woods where Roman had escaped. She switched on the flashlight and cursed under her breath. She shook it, but it remained dark. "Stupid batteries," she muttered.

Maggie followed the fence, calling to Roman and searching under bushes and in the ravine. The terrain was uneven and she lost her footing, gashing her thumb and landing on both knees on a rocky outcrop. As she dusted debris off of her jeans, she decided she'd better return to her car before she became a casualty.

Maggie slid behind the wheel and reached for the ignition. *He's here. I can feel it.* She leaned her head against the steering wheel. *Why didn't he answer me? He must be hurt.* The thought propelled her from the car. The area she had just searched was now engulfed in the long shadows of an early dusk; she didn't dare retrace her steps in the dark. Maggie cupped her hands around her mouth, and yelled "ROMAN!" until she was hoarse.

Maggie leaned against the driver's side door and listened. Had she heard a whimper? She turned her head in the direction of the sound and was about to set off in that direction when her phone rang. Her heart leapt into her throat; maybe John had found him. She dove into the car and upended her purse in the passenger seat, answering her phone just before the call went to voice mail.

"Anything?" she asked.

"No. He's not at my place. I'm going to walk along our favorite routes. Where have you covered?"

"I'm searching the area along the road by the bottom boundary of my property."

"That's pretty steep, and it's getting dark. You need to get out of there."

"He's here, John. I can sense it. I thought I heard him whimper."

"It's windy, sweetheart. I don't think you could hear him whimper."

Maggie shrugged. "I guess you're right."

"If he were there, he'd come to you."

"Unless he's hurt." She hated uttering those words.

John was silent. She knew he agreed but didn't want to acknowledge the possibility. He cleared his throat. "Why don't you drive into town, along the square, and over to Westbury Animal Hospital. I haven't been there yet."

"On my way. And John—we won't give up until we find him."

Maggie got out of her car and called to Roman one last time. She listened carefully but the only answer was the whistling wind. "If you're out here, Roman, we're coming back for you. Hang on, help is on the way."

───────

Maggie drove slowly around the town square, windows down, looking for any sign of a dog huddled in a doorway or shivering in an alley. The square was deserted on this cold Sunday night, and all the shops and businesses were closed except for Pete's Bistro. Maggie angled her car into a spot along the curb.

"Hi, Maggie. What can I get for you?" Pete asked as she pushed through the front door.

"No. I'm not here for food. Roman's lost, Pete," she said. "I came by to see if anyone's reported a stray dog."

"Oh no! That's terrible. Nobody's said a thing. In fact, we've been dead all day. As soon as Frank finishes eating, we're going to close early," he said, pointing to local business tycoon and town council-member Frank Haynes.

"He escaped through a hole in the back fence at Rosemont. Will you keep an eye out?" Maggie asked.

"Of course. I'll look for him on my way home. Do you have any flyers? I'll post one here and take them to the other merchants on the square in the morning."

"Not yet. We've been looking for him since we discovered he was missing. I'll make up flyers tonight and drop them off first thing."

"Put on there that I'll give a free dinner to whoever finds him."

Maggie squeezed his arm.

"You ought to go tell Frank. He finds strays all the time. And someone might turn him in to Forever Friends. He'll get all of his employees at the shelter to look for Roman, too."

"You really think so?"

"I know so. Frank may be a cold fish with people, but he really cares about animals. You'd be surprised."

Maggie gave Pete a quizzical look. He nodded in Frank Haynes' direction.

What is there to lose? She needed to do everything possible to find Roman. Maggie walked over to the table where Haynes was engrossed in *The New York Times.*

"Frank," Maggie said, and noted the flash of irritation as he looked up. "Sorry to disturb your quiet dinner."

Frank stood clumsily. "Not at all. Would you like to join me?" His tone indicated he desired nothing less.

"No. Sit, please," Maggie replied, waving him back into his seat. "I just want to let you know that Roman—John's Golden Retriever—has gone missing. He got out of the fence at Rosemont this afternoon."

Frank Haynes shoved back his chair and jumped to his feet. He pulled his wallet out of his pocket, dropped two fifty-dollar bills on the table, and steered her toward the door.

"Don't you want to wait for your change?" Maggie asked. She'd never known Frank to be careless with his money.

"Absolutely not. Tell me where you've already looked."

"I just wanted you to know in case he's turned in to Forever Friends."

"He'll be microchipped, so we'll know if it's him. I'll help you look now. It's going to be a cold night for him outside."

After a quick conversation on the sidewalk, Frank Haynes headed to his Mercedes sedan. He'd drive along Mill Road while Maggie wove through the streets lining the square. She was pulling into the lot at Town Hall when her phone rang.

"Did you find him?" she asked breathlessly.

"No," John replied. "We're not going to find him tonight. We need to call it quits. I don't want you catching cold. Go home and get some rest."

"I'm not going to catch a cold, and I don't want to rest. I want to find Roman." Maggie paused. "Can he survive outside tonight, in these temperatures?"

John hesitated, and she knew he entertained the same doubts. "He's got a thick fur coat, and he's smart enough to take shelter from the wind. He should be fine." Maggie knew he didn't believe that, and neither did she.

"Will you come back to Rosemont?" she asked.

"I'll stay at my place, in case he comes here."

"Would you like company? I hate to think of you alone. Eve and I could come over."

"No. You need to stay there in case Roman makes his way back to Rosemont."

"Good point," Maggie answered. "I'll sleep in that big chair in the library by the French doors. Eve will bark if he comes to Rosemont. We won't hear him if we're asleep upstairs."

"Thank you, honey."

"I'm going to make up a missing pet flyer tonight. Can you send me a photo of Roman?"

"Yes. Good idea."

"I'll put them up at Town Hall. Pete's offering a free dinner to anyone who finds him and promised to post the flyers all over the square. I stopped at Pete's to see if anyone had mentioned a stray to him. Frank Haynes was there, having dinner. I told him about Roman, and he dropped a hundred dollars on the table and raced out to look for him. Can you believe it?"

"Actually, I can," John replied. "If you or I were missing, it might be a different story. But not with a dog." She could hear John yawn. "We should let him know we've stopped looking for tonight."

"I still have his cell phone, remember? I don't have his home number."

"We've got it in our system at the animal hospital; I can log in to it from here. I'll phone Frank when we hang up."

"Call me if Roman comes home," they both said in unison.

Chapter 3

Maggie gave the lost-dog flyers to Pete early the next morning, and he got every merchant on the square to post them. She pulled into her parking spot, "Reserved for the Hon. Mayor Margaret Martin," and noted that Frank Haynes' Mercedes was in the lot. He was spending more time at Town Hall lately.

Maggie turned toward his office when she got off the elevator.

"Happy New Year, Frank. And thank you, again, for your help last night."

"Any luck? Did he come home?"

"I'm afraid not. We're posting flyers all over town. And we'll keep looking."

Haynes nodded from behind his desk. "I'm really sorry."

Maggie could tell that he meant it. "You're here early. And we don't have a council meeting this week."

"Just attending to some last-minute details before I leave town."

"Really? I didn't know you were going anywhere."

"I'm taking a few days of vacation."

"Good for you, Frank," Maggie replied. "Are you headed somewhere warm? It'd be nice to get away from this weather."

"Yes. Florida. I'm visiting friends," he lied. He was going to Florida, but he didn't have any friends. "And I thought I'd check out those condos that the town pension fund owns in Miami. See for myself where they are and what condition they're in. We need to get those sold. The pension fund needs the cash. Someone has to do something to get the ball rolling."

Maggie bristled at the reproach in his voice. As mayor of Westbury, she was doing everything in her power to restore the town's finances after the recent fraud and embezzlement by former Mayor William Wheeler and probably other co-conspirators, yet to be uncovered. Wheeler's jailhouse suicide had thrown the investigation into turmoil.

"Do you have anything new planned for the upcoming year?" he asked.

Maggie paused. Was he fishing to see if she'd turned in her resignation? It seemed like such a long time ago, even though it had only been a few days. "Nope. I plan to spend the year in the mayor's office, working through the issues facing Westbury." She paused to gage the effect of her words. Did she detect a flash of anger? She couldn't be sure. She hoped so. "Have a nice trip, Frank," Maggie said and turned on her heel.

"One more thing," he called to her. "I've lost my cell phone. I was wondering if you picked it up the other day when we collided on the steps."

Maggie hesitated. Would his phone provide valuable evidence for the fraud investigation? Frank Haynes wasn't a suspect, but he hadn't been cleared, either. And she felt certain that he'd plotted with Professor Upton to manipulate her into resigning the mayoral seat. Just because he'd been so nice about Roman didn't change any of that. She needed time to think this through.

"No, I didn't. Why don't you post a note in the break room?"

Chapter 4

Loretta Nash shivered in the frosty morning while Frank Haynes unlocked the door of Haynes Enterprises. She hung up her coat and settled herself behind her desk without a word to him. Loretta was in no mood to be nice to her employer.

She was logging in to her computer when he said pleasantly, "Happy New Year."

Loretta looked at him over the top of her computer monitor but didn't return the salutation.

Haynes cleared his throat and stepped to the side of her desk. "About the other night. With Delgado ..."

Loretta held up a hand to cut him off. "I don't want to discuss it with you. The subject is closed." She swiveled in her chair to leaf through a binder on the credenza behind her desk.

"I want to apologize to you," he continued.

Loretta remained with her back to him, but she stopped turning the pages.

"Delgado was out of line. He was drunk."

Loretta turned back to him and stared.

"Why did you go to his office with him? When he was obviously into his cups?"

"You sent me there, remember?" Loretta replied.

"Not to go up to his office with him. Surely a beautiful woman like you has had enough experience with men to know what would happen in that situation. Especially dressing like you do, in short skirts and tight sweaters."

"Are you saying I brought it on myself? By what I was wearing? Chuck Delgado almost raped me. I gave him no encouragement whatsoever. I didn't consent to any of it. If you hadn't come in when you did, he would've succeeded."

Haynes raised his hands and gestured for her to calm down. "No. Of course not. It's just something you might think about when you're around men like that."

"I don't intend to be around men like that," Loretta replied in glacial tones. "And I expect you to tell him he's not welcome here," she continued, emboldened by his unexpected apology.

Haynes' shoulders stiffened and she wondered if she had gone too far. "It's not up to you to tell me who can come to my business."

She and Haynes locked eyes. Loretta could taste her fear. She lived paycheck to paycheck and needed this job. She twisted a strand of her long blond hair.

"I'm going away for a few days," he finally replied. "I can't guarantee that he won't stop by."

"I'll keep the doors locked."

Haynes nodded, raking her with critical eyes.

"Where are you going?" she asked as he turned to his office.

"Out of town," he snapped. He shut the door firmly and slumped into his chair. How in the hell had he allowed himself to become entangled with a thug like Chuck Delgado? Ron Delgado was his personal investment advisor and had helped Haynes grow his considerable portfolio. But when Ron brought Haynes into an "investment group" involving his brother Chuck, Haynes should have run the other way—fast. He'd served on the town council with Chuck Delgado long enough to know that he was a sleazy bottom feeder. He had always suspected that the Westbury town councilman had mob connections. Now he was certain of it.

Delgado orchestrated the embezzlement from Westbury's general fund and the town workers' pension fund, commissioned arson fires and what was intended to be a fatal car crash for Alex Scanlon, and who knew what else. *Thank God, no one was killed in that crash. They would have nailed me as an accessory to murder even though I didn't know about it until after the fact.*

Haynes pushed himself out of his chair and began to pace. *Maybe I should go to Chief Thomas with what I know,* he thought for the umpteenth time. But he couldn't—he was in too deep.

He'd never intended to steal from anyone but he'd turned a blind eye to the facts as they emerged. Even if the state offered him immunity for his testimony and he avoided going to jail, his reputation and business interests in this close-knit rural community would be irretrievably tarnished. People would boycott his fast-food restaurants and the business he'd built from the ground up would fail. He'd spent more than twenty years donating to every charity in town and sponsoring most of the sports teams. He wouldn't throw away his stature as the town's leading businessman and philanthropist. And Haynes didn't want to think about how Delgado would even the score if he ratted him out.

He stared at the painting next to his door. The jump drive containing enough evidence to put Chuck Delgado in jail was in the safe concealed by that painting. He didn't need to go to Chief Thomas just yet. He'd continue with his plans for his Miami trip.

Chapter 5

"Maggie," Professor Lyndon Upton said with gusto as he answered his cell phone. "Happy New Year. I'm in California—on the golf course. We're next in line to tee off. Can I call you later?"

"I'll only need a moment, Don," Maggie replied. "I wanted to tell you that I've decided to retain my position as mayor of Westbury."

"Now, Maggie, we talked about that. Won't you be spread too thin with the demands of the town, your consulting assignment, and that handsome veterinarian of yours?"

"I'm not going to accept the consulting engagement. I'm sticking with the town and the veterinarian."

There was a prolonged silence as Upton digested this. "I've already told the client. How do you want me to explain this?"

Maggie held her tongue. She wanted to respond that he could tell the client that she wouldn't work with a conniving backstabber like him. "Say I changed my mind; say you misunderstood my answer."

"They're calling my foursome. Let's discuss this next week when I'm in town for the council meeting," he pleaded. "Don't do anything rash until we can sit down face to face and talk about it."

"That's the other thing I'm calling about, Professor. You won't be attending the council meeting next week." Maggie paused to let her words sink in. "Your services are no longer required. The Town of Westbury has elected to move forward without you."

Upton was quiet and Maggie smiled, picturing him shocked and speechless at the other end of the line. "Have a good game," she said and disconnected the call.

———

Lyndon Upton played a lousy round of golf, marked by an uncharacteristically sour attitude. He settled up his bets and spotted his foursome the first round at the club, extricating himself as quickly as possible.

"I'm needed back at the office," he said as he made his way to the door. "Give me a chance to win it back another time, will you? Enjoy the rest of your afternoon."

Once inside his car, he pulled out his cell phone and saw that he'd missed a call from Haynes Enterprises. He hit redial and asked the pleasant-sounding woman if he could speak to Frank Haynes.

"She knows about us," Upton said when Haynes answered.

"Why do you say that?"

"She just called to tell me she's not taking the consulting job and she's staying on as mayor."

"I wondered. There's been no talk about her resignation. Why do you think she suspects we worked together to convince her to do the right thing—for her and Westbury—and resign?" Haynes asked.

"I told her not to do anything hasty; that we'd talk about it next week when I was in town for the council meeting." He paused, searching for the right words.

"And?" Haynes prompted.

"And she fired me," Upton erupted. "Told me my services were no longer needed; the town would get along without me. Then she hung up."

Haynes sat in stunned silence.

"How could she have found out?" Upton asked. "We were very careful. I didn't tell anyone. Did you, Frank?"

"No. Of course not. But I lost my cell phone."

"When?"

"I'm not sure. New Year's Eve or New Year's Day."

"Did you get my text saying she accepted the consulting job?"

"No," Haynes answered grimly.

"Did you find your phone?" Upton shouted. "Tell me you found it!"

Haynes didn't respond.

"That explains it, then," Upton said. "Someone must have found your phone, read the text, and told her about it."

Haynes stood and began pacing. "It's possible, but don't jump to any conclusions." He didn't add that the most likely person to have possession of his phone was Maggie Martin or that he'd already asked her about it and she'd denied finding it.

"I need to call her right away and explain the whole thing. I need to apologize and make this right. I never should have gone along with this crazy scheme in the first place. I need to clear my name."

"I wouldn't do that if I were you," Haynes said. "There's no way to extricate yourself without implicating me and others that you don't want to get crosswise with." He paused to let the implications of his statement sink in. "I understand your position, Don. Let's give this some time to play out; find out what she knows. Can you keep your powder dry for a while?"

Upton sighed heavily. "I suppose so. Maybe rushing in isn't prudent. What do you plan to do?"

"I'll keep my eyes and ears open. Eventually, something will slip out."

Marc Benson nodded at the receptionist as he strode across the small lobby on his way to Alex Scanlon's office. He and his partner had barely said more than a few words to each other in weeks. Alex was putting in at least sixty hours a week on Westbury's fraud and embezzlement cases. "Has he got anybody with him?" Marc asked over his shoulder.

The receptionist shook her head no, and he kept walking.

The door was slightly ajar, and Marc knocked softly before pushing it open.

"Yes," Alex snapped, without looking up.

"Aren't we cheery this afternoon?" Marc replied.

Alex smiled. "What are you doing here?" He checked his watch. "I thought you'd be rehearsing until your gig tonight."

"We got done early. Everybody was on time and prepared. So I thought I'd stop by and drag you out of here for dinner."

"It's only four forty-five. At bit early for dinner, don't you think?"

"Did you have lunch? Are you hungry?"

Alex pushed his chair back from his desk. "No, I didn't. And I'm starved. But I really shouldn't take the time."

"Yes, you should. You've been pushing yourself unmercifully since you took on the role of special counsel. The town didn't get into this mess overnight and taking an hour off to eat won't make any difference. Get your coat. We'll go over to Stuart's and sit at the bar."

"I suppose you're right." Alex rose and turned off his desk lamp.

"It's nice out. Why don't we walk? The exercise will do us both good."

"You've been working as hard as I have." Alex regarded his partner thoughtfully as they stepped out into the brisk afternoon. "How's it going?"

"Terrific, actually. I've been invited to join the group. Their keyboardist decided not to come back. If I want it, the spot is mine."

"That's great news. But do you want to be part of a group? I thought you intended to focus on your solo career?"

"These guys are true professionals. They don't waste time when we rehearse, and they consistently book well-paying gigs. We're talking about making an album."

Alex stopped and turned to Marc. "I can't believe I knew nothing about this. Congratulations. You deserve it. I'm sorry that I've been so consumed by my work. I should have paid more attention to you. And my family in general. I haven't talked to Aaron in months."

Marc shrugged. "I'm sure your brother understands as much as I do what a huge responsibility being special counsel to the town is right now. I knew that when you took the job. Making any progress?"

Alex quickened his pace. "It's the most frustrating case I've ever worked on. I knew the process of getting documents from offshore banks would be cumbersome, but I didn't think it would be this difficult. I'm stymied at every turn. The research and motion writing are incredibly time consuming. I feel like I'm in quicksand."

"Can't you get someone to help? What's Maggie doing on this? Have you talked to her about it?"

"She'll be able to help assess the documents once we receive them. There's nothing she can do until then. Besides, she's got her hands more than full with trying to balance the budget."

"Why don't you hire someone to help you?"

"Westbury's broke, remember? We're cutting essential services—there's certainly no money for an extra lawyer. I'll need to keep this up until we get the job done."

Marc turned to Alex as they reached the entrance to Stuart's. "We can do this for a while longer, but it can't go on forever."

Alex nodded. "I know." He breathed deeply. "I can smell the steaks from here. Let's eat."

Chapter 6

Roman didn't come home, and although everyone in town was looking for him, no one reported seeing him. John and Maggie kept in
close contact by phone, hoping for Roman's return. With every passing hour, their confidence dwindled. By the morning of the third day,
John was despondent and Maggie was close to tears.

"These things happen, sweetheart. He was a grand dog. I hope a
family somewhere picked him up and he's being spoiled by a passel
of children."

"He had a microchip, didn't he?" Maggie asked.

"Yes, but everyone doesn't check for one. Particularly a stray
without a collar. We've got to accept that he's gone."

Maggie sniffed.

"Don't start; you'll get me going," John chided. "I've got to get to
the clinic. See you tonight."

⁕

John was fully occupied with the medical problems of a pair of over-
weight dachshunds that were the apple of their owner's eye when his
assistant knocked on the exam room door and asked him if he could
step out.

"Emergency?" John asked, heading for the surgery room. He assumed an animal had been hit by a car.

Juan shook his head and grabbed John by the elbow, steering him
to his office. When he opened the door, he was greeted by the sight

23

he longed for—the open-mouthed grin of his beloved Golden Retriever. Roman bounded to the door and leapt onto his master, resting his paws on his chest and licking him profusely. John buried his face in the soft fur.

He drew back and squatted down, examining Roman with practiced, professional hands. Other than a serious collection of burs in his fur, he was in good shape—no nicks, cuts, or signs of frostbite. "Well ... where have you been, fella? You scared Maggie and me to death!"

John stood and for the first time noticed the young man hovering over a cardboard box in the corner of his office.

"John Allen," he said, extending his hand. The young man tentatively shook it. "I'm David Wheeler," he replied, searching John's face for any hint of recognition. Ever since his father's arrest for embezzlement and jailhouse suicide, David had suffered the ignominy of his name.

John brought his free hand to rest upon their clasped hands. "I'm very sorry about the death of your father, David."

David nodded and looked away.

"Did you see the signs around town? There's a reward." John reached for his wallet.

David shook his head. "My mom saw them. I'm glad I found him. I don't know what I'd do if I lost my dog." He looked longingly at the cash that John had extracted from his wallet.

"Whether you saw the signs or not, you're entitled to the reward," he said, passing the bills to the boy. "And I'm very grateful that you took such good care of Roman. Where did you find him?"

"He was in the bushes by the side of the road outside of that big mansion called Rosemont. There was a dead cat and all of these kittens," he said, pointing to the cardboard box containing six tiny gray-and-white kittens. "Roman was acting like their mother. He was licking them and keeping them warm and wasn't letting them run into the street. He picked them up in his mouth—real gentle—and brought them back to this place under a bush. You should have seen him."

John looked at his dog and his heart lurched. As a vet, he saw the goodness of animals in both big and small ways on a daily basis and was constantly moved by the divinity they displayed. He searched for words and, finding none, merely nodded.

"I knew the kittens had to eat, so I brought them home, and he wouldn't leave their side," David said, gesturing to Roman. "I looked online about feeding them and bought kitten formula."

"That was the perfect thing to do," John replied, picking up one of the squirming kittens. "Cow's milk would have made them very sick. You and Roman have done an excellent job. You've saved their lives." David smiled. "What do you intend to do with them?"

"I wanted to keep them, but my mom found them this morning and told me that they'll need more care than we can provide. I work at Forever Friends," the boy said proudly. "I'd take them there, but they can't care for kittens either. So I brought them here," the boy ended and turned hopeful eyes to John.

"You did the right thing. These kittens are only a couple of weeks old. Their eyes are open, which happens at about ten days, and their teeth are beginning to emerge. They'll need to be fed every six hours, and we'll need to teach them how to go to the bathroom." John studied the boy. "Would you like to help? You could stop by before or after school—whatever works best for you. When they're old enough—and if your mom agrees—you can take one home."

David beamed and picked up a kitten with four white paws that was springing up and down, trying to get out of the box. He held him to his chest and the kitten's rumbling purr filled the room. "I'll be here at six forty-five tomorrow morning. You can count on me."

Chapter 7

Maggie kept an eye on her phone all morning; willing it to ring, willing it to be John with news of Roman. She saw the message light blinking when she returned to her office after a trip to the ladies' room and snatched the headset from the cradle. She held her breath when she heard John's joyful voice and fought back tears of relief as she listened to his message. David Wheeler had found Roman and brought him to the animal hospital. Roman was home, safe and sound, with quite a tale to tell. And he'd brought a surprise. Maggie smiled—John was obviously enjoying the bit of mystery he was creating.

She reached for her cell phone and quickly typed:

Are the 2 of you free to join Eve and me for dinner tonight?

His reply accepting her invitation came moments later. As soon as she read it, Maggie realized she didn't have anything on hand that would make a fitting celebratory dinner. Her afternoon was overbooked with appointments, so she'd have to rely on her old standby—takeout from Pete's. She phoned him straight away, and he assured her he had the perfect meal in mind for Westbury's esteemed mayor and his favorite veterinarian. He'd also throw in a couple of good bones for the best dogs in town.

Maggie laughed. "You're quite the salesman, you know—or politician."

"I don't know whether to be flattered or offended by that comment," Pete replied.

"You know I mean it as a compliment."

"Make sure David knows he's entitled to a free meal from me," he reminded her as they rang off.

Maggie's next move was to tell Frank Haynes. He'd been so concerned about Roman, it seemed only fair. His office door was ajar, but he wasn't at this desk. She found him in the break room, waiting for a fresh pot of coffee to brew.

"Great news, Frank. Roman's home."

Haynes looked up and smiled. Was this the first time she had ever seen him genuinely smile?

"That's fantastic. Where did you find him?"

"I don't have all the details yet. John left me a message. Apparently, David Wheeler found him and brought him to the animal hospital."

"Glad to hear it. David's a great kid. He's been working off his community service at Forever Friends and has been doing a terrific job."

Maggie nodded. "Nice of you to give him that opportunity, Frank. It couldn't have been easy for him to have his father arrested for embezzlement and removed from public office. Then to have him commit suicide in jail. No wonder the boy acted out and got into trouble."

Haynes shifted uncomfortably and eyed the coffee pot as the stream of coffee slowed to a trickle.

"Will you be attending the community forums? I'd like as many of the councilmembers there as possible."

Haynes shrugged. "I don't think they're a good idea. You're opening a can of worms, seeking community feedback on our proposed budget cuts. You and Upton think that all this 'transparency' is necessary. I don't. Delgado and Isaac agree with me." He turned and picked up the coffee pot to fill his cup. "You and Upton can conduct them on your own."

Maggie waited for him to face her. "Professor Upton won't be attending." She studied his face for his reaction. "He isn't assisting us any longer."

"When did this happen? Why?" He acted surprised, but she was sure that he already knew.

"Schedule conflict. And, frankly, we don't need him any longer. I'm prepared to see this through, myself."

Haynes nodded slowly and turned abruptly toward his office.

—⁂—

Maggie was setting the table for dinner when John pulled up to her front door. Eve began to bark furiously as Roman bounded up the steps and Maggie knelt to throw her arms around him.

Eve circled the two of them, sniffing Roman and yelping until she got his attention, then both dogs bolted through the front door.

John stood by the open tailgate of his Suburban.

"What are you doing? It's freezing. Come inside."

"Roman comes bearing gifts, I'm afraid."

"Really? Back there?" she said, gesturing to the cargo hold. She raced down the steps as he withdrew a large animal carrier containing the kittens that were now meowing loudly.

"Kittens! Are you kidding me?" Maggie laughed.

"I'm afraid not. It's quite a story. And don't worry—they're not staying. I couldn't turn down dinner with my two best girls, but afterward Roman and his new brood and I will take ourselves home. I don't intend to inflict this motley crew on you."

"I've never had a cat," Maggie cried, hopping from foot to foot. "I always wanted one but Paul was allergic. And now I've got how many?"

"It's a litter of six. But you don't have to take any of them. Roman adopted them—that's why he was missing. David Wheeler found him watching over them in the woods right outside the break in the fence."

"That's incredible," Maggie said, leading John into her spacious laundry room and closing the door behind them.

"They're only a few weeks old and will require a lot of care."

Maggie opened the carrier unleashing a storm of squirming, fuzzy creatures. "Amazing," she said managing to scoop one up as it tore past her.

"I'll take care of them at the clinic until they're old enough to be adopted out. I was going to leave them there tonight, but Roman wouldn't hear of it. He wasn't coming with me without these kittens. I've seen the mother instinct in animals before—male or female. There's no point fighting it."

"Aren't you just the sweetest thing?" Maggie cooed, nuzzling the furry creature in the palm of her hand. She cut her eyes to John. "You can forget about adopting them out. They're Rosemont cats now."

"Slow down there, sweetheart. Going from zero to six cats in under five minutes isn't wise or well thought out."

"Party pooper," Maggie retorted. "We'll be fine—we have an 'in' with the local vet."

John smiled, knowing he'd been defeated. "Let's just see how it goes, shall we? And one of them may already be spoken for."

Maggie arched her brow.

"David Wheeler is going to come by every morning to help me with them, and I promised him he could keep one of the kittens."

"That seems fair," Maggie agreed.

"I'll take them to the clinic with me in the morning, and we'll see what happens."

"I've got a better idea. Leave them here, and you and David can stop by each morning. They're much better off at Rosemont," and her tone indicated the discussion was over.

Chapter 8

That night did not proceed peacefully for anyone at Rosemont. Roman installed himself outside the laundry room door and wouldn't budge. Maggie finally took his supper dish to him there.

Eve was endlessly curious about the squirming fur balls, whose odor confirmed their presence in the laundry room even when they were silent. She barked and scratched at the door and made a general nuisance of herself.

John and Maggie were both starved by the time they turned to the takeout from Pete's. Maggie put their plates in the microwave, ending up with overcooked vegetables and lukewarm entrees. They were too tired to fix anything else and ate without enthusiasm.

Maggie was wiping the counters when John announced that he'd have to go the clinic to get kitten formula and bottles.

"This is going to be a lot of work for the next few weeks," he advised. "They'll need to be fed every six to eight hours, and I'll show you how to teach them to go to the bathroom."

Maggie rolled her eyes. "I'm a mother and grandmother, remember? I think I can tend to these kittens," she said dismissively.

"Don't say I didn't warn you," he replied as he headed to his car.

Maggie closed the door behind him and turned to Eve, who was circling at her feet. "We'll be fine, won't we, girl? You're going to love your new friends, aren't you?"

With Eve at her heels, Maggie was bound for the laundry room when she remembered the bones Pete included for the dogs. She'd use them to get their attention. She retraced her steps and approached Roman, bone in hand. As she hoped, Roman abandoned his maternal instincts and followed her. Once they reached the kitchen, Maggie gave Eve and Roman the bones and the dogs settled down to business.

She eased into the laundry room to visit Rosemont's newest residents. She hadn't counted on the speed and agility of one of the litter. The largest of the bunch—with a salt-and-pepper coat and four white paws—shot out of the laundry room heading for the kitchen.

His siblings followed suit. Maggie dropped to her knees and tried to push them back into the laundry room, but it was like attempting to stop Niagara Falls with her hands.

She rounded the corner to the kitchen in time to see Eve bounding toward them, tail wagging. When the kittens began to crouch and hiss, Eve slowed her pace but continued to advance until the most adventuresome kitten reached out a paw and swiped at Eve's nose. She yelped and tore past Maggie to the far side of the kitchen. Roman abandoned his bone and began corralling the kittens.

Maggie stopped and watched the unfolding domestic scene in amazement. "What a good boy, Roman," she said, approaching to stroke his head. He looked at her with his soft, gentle eyes.

Roman's gaze shifted to the end of the kitchen island where Eve, tail wagging, was making her way slowly to them.

"Oh no, you don't!" Maggie cried. "We've had enough excitement for one day." She leapt to her feet and escorted Eve to her bedroom. "You get in your basket. I'll come back to take you out before bedtime."

Maggie had just returned the kittens to their box in the laundry room when John pulled up.

"How's everything here?" John asked as he brought two large bags of supplies into the kitchen.

"Fine. Peaceful."

John glanced around the kitchen. "Where's Eve?"

"She upstairs in my room."

"Really?" John asked, eying Maggie closely. "What happened while I was gone? Why's Eve banished?"

"Nothing to worry about. It's all good."

"Have it your way. Are you ready to learn how to become a mama cat?"

"Reporting for duty!"

Chapter 9

Frank Haynes drew the wide-brimmed hat low over his eyes, as much to conceal his identity as to shield himself from the searing brightness of the midday sun. He'd only been to Miami once before, with his faithless wife. He hated the place. The sooner he completed his business and got back to the airport, the better.

He took a long pull on his rum and coke. At least he'd found one Cuban influence he could stomach. He couldn't eat any of the food. He'd had indigestion since the moment he stepped off the plane.

On a positive note, the condos were better than expected, given that Delgado selected them to house his whores and number-runners. Westbury would be able to sell them, as is, without much trouble. Liquidating these questionable investments and returning money to the pension fund should ease some of the pressure to find and prosecute those responsible for this mess, including himself. He fished an antacid out of his pocket. Getting involved with Chuck Delgado had been the most idiotic thing he'd ever done. And now Maggie Martin was more determined than ever to get to the bottom of the corruption that had decimated the pension fund and all but bankrupted the town. He needed to make sure that none of the off-shore accounts led to him.

Haynes turned sharply at the sound of his name and stood, leaning toward the tall Latino man in a slim-fitted suit. He motioned for the man to take the seat opposite.

"I thought Ricardo was coming," he stated quietly.

The man shrugged. "He got busy."

"You are?" Haynes replied, extending his hand.

"What does it matter? I'm here with a message from Ricardo."

Haynes nodded and withdrew his hand.

"I have to make sure you keep your part of the bargain first."

Haynes reached under the table to the briefcase at his feet and released the closures at either end, cracking it open to allow a glimpse of the cash inside. The man leaned over to tie his shoe. When he sat up, he spoke softly and slowly.

"Is it all there? You don't want to short us," he stated in a tone that sent shivers down Haynes' spine, despite the sweltering day.

"Of course it's all there," Haynes said. "I'm not an idiot."

The man grasped the briefcase but Haynes did not let go. "Has everything been taken care of? Have all traces of my name and bank accounts been erased from the files of every offshore bank? The town's special counsel will be subpoenaing the records in the next few weeks."

The man smiled. "Relax, brother. Didn't Ricardo tell you they would? As far as the banks are concerned, you don't exist."

"And you've made sure that William Wheeler and Chuck Delgado are the only names and bank accounts that will be found?"

The man inclined his head slightly. "But of course. It's all done, as you directed."

Haynes slid the briefcase over to the man and released his grasp.

The man smiled. "Pleasure doing business with you. Where are you headed from here?

"Back home, as soon as possible."

"What a pity. You should stay a few days and enjoy our hospitality. Get some sun. It'd do you good."

"Perhaps," Haynes replied, and they both knew he would head for the airport as soon as he left the table.

Chapter 10

Loretta Nash unlocked the door of Haynes Enterprises to sign for a package delivered by UPS. Her boss was still "out of town," and she wasn't taking any risks. She deposited the heavy carton on his desk and was retracing her steps to lock the door when Chuck Delgado stepped across the threshold. A pasty gray replaced his usual florid complexion, and despite the cold outside, he was sweating profusely.

She pushed down the fear that threatened to freeze her to the spot and walked around to the back of her desk, putting it between her and this monster who had attempted to rape her just a few days ago.

"Hey, doll," he said as he pulled a soiled handkerchief from his coat pocket to harness a moist sneeze. Loretta recoiled in disgust. "Where's Frankie?"

"He's not here."

"I'll wait," he said, sinking into the sofa against the wall.

"He won't be back today."

"Where the hell is he?" Delgado asked, heaving his heavy frame to his feet.

"I don't know."

"Tell him to call me, okay?"

Loretta stared at him icily.

"What's wrong with you, kid? Sore that we didn't get to finish what we started the other night?" He angled toward her and began coughing so hard that he doubled over. "I'm under the weather, so you're just gonna have to wait," he sputtered.

"You'd better get home and get to bed," she answered, willing him to move to the door.

"It'll be your turn, soon. I promise you—I'll finish what I started," he sneered and exited into the sunless afternoon.

Loretta locked the door before he reached the first step. She made her way unsteadily to the window and released her breath as she watched him drive away. Avoiding him wouldn't be possible, and she couldn't live with the constant fear that he might be lurking around every corner. Loretta knew what she had to do. She'd have no peace as long as Chuck Delgado was a free man. She needed to deliver that jump drive to Maggie Martin.

⸺∞⸺

That evening, while her children were playing with friends at a neighbor's apartment, Loretta carefully retrieved the jump drive from its hiding place in the back of her closet and set out for Rosemont. She drove slowly up the driveway, gathering her courage, praying fervently that Maggie was home alone. Loretta wanted to finish this.

As she rounded the final corner, she noticed the front door closing and a set of taillights disappearing down the far side of the drive. Her pulse quickened. It looked like her timing was perfect; someone had just left. She parked in front of the entryway and quietly closed her car door.

She paused for a moment. There was still time to retreat—to abandon this mission that was sure to destroy Frank Haynes and, with him, her lucrative new job. The genie was not yet out of the bottle. She strengthened her resolve. This was the right thing to do. And Frank Haynes and Chuck Delgado deserved whatever was coming to them.

Loretta walked deliberately up the steps and knocked firmly on the solid mahogany door. A dog began to bark, and a smiling Maggie Martin opened the door.

"I knew you'd be back. You forgot—"

Maggie felt her smile slowly drain away. She stared at the attractive woman where she had expected to see John Allen. There was something familiar about her. Then recognition hit her like a slap in the face. This was the other woman—the woman she had seen pulling out of that upscale Scottsdale driveway in a new Escalade while Maggie sat sweltering in a rental car pulled to the opposite curb, hoping to catch a glimpse of her, trying to make sense of her newfound knowledge that her dead husband had clandestinely maintained a second family. And now *that woman* was standing on the doorsteps of Rosemont.

The woman opened her mouth to speak, but remained silent. She clutched her purse tightly to her side and waited.

Maggie stiffly motioned her to cross the threshold.

The woman extended her hand. "I'm Loretta Nash, Mayor Martin."

"I know who you are." Maggie made no move to take the proffered hand, and it slowly returned to the woman's side.

The two women, from different worlds but with a common intersection, regarded each other warily. Maggie drew a ragged breath. "I can't believe you've the unmitigated gall to track me down."

Loretta made no move to retreat.

"You'd better tell me why you're here," Maggie continued. "Follow me."

Maggie led her unwanted guest into the library and motioned her to a chair in front of the fireplace. Loretta perched on the edge of the cushion and fidgeted with the zipper on her jacket until it became stuck at the halfway point. She turned to Maggie who sat, arms crossed, staring at her.

Loretta cleared her throat. "I work for Haynes Enterprises," she began. "I'm a financial analyst. I don't think we've ever met."

"You're right," Maggie replied. Loretta pulled her jacket closer. "We haven't met, but I know that you and my husband had an affair for years."

The words had their desired effect, and Maggie was secretly pleased. The woman gasped and began picking at the nail on her right index finger.

"How … ?" she sputtered.

"Does it matter?"

Loretta slowly shook her head. "I'm sorry," she began, and Maggie raised a hand to stop her.

"I don't want to hear it. You're not going to come here with a New Year's apology on your lips and leave thinking you've cleaned the slate and made amends. It's not that easy."

Loretta nodded. She swallowed hard and began again. "I understand. I didn't come here to apologize."

Maggie snorted and pushed herself out of her chair.

"Please," Loretta implored. "I came because I need help."

Maggie wheeled on her. "You've got to be kidding. You think I'm going to help you?"

"I'm having trouble with Frank Haynes and Chuck Delgado."

"The whole town is having trouble with them."

Loretta flushed. "For what it's worth, Paul lied to me about you. He said that you were as anxious for a divorce as he was—that you were waiting for his pension to vest before you announced your breakup. You know how convincing he could be. I didn't know how those things worked. I was devastated when he died. And my kids and I lost everything."

"A married man lied to you about his marriage. That's supposed to be surprising? You want *me* to feel sorry for *you*?"

Loretta looked at her hands folded in her lap.

"And how is it that you left Scottsdale and moved here to work for Frank Haynes?"

"A headhunter found me this job," Loretta replied with a hint of pride.

Maggie took a step back and grabbed the mantel for support. So Frank Haynes had recruited Paul's mistress to work for him. This could be no coincidence. He was stirring around in Maggie's past.

She turned back to Loretta. "I can't help you."

"But Delgado tried to rape me."

"Then you need to call the police."

Loretta shifted uncomfortably in her chair.

"You're not welcome here. You need to leave. *Now*," Maggie said, pointing to the front door.

Loretta opened her mouth to protest as Maggie stormed out of the room.

Loretta rose stiffly to her feet and followed her to the entryway where Maggie stood holding the door open. "I am sorry," Loretta said. She stepped out onto the stone steps.

Maggie stopped short of slamming the door.

Chapter 11

"Whoa, what's wrong, honey?" John said into his phone.

Maggie tried again, but choked on her words. "I'm okay, but will you come back?"

John quickly checked his rearview mirror and swung a U-turn in his Suburban. "On my way. I'll be there in under five minutes. Just hang on."

Maggie sagged against the door she had just closed. Eve circled her beloved mistress, acutely aware that something was wrong. Maggie squatted and let Eve shower her with wet doggie kisses.

By the time John pulled into the driveway, she was no longer crying. She flung the door open as soon as she heard his car approach. Eve didn't race out to offer her greeting but remained at Maggie's side.

John took the steps two at a time and wrapped Maggie in his arms. "What in the world happened? Is something wrong with the kids?"

Maggie drew back and shook her head. "No, nothing like that." She looked at him long and hard. "It's time I gave you all the sordid details about Paul."

She led him to the kitchen and poured them both a cup of coffee. They sat next to each other at the French farmhouse table, and John took her hands in his.

"Whatever it is, we're in this together. You know that. You can tell me anything."

Maggie inhaled and rubbed his hands with her own. "I think I once told you that I thought Paul had been cheating on me?"

John nodded.

"I know he was cheating on me because I hired a private investigator to find out where he'd been spending all of the money he embezzled from Windsor College."

John's head snapped up.

"He'd been embezzling for years—over two million dollars." She paused to let the news sink in.

"I never knew anything about it," she added hastily. "He didn't spend any of the money on me or the kids; he never brought any of it home."

"Maggie—I assumed that. I know you'd never be part of anything like that." He scooted his chair closer and put his arms around her.

Maggie released the breath she had been holding. "I quietly settled the college's claim against his estate using the proceeds of his life insurance policy. The board of regents wasn't keen to have the news of his embezzlement exposed since they'd be tarred and feathered over their lax oversight, and I didn't want the kids to suffer the humiliation of having their father's name dragged through the mud."

"Makes sense," John interjected. "I'd have done the same."

"But I was curious about where he spent all the money. By that time, I knew he'd inherited Rosemont—I found ten years of accounting records, money he'd invested repairing and maintaining it. He spent a fair amount here, but nowhere near two million dollars. So I hired a private investigator."

Maggie hesitated and drew a ragged breath.

"And?" John prodded.

"Paul supported a second family. A much younger woman with two school-aged children—not Paul's, thankfully—in a very upscale home in Scottsdale, Arizona." Maggie turned away. "I'm not proud of this, but one September afternoon after Paul died, I flew to Scottsdale to find this woman."

Maggie choked back a sob and John drew her close. "I acted like every cliché in the book. I even got sick in the rental car and, after I saw her, I drove straight home—my return plane ticket be damned."

John brushed a kiss along the top of her head.

"I haven't seen or heard of her since—until this evening. She left here right before I called you."

John held her at arm's length. "What? How is that possible?"

"She lives in Westbury now." Maggie watched as surprise bled into anger on John's face. "She works for Frank Haynes."

Chapter 12

Loretta took the highway exit away from Westbury—away from her apartment—after her encounter with Maggie Martin. She needed time to think without her kids underfoot. Nothing had gone as planned. She never expected, in a million years, that Maggie knew about her and Paul.

Traffic was sparse. She pressed her foot down hard, trying to get as much distance between herself and that humiliating scene as possible. Had that bastard Paul finally told his wife, or did she have her creep of a boss, Frank Haynes, to thank for this?

Thirty miles south of Westbury, she pulled off the highway at a McDonald's to use the restroom. Loretta stood at the sink and let the frigid water race over her hands as she surveyed herself in the mirror. The best things in her life were back in Westbury waiting for her. She wouldn't let Paul Martin or Frank Haynes screw that up for her. *To hell with both of them.* She dried her stinging hands on the coarse paper towel and shoved it into the trash. She would go back to her children and get a new job—away from those creeps Frank Haynes and Chuck Delgado. She'd make a good life for herself and her kids.

An hour later, Loretta collected her children from her neighbor and ushered them through her front door. "Who wants ice cream?" she asked, knowing it was a favorite she never allowed at bedtime. Three-year-old Nicole slumped against Loretta's leg.

"What's the matter, sweetheart?" Loretta asked, smoothing the damp hair back from Nicole's face. She bent down and placed her cheek against Nicole's warm forehead. Nicole sniffed and Loretta fished a tissue out of her pocket and wiped Nicole's nose. "I think someone's catching a cold. You can have your ice cream in bed. In fact, why don't we all have ice cream in bed?"

Loretta trudged up the steps to Haynes Enterprises the next morning. She had intended to start looking online for a new job the prior evening, but Nicole was sick and needed her attention until the wee hours. Loretta was exhausted but determined to get out of Haynes Enterprises at the first opportunity.

She locked the door behind her and hung up her coat. Mr. Haynes would be out of the office doing site visits all week. The work of Haynes Enterprises could wait; she would spend the day looking for a new job.

By three forty-five that afternoon, Loretta was cross-eyed from staring at her computer screen and thoroughly discouraged. Wages weren't as high in Westbury as they were in Scottsdale; she'd have to take a significant pay cut if she were to take any of the available openings. Frank Haynes was overpaying her. And she couldn't afford to make less. It appeared she was stuck right where she was.

Loretta pushed her chair back from her desk and stretched. She was headed to the coffeemaker when the call came in from the babysitter: Nicole was miserable and wanted her mother. Could she please pick her daughter up early? Loretta logged off of her computer and locked up the office. It looked like she'd spend another night tending to a sick child. Would she ever get a break?

Chapter 13

Frank Haynes pulled his Mercedes sedan into his usual parking spot by the employee entrance of Forever Friends. As founder and principal benefactor of Westbury's only no-kill animal shelter, he kept close tabs on the shelter's finances. He was there to review the weekly payroll.

He nodded to the talkative woman who sat at the reception desk and kept moving at a fast clip. Haynes was in no mood to engage in meaningless small talk. He settled himself behind the desk in the tiny administrative office and turned to the payroll records the bookkeeper left for him in a folder in the top drawer. He was surprised to see David Wheeler's name still in the column labeled Intern: Court-ordered Community Service with a notation that he'd spent sixteen hours at the shelter during the past week. The kid had gotten in trouble at school by stealing equipment from the language lab. He'd agreed to let David perform his community service at Forever Friends as a way to make amends in some small way for his own part in the whole debacle that led to William Wheeler's demise. It was at least a step in the right direction, and David had exceeded all expectations at Forever Friends.

Haynes initialed the bottom of each page of the report and returned it to its folder.

"Is David Wheeler still working here?" he asked the receptionist on his way out.

"Yes," she replied, pleased that Mr. Haynes was actually speaking to her. "In fact, he's here now, working in the kennels," she said, tilting her head to the doorway behind her.

Haynes hesitated, then strode around her desk, through the door, and into the hallway flanked by kennels on either side. David Wheeler was at the far end, tools in hand, repairing a loose hinge on one of the cage doors.

"Nice to see you, David," Frank Haynes said, extending his hand.

"Hi," David replied, awkwardly taking the outstretched hand.

"You've finished your community service, you know. You don't have to come here anymore."

David shrugged. Haynes regarded the boy thoughtfully.

"You've done a wonderful job for us. Taken the initiative to clean things up and make repairs. And you're great with the animals. Everyone on staff says so."

David flushed and shifted the screwdriver he was holding from hand to hand. "Everybody is really nice to me here. And I love the animals."

"We can't continue to let you come here as a volunteer," Haynes stated firmly. David inhaled sharply. "We'll need to put you on the payroll," Haynes continued and was gratified to see David smile. "Effective immediately. I'll take care of it. Would you like that?"

The boy nodded.

"So, now that that's settled, tell me about the dog you adopted. The mutt with only one eye? How's he getting along?"

David brightened. Dodger was fine—the best dog ever—smart as all get out—his mother even liked him—and he'd trained him to run an agility course like nobody's business. Haynes abandoned whatever errand was next on his agenda and relaxed against the wall, encouraging David to fill in all the details. When David paused, Haynes interjected, "I'd like to see Dodger on an agility course. It looks like a lot of fun. Can I come watch sometime?"

"Gosh, yes," David replied, unable to conceal his surprise. "That would be really cool. No one's come to watch us—not even my mom. We use the course at the dog park. Do you know it?" Haynes nodded. "People say they've never seen anything like him," David concluded proudly.

"Then I really have to see Dodger in action. When will you be there again?"

"If it doesn't rain or snow, we'll be there tomorrow after school."

Haynes consulted the calendar on his phone and nodded. "I'll see you then."

Chapter 14

Maggie checked the clock on her dashboard as she pulled into her parking spot at Town Hall and saw that she was late again. She hadn't been on time for anything since the kittens moved into Rosemont. She was meeting with Police Chief Andy Thomas and Special Counsel Alex Scanlon—two of the most punctual people on the planet. Maggie sighed and hurried across the icy parking lot to the back entrance.

She heard their raised voices when she stepped off the elevator. Maggie rushed to the reception area outside of the office bearing the plaque that read "Hon. Mayor Margaret Martin." She still got chills every time she saw it. Being elected mayor of Westbury still seemed like a dream. And on days like today, a nightmare.

"Gentlemen," she said. "Let's not carry on like this. I can hear you all the way down the hall."

Alex opened his mouth to protest, and she shot him a reproachful look. She unlocked her office and indicated the chairs opposite her desk. "I'm sorry I was delayed this morning," she said. "I need a cup of coffee before we begin. Can I get either of you anything?" Both men declined. "I'll be right back. Whatever you need to discuss can wait a few minutes."

Maggie loitered in the break room while a new pot of coffee finished brewing. The police chief and Alex normally saw eye to eye on things. She wondered what their disagreement was about. She filled her cup and returned to her office.

"So, good morning, again." The two men sat rigidly in their chairs, studiously avoiding eye contact with one another. "It's obvious we have a problem. Chief Thomas, I'd like to hear from you, first."

"Alex is interfering with our investigation, ma'am," he replied.

"From where I sit, you don't have an investigation," Alex said. "There's nothing to interfere with."

Maggie interceded. "Which investigation are you talking about?"

"The simultaneous fires at my law office and my home," Alex said. "They occurred more than a year ago, and we're still no closer to an arrest. The insurance company investigator concluded they were both arson, but Chief Thomas' department hasn't even gotten that far."

Chief Thomas spread his hands and shrugged. "We don't have the manpower to investigate everything right now. The fraud and embezzlement from the town and the pension fund is our top priority."

Alex snorted. "And how are those investigations coming along? I don't see you making any progress there, either."

"If you'd get me those documents from the offshore banks, I'd have something to work with. Haven't they complied with your subpoenas? Why is it taking so long?" the chief retorted.

Maggie leaned across her desk. "That's enough. We don't need to throw rocks at each other. There are enough people on the outside doing that as it is." She sat back in her chair and addressed the chief of police.

"I agree with Alex—we need to catch the people who set those fires. If the insurance company has determined it's arson, what's the hold up?"

"Their evidence isn't enough to make an arrest. We need proof that will stand up in a criminal court. Special Counsel Scanlon, here, understands that better than anyone."

Alex glanced away.

"We believe the fires were set by professionals. Probably mob connected. We've uncovered nothing to tie this to anybody."

"That's the part that frustrates me the most," Alex interjected.

"I understand, Alex. I really do. It frustrates me, too. And I think your car crash after the candidate's debate was no accident, either. Same deal—a clean crime scene, with no evidence to go on," the chief concluded.

"What are you suggesting we do, Alex?" Maggie said, turning to him.

"I'd like to have the team of detectives report directly to me. Maybe with constant supervision, they'll be more motivated."

"You think I'm not doing my job?" the chief began before Maggie cut him off.

"That's ridiculous, Alex, and you know it. You can't investigate crimes where you're the victim."

"I've done some research on that point of law, actually ..." he began.

"Case closed, Alex. My answer is no. Chief Thomas has my complete confidence. Our resources are stretched to the max, and he's doing an admirable job under the circumstances."

"Thank you, ma'am," Chief Thomas replied and sank back into his chair.

"And he's right, Alex. He needs those records from the offshore banks. Quit digging around in matters that don't concern you and work on the things you can do something about."

Alex's eyes narrowed. "I'm sorry I wasted all of our time," he spat and stalked out of the room.

"That didn't go as planned, did it, Chief? Instead of calming him down, I've thrown gasoline on the fire."

"He's been awfully touchy lately," Chief Thomas replied.

"And who can blame him? He and his partner have been the victims of serious—almost fatal—crimes, and no one is even under suspicion? I'd be at your throat, too."

The chief winced at the rebuke.

"Don't use the fraud investigation as an excuse, either. If you're so undermanned, we can bring in the feds."

"We've been over that before. If we call in the feds we'll lose control over the case. We have ideas about who's responsible. We just don't have solid evidence yet."

Maggie raised her brows. "When were you going to tell me?"

Chief Thomas looked away.

"Don't you think you can trust me? I wasn't living here when the fraud and embezzlement took place. And I can keep a secret. Forensic accountants are ethically bound to keep their clients' confidences." She caught his eye and held his gaze.

He slowly nodded. "Okay. We've uncovered evidence linking Chuck Delgado to two men with arson priors who we know were in the area the morning of the fires."

"Delgado's involvement isn't terribly surprising. He's always struck me as being a sleazy character. So what's the next step?"

"Delgado has been rumored to be affiliated with one of the Chicago mobs for years. He's good at keeping his hands clean, and I think his brother, Ron—the smarter of the two of them—helps with that. I'm not sure if Ron is on the inside or not." He rose and began pacing in front of her desk. "I don't want to nail two cheap thugs from Chicago. They're expendable to the organization. Someone else will take their place before the jail cell shuts behind them. I want to nail Chuck Delgado. He's on the town council, for heaven's sake. We need to clean the corruption out of Westbury's government."

"I agree with you wholeheartedly," Maggie replied.

"I need more time to make my case. I'm betting it's all tied together. The people behind the fires and Alex's accident are behind the fraud and embezzlement."

"What's your next step?"

"I'm tapping our network of informants. It's slow, tedious work with unreliable results. We need to carefully vet all of the tips we receive. Most of them turn out to be false. But they're all we've got at the moment. They'll eventually produce the results we want."

Maggie nodded slowly. She reached for the handle of her bottom desk drawer, where she kept Frank Haynes' missing cell phone. Should she turn it over to the chief? Was that fair to Frank? She paused. "What about other councilmembers? Anything on any of them? Frank Haynes is pretty chummy with Delgado. They usually vote the same way on issues."

Chief Thomas shook his head. "Nothing on anyone else. But we're keeping our eyes peeled."

Maggie released the handle and rose from her chair. "How much longer do you think you'll need?" She crossed the room to where he was standing and walked him to the door.

"Impossible to predict. This case could break wide open at any time."

"Let's hope that it does," Maggie said, fixing him with a stern look as he exited her office.

Maggie shut the door behind him and slumped into her chair. She had hoped to bridge the growing gap between Alex and the chief, but the meeting had only made matters worse. She glanced at her bottom desk drawer. Since Frank Haynes wasn't a suspect, she really should give his cell phone back to him. If she were honest with herself, she hadn't done so already because she wanted to confirm that Don Upton and Frank had conspired to convince her to resign her position as mayor. They had almost succeeded, and the phone might offer proof of their complicity. Still, the prospect of snooping through his phone was distasteful to her. How would she feel if the shoe were on the other foot? She would be livid—would feel violated—if a colleague went through her phone.

Maggie pulled it out of her drawer and pressed the on button. The battery life was at twenty percent. She had to be certain. She'd snoop through his phone until the battery gave out.

Maggie opened the contact list and began scrolling; there was a listing for Lyndon Upton. He and Frank had worked together on the town's budget, so that wasn't surprising. She checked his text messages. There was nothing other than the fateful New Year's Eve message from Upton that she and John had already seen. She finally looked at his list of recent calls. There were a dozen calls between the two men during December. They had been plotting against her, she was certain of it. But conspiring to remove a political opponent from office was the nature of politics. More importantly, it wasn't evidence of criminal activity.

She turned off the phone and replaced it in her drawer. She'd done what she'd wanted to do and uncovered nothing that she didn't already know. She needed to get the phone back to him anonymously, but in such a way that he would wonder if she knew about his duplicity. Frank Haynes should sweat over this. A smile curled around her lips; she had the perfect plan.

Chapter 15

Frank Haynes turned the collar of his cashmere coat up against the biting wind and stamped his feet. Maybe David had decided the afternoon was too cold to bring Dodger to the agility course. Haynes checked his watch. They should be here by now. He turned and was heading to his car when he heard David call his name and an enthusiastic dog of medium build and indiscriminate origin flashed in front of him, then circled back and stood, tail wagging expectantly.

Haynes stooped to greet the exuberant canine. "He's the picture of health," Haynes said to David as he approached. "I would never have recognized him as that poor creature from the shelter. You've done wonders for him."

David shrugged, but Haynes knew that he was pleased by the compliment.

"Let me show you what he can do," David said. "Come on, Dodger!" He led the dog to the start of the agility course, commanded him to sit, and then released him to start. Haynes had seen dogs running agility courses on television, but he'd never seen anything like the scene playing out before him. Dodger flew around the course—turning, jumping, and leaping—with flawless grace and complete abandon. When he was done, he raced into the open arms of his master, who fell onto his back and wrestled with the squirming, licking dynamo that was Dodger.

Frank Haynes opened his mouth to congratulate David but stopped himself, sure that his voice would crack. David Wheeler was so like Frank had been at that age. Haynes couldn't help but wonder if things wouldn't have gone very differently in his own life if he had known about agility courses when he was David's age.

"Most impressive!" he called as he walked over to the pair. "Did you train him to do that?"

"A little. He's a natural. Everybody says so. It's so cold; I don't think any of the other regulars will be out today. But one guy has a dog that's won national awards, and Dodger beats his dog every time. He thinks I should enter Dodger in competitions."

"Why don't you? I bet it'd be a lot of fun. Are there any around here?"

"There's one in Westbury next month. The rest are out of town."

"So will you compete in the one here?"

"It costs to enter," David said. "We don't have the money." David glanced at Haynes. "I know everyone thinks my dad stole all that money from the town, but he didn't. We're broke. I'm saving my pay from Forever Friends for college."

Haynes paused and fixed David with his gaze. He chose his words carefully. "I'll spot you the entrance fees. If you win a monetary price, you'll need to repay me, but if Dodger doesn't win, we'll wipe the slate clean. Does that sound fair?"

David nodded vigorously. "Thanks, Mr. Haynes. And don't worry—Dodger will win! You'll get your money back."

Haynes smiled and put his arm around the boy and squeezed his shoulder. "Good. And if he wins here in Westbury, we'll enter him in other competitions. Same deal."

"Come on, Dodger. We need to practice," David cried as he raced back to the course with Dodger in hot pursuit. David pointed to the first obstacle, and Dodger returned to the course for round two.

Frank Haynes made his way to his car, turning down the collar of his coat and unfastening the top button. The afternoon suddenly seemed warmer.

Chapter 16

Maggie groped for her cell phone to turn off the alarm she set for the kittens' midnight feedings. She shoved her feet into the slippers waiting at the side of her bed, poked her arms through the sleeves of her bathrobe, and trudged down the stairs alone. Eve had long since abandoned her on these late-night treks to the laundry room.

Maggie prepared the kitten formula and carefully squeezed into the room. She didn't fancy a late-night romp through Rosemont, chasing after them—especially the one with four white paws. He was definitely the ringleader of any mischief.

His was the first head to pop out of the blanket-lined box where they slept. She picked him up and began feeding him as he nestled close to her chest. When he was done, she lowered him to the box, but he squirmed free and attempted to jump to the top of the stack of neatly folded towels on the chair by the door. He fell short of his mark, but his claws caught on a towel and he brought the entire stack tumbling to the floor. Maggie sighed. She simply didn't have the energy to do anything about it tonight. The fatigue of these round-the-clock feedings was catching up to her, and she still had the rest to feed.

Maggie couldn't get away from Town Hall in the middle of the afternoon. During the day, she had help. Sam Torres succumbed to the prodding from his wife and reluctantly agreed to take the midafternoon feedings. He stopped in on his way to one of the handyman jobs that occupied his afternoons after he finished his shift in the school's maintenance department. David Wheeler came every morning before school to feed them, too. *What was the saying about raising children? It takes a whole village? Well ... the same holds true for raising motherless kittens*, Maggie thought.

⸺✦⸺

The next morning with coffee in hand, Maggie returned to the laundry room to help David. "John says you're quite good with animals," she observed as she picked up the towels the kitten had pulled off the chair the night before.

David shrugged, but she could tell he was pleased. "He told me you're working at Forever Friends, too. How's your dog?"

"He's amazing," David enthused. "You should see him. I've been training him on the agility course at the dog park. Everybody says he's the best they've ever seen."

"Is that right?" said Maggie, settling against the dryer. "I've only seen it on television, but it looks like the dogs are having tremendous fun."

"They are," David continued. "I'm going to enter Dodger in the agility contest at the old armory in a couple of weeks."

"That's an excellent idea."

"Mr. Haynes is giving me the money to enter Dodger in the competition. If I win, I'll pay him back, but if not, he says that's okay by him."

Maggie paused, digesting this news. Just when she had Frank Haynes firmly painted with a black brush, he went and did something genuinely nice.

"You'd better be on your way to school, and I need to head to work. John told me that you'd like to take one of the kittens when they're old enough to be separated. Have you decided which one?"

"This one here, with the four white feet."

59

Maggie nodded. She had a feeling that the most adventurous one would be a good fit for David.

Frank Haynes wove his way along the sidelines, searching the sea of dogs and their handlers walking the courses and taking trial runs. Two courses had been set up in the old armory. He picked his way around crates, blankets, folding chairs, and beverage coolers to the course where Dodger would be competing. The noise level was deafening and his fine leather shoes were covered in an inch of mud (and probably worse), but instead of being annoyed, he found all of the chaos invigorating.

He searched in vain for David and Dodger and almost tripped over them when he stepped back to avoid being sideswiped by a large Newfoundland running off course.

"Sorry," David said. "I was just coming to let you know we're here."

Frank pulled David to a spot out of the main line of travel between the ring and the entrance.

"How are you both doing today?"

"I don't know, Mr. Haynes. I read up on this on the Internet, but it's a lot different in person. I think Dodger is freaked out by the other dogs and all of the noise."

Frank Haynes bent over to pat their athlete. He didn't want to say a discouraging word, but he had to agree. He glanced up at the boy, who was searching his face with a mournful expression. *Good grief,* Haynes thought. *He's looking to me for words of wisdom and comfort.*

Haynes quickly stood and clapped his hand on David's shoulder. "You'll both be fine. You can't expect to start anything at the top. Hard work makes your success worthwhile. In the meantime, just go out there and have fun." *Where in the world had that come from?* Haynes wondered. Sometimes he surprised himself. He'd been doing that a lot lately.

The cloud lifted from David's face. "You mean it? Because I think we're going to lose your entrance fee."

Haynes dismissed the worry with a wave of his hand. "Don't give it a second thought. Now get ready."

Haynes watched the trials with increasing interest. The dogs were having fun and the communication between handler and dog— limited to voice commands, hand signals, and body movements—was impressive. The first few contestants all had clear runs, but based upon what Haynes had seen at the dog park, Dodger would beat their time by a country mile. He maneuvered himself to the front of the crowd as David and Dodger approached the starting line.

Dodger sailed over the first two jumps and fairly flew off the A-frame. He hesitated on the teeter-totter and lost time, but picked it up going through the tunnel. Haynes clapped his encouragement from the sidelines. Maybe the unlikely duo would pull this off. The weave poles, however, proved very difficult. Haynes couldn't tell if Dodger got through every pole, but he didn't think so. And his failure to pause in the pause box sealed his fate. Dodger was undaunted by his poor showing, but David's shoulders sagged.

Frank Haynes approached them. "Well done, you two."

"You're kidding, right? He did well in the beginning because he's familiar with those obstacles. But he didn't listen to a single command from me when he needed to. I'm not much of a handler," he concluded morosely.

"Nonsense. This is your first contest. And you've had no coaching. You can't expect to do this without a lot of practice and some training for both of you."

"Are there classes we could take?" David asked, hope creeping into his voice.

"Of course there are. Let me check into it, and I'll let you know. And don't worry about the cost. I think Forever Friends should sponsor you, since you're both affiliated with us. You'll be our sports team, so to speak. This'll be good publicity," Haynes said, warming to the idea.

"That'd be cool."

"Leave it to me," Haynes replied. "Now, let's gather up our future champion and get out of here. I'm buying you lunch."

Frank Haynes thought he was well acquainted with the size of a teenage boy's appetite, but if all of his paying customers ate as much as David, his profits would triple. After feeding David an astounding number of hamburgers, he placed a call to John Allen.

"John. Wondering if I could get some advice."

"Hello, Frank," John answered. He didn't trust the man—especially now that he suspected Haynes of conspiring to manipulate Maggie into resigning the mayoral seat—but his dedication to animals couldn't be denied.

"How would you go about training a dog to compete in agility contests?"

John had to hand it to him—Frank Haynes never ceased to amaze him. "Are you thinking of entering your dog, Sally? Border collies are naturals at the sport. It would help with her weight issues."

"I'm asking for a friend. But now that you mention it, I might take it up myself. How would I start?"

"The best place is a group class. They've got them going on regularly over in Springerville."

"None here in Westbury?" Haynes asked. David probably wouldn't be able to take part in a class out of town.

"Not that I know of. But I'm in touch with the instructor, and if there's enough interest here, I'm sure she'd offer a class. Let me post a notice in my reception area and make some calls."

"That'd be great, John."

"Give me a week."

"Put me on the list. And David Wheeler and Dodger."

"I didn't know they were into agility."

"You should see them at the dog park, John. Dodger is incredible. And David is great with animals. That's why I'm asking about training."

"I've seen that side of him recently. It's nice of you to help him, Frank."

"It's the least I can do, considering what happened to his father."

Both men were silent. "William appreciates it, Frank; I'm sure he does," John said quietly.

Frank Haynes swallowed the lump in his throat and wished John a pleasant day.

Chapter 17

Loretta approached the closed door of Frank Haynes' office with trepidation. He'd been acting strangely lately—harsh and morose one minute and cheerful to the point of giddiness the next—and it had gotten worse since he returned from his vacation to Florida. She'd asked him about his trip, and he'd shut her down, fast, saying it had nothing to do with Haynes Enterprises.

She sighed and summoned her courage as she raised her hand to knock. This would be the fourth time in the last three weeks that she'd left early to pick Nicole up from school. Her daughter just couldn't shake this bug that had gotten hold of her.

Loretta knocked lightly and recoiled at the gruff "what" that greeted her when she poked her head around the door.

"Sorry to disturb you, Mr. Haynes. My daughter's school just called. Nicole is sick, and I need to leave early to pick her up and take her to the babysitter."

"Again?!" Haynes exploded. "You're gone more than you're here! Haven't you taken this kid to the doctor?"

A wave of anger traveled from her toes to the top of her head. She was sure she must be beet red. "Of course I've taken her to the doctor. And I've followed all of the doctor's instructions to the letter. But she's getting worse every day. I'm not sure what to do now." To Loretta's horror, a sob escaped her lips. "I know I've been gone a lot. I'll drop her at the babysitter and come right back."

Haynes waved her away. "See that you do. I can't keep paying you for time that you're not working."

Loretta paused, searching for a response that wouldn't get her fired.

Haynes looked up from his desk. "Get going. The sooner you leave, the sooner you'll be back."

Loretta pulled his door shut firmly, stopping just short of slamming it. She grabbed her purse and her coat and headed to her car.

———

Nicole, indeed, was not feeling well when Loretta arrived in the nurse's office. "Her hands and feet are swollen," the nurse said, "and her eyes are puffy. This isn't a normal cold. I'd take her back to the doctor, if I were you." She stared at Loretta.

Loretta examined Nicole closely and nodded. "I've got to go back to work now."

"Some things are more important than work," the nurse admonished.

Loretta spun on the woman. "Do you think I don't know that? Do you think I'm not concerned?" The nurse took a step back. "Well, I am. But I also need to keep my job. I'm a single parent, you know."

"Surely your boss will understand about a sick child," the nurse began.

"You don't know Frank Haynes," Nicole retorted. "Come on, sweetie. Let's get you home and into bed." Loretta grabbed Nicole's backpack and took her hand. She turned back to the nurse. "I'll take her to Urgent Care as soon as I get off work."

———

Loretta arrived back at Haynes Enterprises shortly before five o'clock. She'd been gone for almost two hours, so she would need to work until seven to make up the time. With any luck, she'd have Nicole checked in to Urgent Care by eight. Thank goodness her babysitter needed the extra money and was available to keep her kids extra hours, but the unbudgeted expense was wreaking havoc on her finances. She'd maxed out the cash advance on her credit card.

Loretta threw her coat onto the coat rack and slid into her chair. Everything on her desk was as she'd left it. Frank Haynes' door remained shut. She wondered if he'd even left his office while she was gone.

Loretta had just finished preparing the bank deposit when his office door opened and Frank Haynes appeared, briefcase in hand. He shrugged into his overcoat and switched off his office light.

"How's your daughter? What's her name again?"

"Nicole. And she's worse. We don't know what's wrong with her. I'm going to take her to Urgent Care tonight. But don't worry," Loretta added hastily, "I won't miss any more work."

Haynes cleared his throat and studied his shoes. "All right, then. Let's call it a day. You need to get your kid to the doctor. You can finish that up tomorrow."

Loretta regarded him closely. It wasn't like Frank Haynes to consider anyone else's feelings. "Thank you, Mr. Haynes," she said as she rose. "I really appreciate this."

—◦◦◦—

Loretta and Nicole entered the Urgent Care clinic shortly before seven o'clock. The waiting room was packed with others who, like Loretta, needed to wait until after work to attend to their ailments. She signed Nicole in and looked for two chairs together. A middle-aged man in work boots and a rugged jacket caught her eye and motioned for her to take his seat and the empty chair next to him.

"Thank you so much," she said as she and Nicole settled in for what appeared to be a long wait. The man nodded and took a single seat on the other side of the waiting room.

Loretta reached into her purse and took out the *Angelina Ballerina* book that was Nicole's favorite. Nicole nestled against her mother and was soon lulled to sleep by the rhythm of the familiar story. Exhausted herself, Loretta closed the book and enjoyed the short break of doing nothing.

The waiting room eventually began to clear and mother and daughter were called into an exam room at eight fifteen. The young nurse apologized for the wait, took notes on a tablet as Loretta cataloged Nicole's recent complaints, and took her vital signs.

Nicole lay back on the examining table and was soon asleep. Loretta foraged in the stack of well-worn magazines in the rack on the wall and was thumbing listlessly through a six-month-old copy of *Highlights* when the doctor knocked and entered the room.

He read the nurse's notes on his tablet. "Do you mind if I wake her?" he asked, turning to Loretta.

"Go ahead."

"Hi, Nicole," he said, gently touching her shoulder. "I'm here to examine you. Can you sit up for me, please?"

Loretta rose and helped the drowsy child remain upright.

"This may be a bit cold," he said as he put the stethoscope under her blouse and listened to her breathing. "Can you open wide?" he asked as he looked at her throat. "What a good patient you are," he praised. "Best one all night." Nicole smiled. "I'm going to look into your eyes, now. The light is real bright, but it won't take me long." He finished his examination.

"Okay, good job," he said to Nicole. "You can lay back down while your mother and I talk." He turned to Loretta.

"She's a bit congested, which is consistent with the cold you mentioned. Her throat looks fine. Ordinarily, I'd say there's nothing else wrong with this child. But she's unusually lethargic and the swelling is a concern."

"So what do we do?" Loretta asked.

"I'd recommend a urine test and a blood test," he said. "They'll give us more information to go on."

"What could it be?" Loretta asked, unable to conceal her alarm.

"I honestly think she has nothing more than a lingering cold. Anything else would be very rare. Let's not worry about that until we get the results of the tests."

"Okay," Loretta replied. "Do you do that here?"

"We can," he said. "But the tests will be much cheaper if you have your primary care doctor do them."

Loretta nodded.

"We've got your doctor's information here," he said, pointing to his tablet. "I'll send my report to him before I leave tonight."

"Thank you, Doctor," Loretta said as she reached over to rouse Nicole.

"Get her in to see your primary as soon as possible, and go home and get some rest," he said kindly. "Moms need to take care of themselves, too."

Chapter 18

True to his word, John collected enough names to persuade the agility trainer to start a class in Westbury. The first class was scheduled for the dog park on Saturday morning at eight o'clock.

Frank Haynes groaned when his alarm went off at six thirty that Saturday. He pushed himself out of bed and could see that Sally, his border collie mix, had no interest in leaving her warm bed, either.

"Come on, girl," he cajoled. "This is for you. It's gonna be fun."

The dog thumped her tail tentatively.

Haynes clapped his hands, and she dutifully rolled out of her blanket and followed him to the kitchen.

David and Dodger were already streaking around the agility course when Frank Haynes and Sally arrived shortly before eight. Haynes thought he recognized an assistant manager from one of his restaurants and nodded at the woman, who beamed in return. He hoped he wouldn't be called upon to remember her name.

The instructor quickly took charge, issuing orders in equal measure to the dogs and their handlers. Haynes was pleased to see that David hung on her every word and easily implemented her advice. He and Sally, however, were another matter. At the halfway point in the lesson, the instructor divided the group in two. He and Sally were consigned to the remedial group. Even so, it was invigorating to be up and outside on a Saturday morning, instead of drinking his fifth

69

cup of coffee while pouring over the cash flow statements of Haynes Enterprises. And Sally was having fun.

The instructor reunited the groups to hand out homework for the next week. Frank knew he wouldn't look at the assignments. David, however, was studying the paper she gave him and asking questions. He turned to Haynes. "This doesn't seem too hard. Dodger's got most of this down already."

Haynes smiled. "I'm not sure Sally and I are cut out for this."

"Don't be discouraged," David replied. "This was only your first time." He knelt to pet Sally. "Border collies are naturals at this agility stuff. You just need to practice with her." He brought his head up and looked at Haynes. "Why don't we practice together, Mr. Haynes? I can help you with Sally—just to get you two started."

Haynes opened his mouth to dismiss the idea, but something in the boy's expression stopped him. When was the last time anyone offered to help him with anything? "All right," Haynes said slowly, a smile stealing across his lips. "You're on. But you'll need to start calling me Frank. Have you had breakfast?" he asked, knowing that this boy could down another full meal even if he'd already eaten at home. David shook his head. "Let's head over to Pete's Bistro. They have the best pancakes in town."

Chapter 19

Maggie walked David to the kitchen, where the kittens were now holding court. Roman gently nosed them off the countertop. The kitten with four white paws, however, had other ideas. He leapt back to the countertop and streaked away with Roman barking and running along the floor in hot pursuit. The kitten came to a screeching halt, boxing himself in between the toaster and the coffeemaker, and Roman picked him up with his gentle mouth and placed him on the tile floor where David scooped him up.

The adventuresome kitten also liked to bait Eve, noiselessly sneaking up on her as she lay snoring in her basket in the corner of the kitchen. The kitten would pounce on her then bolt before Eve could uncoil herself from her cozy perch. Eve chased him the first time, but now she gave all the kittens a wide berth. She'd experienced enough whacks on her nose from their razor-sharp claws to know that they didn't fancy being chased through the house by a slobbery-mouthed dog.

"He's almost old enough for you to take home," Maggie said, handing David a bottle while the kitten squirmed against his chest. "Have you named him yet?"

David nodded as the kitten nursed greedily. "Namor," he said, sliding his eyes to hers.

"That's an unusual name. Sounds exotic—almost Egyptian."

"It's Roman spelled backwards," David said. "I thought it was fitting."

Maggie grinned. "Indeed it is. Very clever of you, David."

She picked up one of the other kittens and started giving her a bottle. "I was going to keep the others, but I think Sam Torres is getting attached to that one," she said, indicating the smallest one of the litter. "When he started coming here in the afternoons to feed them, you'd have thought he was going for a root canal. I could tell he was annoyed and only agreed to help because Joan put him up to it. But these little guys get under your skin, don't they?" She nuzzled the one she was holding.

"I need to name the ones I'm keeping. Any suggestions?"

David shrugged.

"So, how did Dodger do in his agility contest?"

"We started out pretty good, but it all fell apart fast. Frank—Mr. Haynes told me to call him that—said that Forever Friends will sponsor us, and he's paying for us to take lessons."

"Really?" Maggie replied.

"Yep. And the classes are great. Dodger and I are learning a lot. We'll be so much better at our next competition. Even Frank and Sally are taking lessons."

"You don't say." And this time Maggie couldn't hide her astonishment. "I never thought Frank Haynes would tear himself away from his business to pursue a hobby."

"She's a sweet thing, Sally is. And with training, she might be almost as good as Dodger. I'm helping them practice between lessons."

What an odd couple these two must make, Maggie thought. *David Wheeler and Frank Haynes. But it appears the alliance is good for both of them.*

After they finished feeding the kittens, Maggie picked a large box off of the kitchen counter. "I'll walk you to the door."

"Here, let me take this for you, ma'am," David said. "Where does it go?"

"Up in the attic, I'm afraid. You don't have to do that. I can manage."

"Don't be ridiculous," he replied, already halfway up the stairs to the second level. "Just show me where to put it."

Maggie followed him up the first set of stairs, then led the way to the attic, making sure that the doorstop was firmly in place before they ascended the final set of steps. Sam had fixed the knob after that disastrous day just a few months ago when she'd been locked in the drafty old attic, but she was still leery of it.

"Wow! Look at this place," David said as he set the box where Maggie indicated. "What's in here? I bet there's all sorts of cool stuff."

"I haven't had a chance to get through it yet." She turned to survey the attic. "Just moving things around and cleaning it up will be a huge task. But I agree—we'll uncover some interesting things." She pointed to the secretary in the corner where she'd found a treasure trove of tarnished silver during her fateful confinement. "That large cabinet—next to the broken-down hat rack—is full of old sterling silver pieces. I'm dying to bring all of them downstairs. They have to be cleaned and cataloged."

"If you could use some help, I'm good at odd jobs."

"Really?" Maggie said, turning to him. "Rosemont is full of odd jobs that need to be done. Do you have time?"

"We've got a three-day weekend next week. I could get started then, and I can work over spring break."

"You and your mom won't be going anywhere?"

David shook his head.

"You're on! We'll bring all of the silver downstairs and spread it out on the dining room table."

"I'll see you on Saturday. Frank and I always go to Pete's for breakfast right after our agility lesson."

Would wonders never cease? Maggie thought.

"I'll come over as soon as we're done."

Chapter 20

David arrived midmorning on the gray and cheerless Saturday. "This looks like the perfect movie set for a haunted attic," Maggie remarked as she turned on the lights. David took a step back. "I'm kidding. There're no ghosts at Rosemont," and as she said it, she wasn't so sure.

"Let's clear a path to that secretary in the corner," she said, pointing with her flashlight.

"That cabinet thing?" David asked.

"Yes. It's called a secretary. Anyway—that's where I found all of the silver. There may be more up here, too. I didn't find any downstairs in the butler's pantry, which is where it would have been stored back in the day."

David shrugged. It was clear he had no knowledge of such things.

"The butler would have been responsible for keeping it polished and accounted for. It would have been kept in a locked cabinet," she continued. David moved boxes and slid furniture aside as they made their way to the secretary.

The key remained in the lock where Maggie had abandoned it, and she slowly opened the doors. The sight still made her gasp.

"Where do you want it?" David asked, reaching in to begin loading his arms with pitchers.

"We'll take it all down to the dining room. I've cleaned off the table and padded it with blankets so nothing scratches the wood."

Maggie swiftly reached over and took two pitchers from him that he was holding by the handles with one hand, allowing them to knock against each other. "I know this stuff isn't breakable, but it can dent and scratch. We have to be careful with it."

"Are we taking it all downstairs a piece at a time?" He wasn't able to conceal his incredulity.

"I brought some empty boxes and towels up here. We can cushion each silver piece in towels so it doesn't rub against anything else. How would that be?"

David nodded and they got busy, Maggie handing a piece of silver to David, David placing it carefully in a box, and Maggie checking and eventually redoing everything David did. Although it took all morning, they finally moved the contents of the attic secretary to the dining room table.

Maggie was thrilled with what they'd found so far: an ornate tea set, a chocolate pot, a large flatware set bearing a family crest, and a dozen demitasse spoons, each engraved with a sign of the zodiac, along with trays, pitchers, and serving pieces of every description. Her fingers itched to pull out the silver polish to start restoring them to their former luster.

"That's everything from the cabinet," David said. "Do you want me to look in that stack of boxes next to it, to see if there's any more?"

Maggie tore her attention away from the array on her dining room table. "That'd be a good idea," she answered. "Do you need me to go back up with you?"

"No. I've got it. And I know to be careful. I'll make sure we brought all the silver down here, and I'll organize stuff for when I come back on spring break. That's if you still want me," he added hastily.

"Of course I do," Maggie assured him. "You've been extremely helpful, and I appreciate how careful you've been with all of this."

"It looks pretty cool. Hard to believe anyone ever really used all of it." He paused, eying the table. "Glad I wasn't a butler," he continued, and Maggie laughed. "Me, too. You go do your thing in the attic. I'll start polishing all this."

Maggie tuned to the classical music station on her radio—somehow, that seemed fitting for the task at hand—while David returned to the attic. He found two additional boxes of silver, which he ferried downstairs to Maggie. He spent the rest of the afternoon in the attic moving the furniture to the area in front of the windows and arranging boxes and trunks in neat rows along the far wall. In the center, he created an area of items comprising the miscellany of lives lived at Rosemont: dress forms and golf clubs, curtain rods and tennis rackets, plant stands and drying racks. He never noticed, in the dim light of the incandescent bulbs, the folder labeled *F.H./Rosemont* that slipped to the floor and was trapped underneath an old steamer trunk.

Maggie had barely made a start on the items covering the table and would soon be out of polish. She was heading upstairs with cookies and a soda for David when she spotted John's Suburban swinging to a stop by her front door. She opened it as he stepped out of the car.

"Just checking on my best girl. You've got some bad history with that attic. I wanted to make sure we didn't have a repeat of that unfortunate incident."

Maggie smiled and wrapped her arms around him. "Aren't you the most thoughtful fiancé? Everything's fine here. You won't believe what we've found up there!"

John steeled himself for a lengthy discussion on vintage silver—a subject he had no interest in, but one he knew she loved talking about. "I have a suggestion," he said, brushing a kiss along her hair. "Why don't you call Judy Young to come over after she closes up

Celebrations? She's an antiques buff. I'm sure she'd be excited to hear all about it."

"And you wouldn't, would you?" Maggie asked, rocking back to look at him closely.

"You've got me there. It's not one of my core interests."

"Your loss. Lots of fascinating stuff there. But now my lips are sealed. I need to run out for more silver polish. I'll swing by Celebrations and talk to Judy. I may need her expertise."

"Is David still here?"

"Yes—working like a maniac. He wouldn't even stop for lunch. I was just taking him a snack."

"Let me see if he needs a hand," John said. "And I think it's time to let him take his kitten home. I talked to his mother today, and she agreed."

"Wait till you hear the name he's chosen for him," Maggie said as they climbed the stairs.

"What do you think, Ms. Martin?" David asked, turning as he heard her footsteps on the stairs.

"You've done a marvelous job," Maggie said, stepping into the attic.

"Hey, David," John said, extending his hand. "How would you like to take your kitten home today? Your mother says it's okay."

David beamed.

"Let's go get him. Maggie tells me you've picked out an unusual name?"

"Namor," David said proudly. He paused and watched John's puzzled expression change to a grin. "Very fitting. Roman would like that. Let's go get Namor. I've got a cat carrier for you and some food, litter, and a litter box—to get you started."

"Thank you, Dr. Allen," David said as he rushed down the stairs to the laundry room.

Namor, however, was not quite ready to leave Rosemont. He shot out of the laundry room as soon as David opened the door and tore through the kitchen heading for the stairs. John got a hand on him as he rounded the turn at the second-floor landing, but Namor wriggled free and made a beeline for Maggie's room, with Eve in hot pursuit. Maggie snagged Eve's collar and managed to drag her out of the bedroom and close the door.

She turned to John and David who were now standing in the hallway outside of her room. "That sure happened fast," she exclaimed.

"Sorry, Ms. Martin. I didn't expect him to be that fast."

"At least we know where he is. Let me put Eve outside before you go in there," she said, gesturing to her room.

"I'll get the carrier and some cat treats, in case he's hidden himself away somewhere," John said.

Namor, as feared, was nowhere to be found. The three of them looked high and low, in every nook and cranny, with no sign of the kitten.

"He couldn't vanish into thin air," Maggie sighed in exasperation.

"Let's get a flashlight," John said.

David wrapped his arms around himself and shifted from foot to foot. "You don't think he went up the chimney, do you?"

"No," John turned to the boy. "He's here, and we're going to find him. Cats have an uncanny aptitude for hide-and-seek. Don't worry—he's not lost. In fact, I'll bet he's enjoying himself immensely right now."

David straightened and nodded.

Maggie retrieved the flashlight from the drawer in her nightstand and handed it to John. "I'll go downstairs and get two more."

Twenty minutes later, Maggie was on her hands and knees, shining the light under her bed for the third time when she noticed a slight bulge in the fabric lining the bottom of her box spring. "John," she called. "Can you come and look at this?" And as she said it, the bulge changed shape.

"Yep," she said, rocking back on her heels. "That silly cat has gotten himself into the box spring!"

John laughed as he took the flashlight and trained it under the bed. "You're right. There he is."

David let out a low whistle. "Here," he said. "Let me see if he'll come out to me." He lay on his back and reached a long arm under the bed until he touched the lump. "It's him all right. C'mon, Namor," he coaxed. "Get out of there."

"Is he moving?" John asked.

"He's trying to. I think he's caught on something."

"We'll have to take the bed apart," Maggie said, dismantling the mound of decorative pillows.

David and John slid the mattress to the floor. Namor began caterwauling as they shifted the box spring off the bed frame.

"At least we know his lungs are good," John observed.

Namor began thrashing, his sharp claws tearing the batting that sealed the underside of the box spring.

"Let's cut him out before he does any more damage to himself or my bed," Maggie said, inserting a pair of scissors near the spot where Namor flailed and swiftly cut the fabric.

Namor shot out of the opening and David tackled him as he attempted to streak past.

"You rascal," David said, holding him tight. He placed Namor into the cat carrier and closed it securely. "Sorry about that, Ms. Martin."

"You've got a cat with quite a personality," John observed, and they all nodded in agreement.

The bell jingled as Maggie walked through the door of Celebrations shortly before closing time. Judy Young was at a table near the back, mediating a dispute over wedding invitations between a bride-to-be and her mother. She smiled at Maggie over her half-moon glasses.

"I think you've narrowed it down to these two?" she asked, gathering up two samples. "Why don't I let you take them home tonight to think about it? Can you have them back to me by noon on Monday? Good. Then it's settled." She rose and the two women followed suit.

"Either one will make a perfect choice," she said as she ushered them out the door.

Maggie burst out laughing as Judy turned to her. "Look who's the diplomat. Long day?"

Judy stretched. "Long and slow. Other than a handful of people buying birthday cards, it's been dead. And those two have been here for over four hours. They looked at every invitation in every book. They don't have the same taste or vision for this wedding, and neither of them can make a decision to save their life. God knows how they're going to plan a wedding." She patted Maggie's arm. "But you didn't come here to listen to me complain. What are you looking for?"

"Advice, really," Maggie said.

Judy arched her brow.

"Remember when I got locked in my attic? Did I tell you I found an old secretary full of vintage silver?"

Judy's head snapped up. "I remember you getting locked in. But you never mentioned vintage silver!"

"I've had it all moved downstairs, and I've started polishing it. In fact, I ran out of silver polish and just bought more. You should see this stuff—incredible!"

Judy's breathing quickened.

"John said to call you. That you're the local expert."

"He's right!" Judy said, flipping the Open sign on her door to Closed. "Let's get out of here. My day is suddenly looking up!"

Chapter 21

"Hey, John," Judy Young said, never taking her eyes from the treasure spread out on the massive dining room table at Rosemont.

"I can see I'm not needed," John said, winking at Maggie. "I'm on call tonight at the emergency animal hospital, so Roman and I will just head on home."

"Coward," Maggie said, walking them to the door.

"You better believe it. You won't get rid of her before midnight."

"That's fine by me. I'm lucky that she's knowledgeable and interested."

"What was it my grandmother used to say? Always count the silver?"

"I'm not worried about Judy," Maggie said.

John leaned in to kiss her. "Call me if you get lonely later."

Judy was circling the table like a lion stalking its prey when Maggie returned to the dining room.

"Incredible, isn't it?' Maggie asked.

"I'll say. You've got quite the collection. And it's from different periods. Mostly Victorian, but that little creamer in the center—next to the teapot—is almost certainly Revolutionary War era."

"Really? I thought it was too unadorned to be a contemporary of most of this stuff, but I had no idea it could be that old."

"If it's Paul Revere, you can probably retire. Let's take a look," she said as Maggie handed the piece to her.

"Nope. Sorry. But it's got a stamp and the patina is consistent with the era. Here," Judy said, handing the piece back to Maggie. "Hold it while I snap a photo of the mark with my phone. I'll go online and do some research."

"You don't have to do that," Maggie protested.

"I want to do it," Judy stated firmly. "This is the most fun I've had in ages. Makes me wish I had an attic full of old junk."

"Did you see this flatware?" Maggie asked, pointing to the side-board.

"Holy cow—how many pieces are there?"

"One hundred and fifty-five. I don't even know what some of them are supposed to be used for," Maggie said. "I know this is a tea-spoon, of course, and one of these must be a soup spoon, but what about this other spoon? It's almost the same size and shape as the soup spoon. Why are there two similar, but slightly different shapes?"

"Good question. Very observant of you. The smaller of the two is a bouillon spoon. You've also got both teaspoons and coffee spoons. See? The coffee spoons are a bit smaller."

"You're right. I hadn't noticed that. There're also fish forks and knives. The original Mrs. Martin must have been a very particular hostess to have owned all of these specialized pieces."

Judy turned one of the soup spoons over in her hand, examining the decoration on the handle. "I'm not sure that Mrs. Martin ever used this," she said.

"Really? Why do you say that?"

"Take a look at this. It's a family crest. I don't recall hearing about a Martin family crest. But I do remember the story of a wealthy Eng-lish family named Donaldson who lived in a mansion that stood where the high school is now. They made their money in banking and lost everything in the Great Depression. The story has it that the old couple jumped out of a third-story window on the night before they were to lose their home to foreclosure. A joint suicide."

Maggie shivered. "That's gruesome. Why would the Martins have the Donaldson's flatware? Maybe they bought it at a tag sale?"

Judy shook her head. "Not likely. The Martins wouldn't buy at a tag sale. It wouldn't conform to the Victorian sense of propriety and status."

Maggie nodded. "What, then?"

Judy leaned against the sideboard and contemplated the object in her hand. "They were probably friends with the Donaldsons—maybe very good friends. There weren't that many rich people in town. Maybe they stored the flatware in the attic for the Donaldsons so that their bill collectors wouldn't get it."

"Makes sense," Maggie agreed. "Flatware is easily portable—they could liquidate a piece at a time. It wouldn't be like trying to sell a tea set. And there are a few pieces missing."

"And when they killed themselves, the Martins just left it there. What else could they do? They couldn't use it."

"Yes," Maggie agreed. "They couldn't sell it, either, because they wouldn't want anyone to know that they had been helping the Donaldsons conceal assets from creditors."

The women exchanged a conspiratorial glance. "I'd use these, if I were you," Judy said. "Just think of them as the ultimate conversation piece."

Maggie shook her head. "I don't know about that. I'm finding them a little bit creepy and depressing. Plus, I really don't like that crest. It looks like a raven perched on rocks."

"You need to get it appraised and insured. In fact, you should do that with all of this as soon as possible. You've got a small fortune spread out here."

"I was thinking the same thing," Maggie said. "I'm really glad you came over tonight."

"Let's see what other treasures await," Judy said with a gleam in her eye. "Look at these demitasse spoons with the zodiac symbols engraved on their handles. Do you know why they did this?"

"No idea," Maggie smiled, drawn in by Judy's enthusiasm.

"The Victorians were fascinated with astrology, of course, but they also would have used these to mark the seating arrangement. Any hostess worth her salt would have known the sign of each of her guests."

It was almost midnight when they finished their first pass around the table. Maggie was exhausted, but Judy seemed to gather steam as the night wore on. "We've got a lot to do tomorrow," Judy said as Maggie ushered her to her car.

"Nonsense. You've done enough already—I wouldn't dream of interfering on your day off." Maggie stated firmly. She was happy with her newly uncovered treasures, but she wanted to relax and spend the day with John. This stuff had been in her attic for almost a decade—a few weeks on her dining room table wouldn't matter.

"Nothing I'd rather do," Judy replied in tones that indicated she would not be denied. "We need to catalog what you've got, and you'll need to call your insurance agent first thing Monday morning. They'll send an appraiser out here. We'll start right after early church. Have the coffee on. See you tomorrow," She patted Maggie's arm. Maggie stifled a yawn and waved as Judy pulled away.

Chapter 22

Maggie opened an eye and looked at her bedside clock. *Ugh,* she thought. *Time to get up and feed those kittens.* "Come on, Eve, we've got to get moving."

She snatched her cell phone from the nightstand and headed downstairs. She checked for messages after she'd fed Eve and the kittens and found a text from John:

Tied up at ER. No church for me. Will call later.

Maggie sighed and wandered into her dining room. She flipped the switch to the chandelier and the room jumped into brilliance, the silver spread out on the table acting like a giant mirror. *What a remarkable find,* she thought. *And what remarkable tales Judy Young will be telling about it.* Maggie didn't want word to get out. At least not until she had it all insured and safely stored.

There would be no going back to bed for her. She'd get ready for church and be there in time to stop Judy before she got started.

Maggie entered the parking lot at church forty minutes before the start of the first service. Judy pulled in behind her.

"I've never known you to be here so early," Judy called. "You normally slink in during the first hymn."

"I'm not that bad," Maggie protested. "I'm in my pew at least thirty seconds before the processional."

"What's up?" Judy asked, looking pointedly at Maggie.

"I wanted to catch you," Maggie stopped and pulled Judy aside. "I don't want anyone to know about the silver. Not yet. I was thinking about what you said. I want to get it insured and have most of it stored before we let anyone know it's at Rosemont."

"I was thinking the same thing," Judy nodded. "I know I'm a blabbermouth, but I wasn't going to say anything. You should talk to Sam Torres about installing a safe."

"Good suggestion. He and Joan are going to stop by this afternoon to pick up their kitten."

"That'll leave you with how many?"

"Four. David Wheeler took one, too."

Judy shook her head. "You've got your plate full."

Maggie stifled a yawn. "I hope I don't fall asleep during the sermon. Someone kept me up very late last night."

She managed to stay awake during the service, aware of Judy's watchful eye on her. She wasn't concentrating on the pastor's message or thinking about the silver, however. She was wrestling with the standstill in the investigations that were frustrating both Special Counsel Scanlon and Chief Thomas. She'd call her daughter in California this afternoon. Susan wasn't a prosecutor, but her instincts as a high-powered litigator were dead on and her insights were invaluable. Susan would offer practical solutions. Talking things through with her always helped Maggie organize her thoughts.

Maggie abruptly realized that the people on either side of her were standing. She reached for her hymnal and joined in the final hymn.

Judy intercepted her as soon as she shook the pastor's hand and stepped away. "Let's skip the social hour and get back to work, shall we?"

"Sure," Maggie said as she and Judy headed to their cars. They were halfway there when Maggie heard her name being called from behind. She turned to find Glenn and Gloria Vaughn hurrying toward her.

Maggie motioned for the elderly couple to stay where they were.

"Darn it," Judy muttered. "You're sunk now."

"Sorry," Maggie said over her shoulder to Judy. "Why don't you go change, and I'll call you when I'm on my way home?"

"Just try to keep it brief, okay?" Judy grumbled.

Maggie smiled at Glenn and Gloria, newlyweds at seventy-seven and eighty-two, respectively, and accepted a hug from each of them.

"How's the best mayor in the United States?" Glenn asked.

"I wouldn't know," Maggie replied.

"Spirits a bit low, dear?" Gloria chimed in.

"Things aren't exactly coming up roses in Westbury—or hadn't you heard?" she laughed.

"You helped us get Fairview Terraces out of foreclosure. Don't you forget that," Glenn stated sternly. "This mess didn't happen overnight, and it won't get fixed overnight. You're on the right track."

Maggie squeezed his arm. "That's just the vote of confidence I need right now. As for Fairview Terraces, I think that your ideas to rent out the recreation hall to the Westbury West Coast Swing Society and sponsor a farmers market on your campus put your finances in the black."

Gloria beamed. "He did a great job, didn't he?"

"We didn't call you over to brag about me," Glenn said.

"We heard you have kittens to give away," Gloria interjected.

Maggie laughed. "Word gets around in a small town, doesn't it? Are you looking to get a new cat?"

Glenn put his arm around Gloria. "Tabitha finally went to her reward a couple of weeks ago."

"I'm so sorry," Maggie replied.

"After seventeen wonderful years," Gloria said. "She was a terrific companion."

"Gloria's been miserable without her. I became quite fond of having a cat around, too. So we thought we'd adopt a stray. If you have some you'd like to find homes for, we'd love to help."

"Actually," Maggie said, thinking, "That would be terrific. And they've just been weaned, so your timing is perfect. I started out with six kittens and two have been spoken for. I was going to keep all four of them, but that's a bit much. Why don't you stop by to see if any of them strike your fancy?"

"How about this afternoon? Will you be home?"

"That'll be fine. I'm not going anywhere."

So much for a quiet Sunday afternoon at home, Maggie thought, shaking her head as she made her way to her car.

———

Eve began barking while Maggie was upstairs, changing out of her church clothes. She quickly shrugged into an oversized sweater and her favorite pair of old jeans and raced downstairs to open the door for Judy.

"That wasn't too bad," she said, sweeping past Maggie, bound for the dining room. "I was afraid you'd be stuck there for over an hour. People always want to corral you to suggest this or grumble about that. I feel sorry for you, I really do. As mayor, you can't be off the clock, even at church on Sunday morning."

"That's for sure," Maggie replied. "I don't dare run out to the grocery without my full hair and makeup, either. It gets to be a bit much."

Judy didn't respond. She was already lost in the magical world represented by the objects on the dining room table. She pulled out her laptop and opened a blank spreadsheet. "I set this up while I was waiting for your call. This will be our inventory record," she stated proudly.

"Wow," Maggie replied. "You're so organized. This is really helpful."

"Let's get started. We'll begin with this nine-piece tea set. Hand me the teapot, will you?"

Maggie complied. "Careful—it's surprisingly heavy."

"Must be solid silver. This will be worth a fortune in silver content, alone." She turned the elaborate item over in her hand and studied the silversmith's mark. She let out a low whistle. "Maggie," she said breathlessly, "this is Martin-Guillaume Biennais. Do you know how valuable this is?"

Maggie shook her head. "Never heard of it."

"*Him*," Judy corrected. "He was a French gold and silversmith in the late eighteenth century. He made items for Napoleon."

Maggie's eyes widened.

"I've seen his work in the Metropolitan Museum of Art. I can't even guess what this is worth."

Both women stared at each other.

"Do you have a good camera?"

"John does. And he knows how to use it."

"Good. We've got a job for him this afternoon. We'll need photos of all of this. And you need to rent a safe deposit box for this." She held Maggie's gaze. "I don't care what's on your schedule. You need to get this out of Rosemont and into a vault."

"Don't worry, I'll do just that." *And I'll go to a bank in a nearby city.* She didn't trust her local banker to keep quiet. Some secrets couldn't be kept in a small town.

By the time John arrived to photograph the collection, they had cataloged valuable items by Tiffany, Gorham, and Lunt, as well as lovely pieces that bore no mark.

"Quite the haul," John remarked as he set to work. "Who'd want to polish all this? No wonder it was in the attic."

Judy shot him a reproachful look.

Maggie addressed them both. "It's obvious we've uncovered a significant collection of vintage silver, possibly worth a small fortune. I'm not sure what I want to do with it, or even if it's all mine. They say possession is nine-tenths of the law, but I'm not so sure when you're talking about items of this value."

John put his camera down.

"We're the only three people who know about this—other than David Wheeler. And he took little interest in it and has no idea of its value. For now—until we can sort this all out—I don't want to breathe a word of this to anyone."

"Of course not," Judy agreed. "I won't tell a soul. And you shouldn't be alone at Rosemont with all of this spread out." She glanced at John. "Someone should stay here with you until all of it is secured."

John smiled. "That's the best suggestion I've heard all day."

"It's settled, then. Let's shut the doors to this room and keep this secret to ourselves, for now."

Chapter 23

Eve began barking furiously, and Maggie was halfway to the front door before she heard the knock. She glanced at the grandfather clock in the entryway and couldn't believe it was almost three o'clock. Her oldest and dearest friends in Westbury, Sam and Joan Torres, stamped their feet against the cold.

"Is this a good time? You look like you're in the middle of something," Joan said, eyeing her tarnished apron.

"Perfect time," Maggie replied brightly, avoiding the implied question. "The kittens are in the laundry room. Follow me."

She turned and led the way past the closed dining room door, through the kitchen, and paused outside the laundry room. "It's quiet in there, so they must be asleep. As soon as I open this door, they'll wake up and start to scatter. They've gotten so much faster than the last time you saw them, Sam" Maggie said. "Get in there as fast as you can."

Sam cracked the door, and he and Joan slipped through. As predicted, the laundry room erupted into a scene of flying fur and plaintive meowing.

Maggie eased into the room behind them. "I think you've got a favorite, don't you, Sam?"

Sam started to protest and Joan laughed. "He's got a favorite, all right. Don't try to fool us, Sam Torres," she said, wagging her finger at him. "He's told me all about the one with gray stripes and black hind feet. That one, I think." She pointed to a kitten as it bounded over to Sam.

Sam scooped him up and cradled him against his chest. Both women laughed. "Okay—I admit to being partial to this guy. But you can pick whichever one you want, sweetheart," he said, turning to Joan. Sam handed her the kitten, and he nuzzled Joan's neck, coming to rest under her chin. Joan beamed.

"It looks like this one's smart enough to know he'll find the perfect home with both of you," Maggie said.

"Sweetheart?" Sam asked, hopefully.

"He's the one," Joan said. "We've got a carrier in the car. Let's get him home. We need to change and head over to Fairview Terraces. We're teaching lessons at four and dancing starts at five. I thought you and John were going to join us. With a little practice, you'd both be good. And it's tons of fun," Joan turned to Maggie as Sam slipped out the door to retrieve the carrier.

"We will," Maggie hastily assured her. "It's just been too hectic."

"You're not working twenty-four hours a day, are you? All work and no play, you know."

"It's not that," Maggie replied. "Caring for these kittens has eaten up all of our free time. Once they're a bit older, we'll have time to attend."

"I'm holding you to it," Joan said as Sam returned with the carrier. She extracted the kitten, claw by claw, from her sweater and placed him, protesting mightily, into the carrier.

"Thank you," Sam and Joan said in unison.

Maggie smiled. "I'm thrilled he's going to a loving home."

They exited the laundry room without allowing any additional escapees, and Maggie walked them to the door. "I've got some projects here that I'll need help with," she said to Sam. "Can you stop by next Saturday?"

"Whatever you need," he replied. "See you then."

Maggie was closing the front door when she glimpsed another car approaching through the trees that lined the long, winding driveway up the hill to Rosemont. She paused in her doorway as Glenn Vaughn's old Cadillac came into view. She waived as it pulled to a stop and Glenn got out and went around to the passenger side to open the door for Gloria. Maggie smiled. It was heartwarming to see the old-fashioned chivalry of these newlyweds.

"What in the world are you doing, standing around in the cold?" Gloria fussed as they climbed the steps to the entryway.

"Sam and Joan just left with their kitten," Maggie replied. "I was closing the door when I saw you."

"Busy afternoon for you," Glenn remarked.

"I'm happy to get some of these guys adopted out," Maggie replied. "They're very cute, and I've had lots of fun with them, but six cats is a lot."

"Too many," Gloria agreed.

"But you don't have to take one," Maggie hastily added. "Only if you find one that you'd really like to have."

She retraced her steps to the laundry room and abandoned all hope of getting the elderly couple to quickly slide through the doorway. This time, however, it wasn't necessary. The kittens were occupied dismantling a stack of paper grocery bags and paid no attention to the new visitors.

Glenn and Gloria stood quietly and watched the inquisitive group. A tiny white kitten with gray tips on her fur finally broke away from her siblings and cautiously approached Gloria. She wound around Gloria's feet in the familiar figure-eight pattern that cats favor and allowed Gloria to pick her up. Gloria cradled her gently, stroking her between the ears and along her back. She began to purr and Gloria nodded to Glenn.

"Whatever you think, my dear," he said quietly.

Gloria turned to Maggie. "I've always thought that cats pick their owners, not the other way around."

Maggie nodded. "There's some truth to that."

"This little gal has picked me, so I think we're all set. How much is she?"

"Nothing, of course," Maggie replied. "I'm just thrilled you're adopting her. Let me get you a cardboard box to take her home in."

Gloria shook her head and held up the large canvas satchel she carried on her arm. "Not necessary. This will do fine."

She placed the cat in her bag, and she and Glenn turned to leave. "We've got to run. We're going to the dance at four," Glenn said. "As I remember, you're a very good dancer. Why don't you and John join us?"

Maggie smiled. "Joan was just asking, too. Things have been a bit crazy lately," she said, gesturing to the kittens. "How's it going? Is attendance good?"

"Terrific," Glenn replied. "Westbury West Coast Swing Society has renewed their lease for another year, and we even raised their rent." He proceeded down the front steps to open Gloria's door.

"Thank you for our cat, dear," Gloria said, patting Maggie's arm. "We'll be a very happy family."

Chapter 24

Maggie and John were both visibly relieved when Judy Young closed up her laptop and announced she had to get going. "I'll tidy up this list tonight and email it to you. Give it to your insurance agent first thing tomorrow, before you go to Town Hall," she said, peering at Maggie over her glasses.

"I promise," Maggie assured her. "And I can't thank you enough for all your hard work and expertise. I had no idea."

"Believe me, the pleasure was all mine. Most fun I've had in I-can't-remember-when."

John and Maggie collapsed in the wing chairs flanking the living room fireplace as Judy's car pulled away.

"You've hit pay dirt, my dear," John reached over and took her hand.

"I know. I can hardly believe it." She turned to him. "I almost forgot it was up there, what with all that's been going on."

John nodded.

"Great suggestion to get Judy over here. I would have eventually called my insurance agent, but who knows how long I would have left it all sitting out in plain sight. Makes me nervous, to be honest with you. Are you on call tonight?"

John shook his head. "I need to run by the emergency hospital to check on a patient I treated late last night, but that's it. Why don't I do that now and come back here to take you to dinner."

"And leave this stash? No way,"

"Then I'll pick up a pizza from Tomascino's."

"Nothing I'd like better," Maggie replied, pulling him to his feet. "If we don't get moving, we'll never get up. You go check on your patient, and I'll call Susan—after I set that silver chocolate pot aside to give to Judy. It was her favorite piece and will make the perfect thank-you gift."

"You're a class act, Maggie Martin. That's one of the many reasons I'm so crazy about you."

"Mom?" Susan answered on the fourth ring, sounding groggy.

"Oh, honey. Were you asleep?" Maggie asked.

"Taking a nap. What time is it?"

"It's one-thirty, your time," Maggie replied.

"I should get up; I've got stuff to do. What's up?"

"We made the most amazing discovery here at Rosemont."

"Do tell," Susan demanded, and Maggie pictured her daughter sitting straight up in bed, now fully alert.

"Remember when I got locked in the attic?"

"Of course I remember, Mom." Maggie imagined the eye roll that Susan would be giving her. "You were in that cold, creepy attic all afternoon and planned to tie old draperies together to climb out the window if no one found you. The thought of you doing that still gives me nightmares."

"Thank goodness I heard Frank Haynes drive up and was able to get his attention. I know the police tell you never to hide a key outside your house, but I'm sure glad I had one hidden that day. I'll always be grateful to him for rescuing me—no matter what else he's done. Anyway, did I mention I found that old secretary full of vintage silver in the corner?"

"You mentioned it—and?"

"We brought the silver downstairs this weekend. I got David Wheeler to help me. Tons and tons of stuff. I was polishing it yesterday afternoon when John stopped by and suggested I ask Judy to take a look at it. Turns out she is quite an expert on antique silver."

"That's cool, Mom." Maggie could tell Susan's enthusiasm was starting to wane. *These modern girls don't want to fuss with anything that requires much upkeep. Who could blame them?*

"Turns out some of it may be incredibly valuable. Maybe even priceless," she expounded, feeling guilty if she was exaggerating to seize her daughter's attention.

Her words had their desired effect. "No way! That's incredible." Maggie could hear Susan settle down for a prolonged chat. "Tell me everything."

Maggie slipped into the laundry room and, with one hand, removed a load of dry socks and towels from the dryer while she held her phone to her ear and launched into the story. She transferred a load of clothes from the washer into the dryer and never noticed the trio of bright green eyes following her every move. Before she'd closed the door behind her, one of the kittens abandoned her perch to investigate.

Maggie and Susan spent the next forty-five minutes discussing the silver and speculating on its origins before Susan inquired about the status of things at Town Hall.

Maggie sighed.

"That good, huh?" Susan remarked. "Has anything happened?"

"No. And that's the problem. We can't seem to make progress on any of the investigations. We're running into road blocks everywhere we turn."

"These things take time, Mom. Especially financial fraud on the grand scale that you're dealing with. You know that."

"I do. But Chief Thomas and Alex are feuding, which makes it all so much harder. And they're coming to me to take sides. No matter what I do, I can't win."

"What are their gripes?"

"Alex is frustrated that there's no progress on the investigations into the arson fires or his accident. Chief Thomas is mad at Alex because he's interfering in the arson investigations. The chief is taking his time, hoping to catch bigger fish than the guys who set the fires. He thinks the mob is involved, and he wants to make arrests at the top of the food chain."

"Makes sense. And Alex can't be part of an investigation where he's the victim. He knows better."

"There's more. Chief Thomas is frustrated that he hasn't received any of the documents from the offshore banks Alex subpoenaed months ago. Now that William Wheeler is dead, the chief has no one to turn state's evidence. He's at a standstill and needs those documents to get going again."

"What does Alex say to that?"

"That he's working on it and that enforcing a subpoena internationally is very complex."

"He's right. Does he have anyone helping him?"

"His paralegal. She's wonderful, but every time I see her, she looks like she hasn't slept for a week. And the town's in a hiring freeze."

Susan was silent, thinking. "You've got too much work for too few people."

"That's obvious," Maggie snapped and instantly regretted it.

"Don't go getting testy, Mom. I have a suggestion."

"Sorry, honey. Let's hear it."

"You've still got the law firm on retainer, don't you? Stetson & Graham? I'll bet they haven't done much to earn that retainer since you appointed Alex as special counsel. Time for them to earn their keep."

"You think so?" Maggie asked, intrigued by the idea.

"I know so. Not Bill Stetson. He'd try to take over and would irritate Alex. You need an associate with experience. Someone who can take over the research and motions that Alex has to contend with. That'll help clear this log jam."

"Brilliant idea. Thank you, honey. How did you get to be so smart?"

"I must take after my mom," Susan said. "And one more thing. While we've been talking, I figured out what you should name your three kittens."

"You have?"

"I hope they're all girls, but even if they're boys, you should call them Blossom, Bubbles, and Buttercup."

"Those are sweet names. Why do they sound vaguely familiar?"

"Remember the PowerPuff Girls on Cartoon Network? They're the names of those big-eyed little girls with superpowers that zoomed around protecting the mayor of Townsville, USA," Susan stated proudly.

"That's it. You used to babysit for kids that loved that show." Maggie laughed. "You're right—those names are perfect. I could use someone with superpowers to help me."

"So it's settled?"

"It's settled. And the three kittens I'm keeping are all girls, so it'll be fine. Once again, Susan to the rescue."

"Aaron's picking me up in twenty minutes, and I haven't showered yet. Gotta go. I'll call you tomorrow."

Maggie picked up her laundry basket and entered the laundry room. She was greeted by a duo of bright-green eyes and no clean laundry anywhere. She blinked. *Where in the world was the laundry I placed on top of the dryer? And where is that third cat?*

Maggie searched high and low, to no avail. *The kitten must have escaped when I left the room and is now wandering all over Rosemont, getting into heaven-knows-what*. Maggie was closing the door when she heard a soft mewing coming from somewhere below her feet. She stood still and listened. After what seemed like an eternity, she heard the sound again.

Maggie stepped back into the laundry room. "Where's your sister?" she asked the less adventuresome pair, peering at her over the side of their box. Maggie got down on her hands and knees and waited. This time, she was able to trace the sound to an old grate in the wall positioned just above the floor. One of the bars of the grate was bent, creating an opening just large enough for a kitten to slip through. She was definitely in the ductwork behind that grate.

Maggie quickly retrieved a flashlight from the kitchen and shone it into the grate. She was able to make out a string of socks—her recently laundered socks—leading back and out of sight. The kitten was nowhere to be seen, but she could hear her meowing unhappily.

Procuring a slice of cheese from the kitchen, Maggie tore off a small chunk and placed it inside the grate. She didn't have long to wait for the kitten to follow her nose to the treat. She reached two fingers through the grate and stroked her fur while the kitten ate the snack. Maggie placed a piece of cheese outside the grate but the kitten wasn't able to go back through it. Maggie tried to pull her to safety until the kitten squirmed free of her grasp. "Stay right here," Maggie admonished sternly. She secured the other kittens in their box and went in search of a screwdriver and a letter opener.

When she returned, the wayward kitten was nowhere to be seen. Maggie unscrewed the grate and used the letter opener to pry it loose from the wall. She placed a piece of cheese on the floor outside the opening to the vent but the kitten didn't approach. She sat quietly and listened. She was sure she could hear her, crying faintly, somewhere along the long, dark pipe. Maggie rolled onto her stomach and shone the flashlight into the duct. She could see the kitten, almost ten feet away. Beyond that was another grate that opened to the breakfast room. Maggie cooed to the kitten and tore off pieces of cheese and flung them in her direction. Wary and scared, the kitten wouldn't budge.

Maggie rocked back on her heels to think. If she couldn't coax her out, maybe she could force her from the other direction. "I'm coming back for you; don't be afraid," she whispered as she pushed herself to her feet and headed off to her bathroom. Grabbing her hairdryer, she ran to the breakfast room and found the grate that lay at the other end of the duct. She positioned her hairdryer on the floor, setting it upright between a large can of beans and a bottle of olive oil that she'd snatched from the pantry. She set the hairdryer at the coolest temperature and aimed the airstream into the duct.

Maggie raced into the laundry room just in time to see a very disgruntled kitten scamper from the duct. "Success!" she cried as she scooped her up, delighted that her plan had worked. She deposited the kitten in the box with her sisters and took them into the kitchen.

"You'll have to stay here until Sam Torres fixes that grate. In the meantime," she said to the three earnest faces staring at her, "don't get into any trouble."

Chapter 25

Maggie stole a glance at her cell phone, propped inconspicuously against the base of the microphone in front of her. Seven fifteen. They had another forty-five minutes to go.

She was presiding over a citizen's forum to solicit public input on budget cuts. So far, every suggestion—whether to shorten the library's hours or restrict the bus schedule—had been met with vehement opposition. She'd directed one man to sit down when he started ranting about abolishing the government entirely. Several times she'd reminded the townspeople that they were asking for *suggestions* and each would be thoroughly investigated before any change was adopted. They'd have to hold more public meetings before any services were reduced—the idea of another of these meetings made Maggie's head spin.

She glanced at the empty seats. Councilmembers Frank Haynes and Chuck Delgado had both come up with last-minute excuses to be absent tonight, leaving Maggie and Councilmembers Tonya Holmes and Russell Isaac to suffer through this interminable evening. She looked to Isaac, who glared at her in return. She could hardly blame him. After the disastrous public meeting when a riot had broken out over proposed pay cuts, she wanted to make sure that the public had an opportunity to comment before they brought anything to a vote. Hadn't her trustworthy advisor Professor Lyndon Upton suggested this approach? Except that now she didn't believe he was trustworthy at all.

Maggie hadn't been paying attention and was pulled back into the present when Councilmember Holmes answered a question into her microphone. She shot Tonya a grateful smile.

As she returned her attention to the bullet points on the agenda in front of her, she noticed that she'd missed a text from John. Maggie pretended to adjust the position of the microphone and pushed the button to read his message.

In a booth at Pete's. Tonight's special is your favorite. He's saving some for you. Join me when you're done. We've got something big to discuss.

Maggie's brow creased. There was nowhere she'd rather be right now than with John, but what did "something big to discuss" mean? Maggie looked up to find all eyes on her.

Tonya Holmes cleared her throat. "As Mayor Martin has said repeatedly, these discussions are only preliminary."

Maggie leaned forward and spoke into her microphone. "I understand—the entire council understands—that budget cuts create hardships. We've already made deep cuts. The only things left will negatively impact a lot of people." Maggie paused and scanned the crowd. "We've got some hard choices to make, and we want to be as well informed as possible when we make our decisions. That's why we're holding these forums." She consulted her watch. "We have time for two more comments from the floor before we adjourn."

———

Maggie exited the council chamber by the rear exit. She was in no mood to get pigeonholed by a disgruntled constituent. Russell Isaac and Tonya Holmes followed closely on her heels.

"Another wasted evening, Mayor," Isaac remarked.

Maggie spun on him. "Then you come up with something, Russ. It's easy to sit back and take pot shots at people, harder to come up with useful ideas. You ran for this seat. You must have something to suggest."

Isaac smirked. "I'll save it for when I defeat you in the next election," he said. "Right now, I'm enjoying watching you twist in the wind."

"For God's sake, Russ!" Tonya cried. "The town is on the brink of bankruptcy. This isn't the time to be licking old political wounds and acting like a sore loser. If you've got ideas to help, you should put them forward. That's leadership," she said, staring pointedly at him.

Isaac delivered a rude gesture to both of them and strode out the exit.

Maggie turned to Tonya. "If the town wasn't in such dire circumstances, I'd find that funny. He's acting like he lost the race to be seventh-grade class president."

"I'm relieved that Haynes and Delgado weren't here tonight. They'd side with Isaac, and we'd never hear the end of it." Tonya turned to Maggie. "I'm awfully glad you're here. If I didn't have someone on my side—the townspeople's side—I don't think I could carry on."

Maggie flushed from her shoulders to the top of her head. *To think that I almost resigned my position as mayor on New Year's Eve.*

"Maggie," Tonya said, taking her arm. "Are you okay? You looked like you were a million miles away in there. And where's Professor Upton? I thought he was supposed to be here."

"Something came up and he's not going to be assisting us anymore."

"When did this happen? I didn't particularly like the guy—he was pompous and condescending—but he knew his stuff."

"I talked to him after the first of the year. We'll be fine without him. We can implement the necessary changes without his help." She swiftly changed the subject. "Did you hear about the kittens I'm fostering? In fact, would the Holmes like a cat?"

Tonya held up her hands and backed away. "Oh no, you don't. I've got my hands full with George, the kids, two dogs, three fish, and a hamster. If you try to foist one of those kittens off on me, I'll resign and leave you all alone with these creeps."

"Understood." Maggie laughed. *Although, that might be just what I deserve, since I almost did that to you,* she thought as they headed to their cars.

Maggie waved to Pete as she sailed through the door of his restaurant at eight fifteen. She found John in a booth in the corner, deeply engrossed in a medical journal.

"I hope you went ahead and ate," Maggie said, sliding onto the bench next to him and planting a kiss on his cheek. "I'm sorry that I'm so late. It was really nice of you to ask Pete to save me a serving of the special."

John set his journal aside and drew her close, kissing her on the lips. "I can't let my best girl miss out just because she's a bigwig and busy running this town."

Maggie laughed. "Is that what I am? You're the only one who thinks so."

"Hard day?"

"These community forums are so contentious. I'm not convinced that we made any progress. There may not be any way to get public buy-in on budget cuts. Maybe it wasn't such a good idea."

"I don't believe that. Not for one minute. You knew that things would get worse before they got better. You've thought this through from every angle. You're doing the right thing." John ran his hand up and down her arm, like he was a football coach sending his quarterback into the huddle with a new play. "It's too early to assess how things will turn out. Quit second-guessing yourself."

Maggie smiled at him. "How in the world did I get so lucky as to land you? You always know the right thing to say."

John blushed, and she knew he was pleased. "So—you've got me intrigued. What 'big thing' do we need to discuss? Is everything okay?"

"Yes, of course it is." John turned to her. "Did I worry you with that?"

Maggie shrugged. "Maybe a little."

"What we need to discuss," John said, as the waiter delivered their salads, "is when—and where—we're going to shop for your ring. You've been engaged for weeks and the entire world doesn't know about it yet."

Maggie almost bounced in her seat. "This is big," she replied. "As for when—I'll clear my calendar. We'll go as soon as you can take the time. As for where—we'll have to go to Burman Jewelers. If we don't buy local, we'll be ridden out of town on a rail."

"Let's go Saturday. I only have appointments until ten. I won't book anyone else. And we can get your ring anywhere you'd like—you shouldn't buy local unless you really want to."

"I do," Maggie said. "If they're honest and reliable. And reasonably priced."

John laughed. "Don't worry about the price. And I've known them for years—they're terrific people. Do you have any idea what you'd like?"

Maggie smiled impishly. "Sorry to say this, but I want a big, honkin' diamond. I don't want to put reading glasses on to see my stone."

John pretended to cringe. "I figured you'd come with a high price tag."

Maggie laughed, patting his forearm. "I don't want you to break the bank. Seriously, John, we'll stick with what you can afford."

"Very considerate of you. I think I can scrape up enough to get my girl a ring," John said, wrapping his arm around her shoulder. "I'll call Harriet Burman tomorrow to bring in some stones for you."

"That sounds wonderful!" Maggie leaned in for a kiss, and John grasped her hand, playing with her fingers.

"I've investigated. You pick your setting, and then you pick your diamond. Or diamonds, if you want. I want you to love this ring as much as I love you," he said, kissing her ring finger. "that's why I didn't present you with a ring when I proposed. You need to pick it out."

"Could you be any more perfect? I can't wait until Saturday! Since you didn't mention a ring when you proposed, I've been trying to figure out how to bring it up. I even thought that maybe you didn't want to do an engagement ring, but Susan said that was ridiculous."

John snorted. "You've been plotting with Susan to convince me to buy you an engagement ring? Now I really feel bad."

"You have nothing to apologize for—everything was so chaotic for us after Roman disappeared."

"Still—I'm an idiot. I should have at least said something. I'd better come through with lots of carats now."

"Susan will like what you're saying—that girl's even set up a Pinterest board of styles for me to consider."

John shook his head. "You two have me outnumbered."

Chapter 26

The doorbell rang at precisely ten o'clock. The appraiser recommended by her insurance company was on time. She opened the door to a tall man wearing a heavy black overcoat and a neat fedora. "Gordon Mortimer," he said, extending his hand. "Ms. Martin, I presume?"

"Yes," she said, shaking his hand. "Come in. Let me take your hat and coat."

"Thank you, madam," he said, handing them carefully to her. He took a handkerchief out of his pocket and polished his oversized glasses.

His receding hairline and salt-and-pepper mustache suggested he was in his fifties, but his slim build and smooth forehead gave the impression of a much younger person. Maggie turned to him, "Would you like something to drink? Coffee or water?"

"No, thank you, madam. I'm anxious to get started. Your call was most intriguing."

"How long have you been an appraiser?" she asked as she led the way to the dining room.

"My entire life, really. My father was an antiques dealer and appraiser. I grew up in his shop. I worked for him—except for a stint at Sotheby's in London—until he died several years ago and left the business to me. Buying habits have changed—very few people appreciate true quality anymore—so I closed up the store and have devoted myself to appraisals."

"And you have expertise in vintage silver?"

"Indeed I do. I was the head of the department at Sotheby's before I returned to the family business."

Maggie nodded. She threw open the double doors leading into the dining room. "Here's what we found in the attic."

Gordon Mortimer reached out a hand to the doorframe to steady himself. He swallowed hard and turned to her. "You've got quite a collection here. You found all of this in the attic?"

Maggie nodded.

"I'll photograph and make notes on each piece." He set his satchel on the floor and removed an expensive-looking camera and an electronic tablet. "May I move things around a bit? I want to group the pieces."

"By all means," Maggie said. "Do what you need to do. We've already photographed things, if that would be helpful." By his expression she could tell he didn't think their photos would be useful.

"I have my own way of doing things, madam."

"Of course," Maggie replied. "I'll leave you to it. How long do you think you'll be?"

"All day, I'm afraid. If it's all right with you, I may need to work into the evening."

"Certainly," she said, although she hadn't planned to spend the day at home. She didn't have any appointments but hated to be away from Town Hall. She turned to look at him as he began inspecting the items at the far end of the table. Surely she could leave him alone to complete his work. They had photos of everything—he wouldn't steal anything. Judy Young's admonishments, however, rung in her ears, and she decided to remain at Rosemont.

Maggie was halfway to the library when she heard a startled yelp from the dining room. She retraced her steps and found a red-faced Gordon Mortimer leaning over the table, frantically grabbing at Bubbles who was racing in and out of the maze of silver pieces. He got a hand on her, but she wriggled free and streaked down the table. Maggie flung her arms out, and Bubbles did an about face, tearing back to the appraiser who fielded her like a major-league ballplayer catching a ground ball to first base.

He stood and held the squirming creature out to Maggie. "That cat was in one of the serving dishes, madam. I didn't see it—it just exploded out of there."

Maggie stifled a laugh. "My apologies. I have three new kittens, and they're curious about everything."

Mortimer fixed her with a disapproving stare.

"I thought I'd kept them out of here. I'm sorry that she disturbed you." She could see that his feathers were still ruffled. "I'll be in the library if you need me."

Maggie emailed her assistant to say that she would be working at home, and to contact her if anything required her attention. Next, she searched online for a bank in one of the neighboring cities that advertised large safe deposit vaults. She found two candidates and quickly settled on one that was only ten minutes further down the highway than the airport. She finalized the rentals online. Bubbles sat on the credenza by the printer, batting at the pages as they emerged while Buttercup strolled across her keyboard whenever Maggie lowered her elbows.

By midafternoon, Maggie was tired of all the "help" from her kittens. Her curiosity was also getting the better of her. She rapped lightly on the dining room door and stepped inside. She waited patiently for Mr. Mortimer to finish typing.

He looked up at her and removed his glasses, running his hands over his eyes. "You've got some remarkable pieces."

Maggie smiled. This was exactly what she'd hoped to hear. "You're tired. And probably hungry. I was just about to make myself a sandwich. May I fix one for you as well?" Mortimer started to shake his head. "You've got to eat," she insisted. "You'll work better if you do. And you can tell me what you've learned so far."

"All right. That's very kind. Thank you. Let me finish this entry, and I'll be right there."

Maggie was slicing an apple and setting two turkey sandwiches on plates when Gordon Mortimer entered the kitchen.

"Ordinarily, I'd suggest that we go out to lunch. But I don't want to leave a collection this valuable unattended," he said.

Maggie carried the plates to the farmhouse table, where she'd set two glasses and a pitcher of iced tea. "Sorry I can't produce something more elaborate," she said a bit sheepishly. "I don't keep much food on hand."

"This is more than sufficient, madam," he said in his formal way.

"Any preliminary conclusions on value?"

"I'd say you have at least half a million in there. Not counting the Martin-Guillaume Biennais pieces. I need to consult my contacts at Sotheby's on those."

Maggie stared, dumbstruck. "I had no idea," she finally sputtered. "I thought we might be talking about a hundred thousand, tops. Are some pieces significantly more valuable than others? I've just leased four large safe deposit vaults and will store as much there as I can. But I don't think it'll all fit. I also plan to purchase a couple of cabinet safes."

"I was going to suggest you do just that. The Martin-Guillaume Biennais needs to be in the vault, of course. And some of the other pieces. All of it isn't of extraordinary value. When I'm done, I'll prioritize what to take to the bank. And I can help you move the rest of it back to the attic. It's been safe there for almost a hundred years—it should be fine a few more weeks."

"Thank you. That's most kind, but you don't have to do that. I can hire the local boy who carried it all downstairs for me."

Mortimer looked at her sharply. "I wouldn't let anyone know about this."

"I can trust this boy," Maggie said as she cleared their plates.

Mortimer shook his head. "You may be able to trust him, but he could innocently let it slip to someone that you can't trust. Insurance theft claims are full of such reports. You should keep this as quiet as possible," he almost scolded.

Maggie knew he was right. "That's very kind of you. I'm grateful for your help."

"Maybe you have some other valuables in that attic. I can take a quick look around before I leave."

Maggie nodded slowly. "Yes. I'd appreciate it very much." She turned to look out the window. "I can hardly believe all of this. Who knew what was waiting up there for me?"

———

"You won't believe it," Maggie said when John called that afternoon. "Judy was right. He thinks it's worth at least half a million. And that's not counting the Martin-Guillaume Biennais."

"The what?"

"You remember—the French guy that designed gold and silver pieces for Napoleon. The one whose work Judy said is in the Met? Mr. Mortimer thinks it's genuine, and it's in pristine condition. He needs to research the value of it and a couple other pieces."

John whistled. "I guess you hear about this type of thing happening to people. What will you do with it all?"

"I'd like to keep a few of the pieces to use. I'll see if Susan or Amy would like a piece or two. And I'm giving that chocolate pot to Judy, no matter what it's worth. The rest of it I'll sell. The appraiser has connections at Sotheby's, so I'll auction through them."

"Sounds sensible."

"In the meantime, I've rented safe deposit boxes in Ferndale and will take as much of this over there in the morning as I can. The appraiser said he'd help me prioritize which pieces are the most valuable."

"That's helpful. And I think you're doing the right thing by taking it out of town. You don't want people around here talking about it. You shouldn't tell Judy what the appraiser said, either. She means well, but it'll be all over town before you know it."

"I agree."

"What about the rest of it?"

"The appraiser and I are going to haul it back up to the attic. I'll store it there until I can purchase cabinet safes. He said that's what the insurance company will tell me to do."

"I just finished with my last patient, so I'm on my way to help. Your history with that attic and men isn't something I want repeated."

"You're being ridiculous," Maggie said. "But we can use the help."

Maggie carefully wrapped and boxed the silver that was being returned to the attic, and half an hour later John and Gordon Mortimer placed the last box in the far corner.

"That should be secure. Someone would either have to know where it was or have a lot of time to search to find it," Mortimer said, brushing dust from his trousers. He turned and made a careful pass through the attic.

"These items piled up in the middle are of no significant value. You could get an antiques dealer to give you a reasonable price for the lot," he said to Maggie. "The furniture along the wall, however, is a different story. I suspect you've got some nice pieces."

"Will you come back to appraise them?"

"I'd love to. And I'd appreciate it if you could remove these items in the middle and pull the furniture out so I can examine all of it properly."

"Will do. I'll call you when we're ready. We're getting married in June, so maybe sometime this summer? After the wedding."

"No rush. You'll be busy dealing with the silver, I should think."

"Let's slide this old steamer trunk over, in front of the boxes. Just to be safe," John suggested. The two men slid the trunk into place, and neither of them noticed the file folder labeled *F.H./Rosemont* now lying in the shadows.

Chapter 27

"Mayor Martin," Bill Stetson said, extending his hand.

"I'm sorry to barge in on you without an appointment," Maggie said.

"Don't be ridiculous," replied the senior partner of Stetson & Graham, the town's outside counsel for as long as anyone could remember. "You never need an appointment here. The town is our most important client."

"I wouldn't let the others hear that," Maggie chided.

"To what do I owe the pleasure?"

"I'm here to solicit help for Alex. The fraud investigation is bogged down in procedural red tape. We're trying to get documents from those offshore banks. Until we get our hands on those records, we're dead in the water."

"I've heard rumors," he said.

"We're in the middle of a hiring freeze, so I can't put anyone else on the payroll to help him. But we've got your firm on retainer, and since Alex has taken on the role of special counsel, we haven't drawn on your firm for services."

"The retainer is a fixed amount, whether you use us or not," he was quick to remind her.

"I understand that," Maggie replied. "But given our long association—and in light of the dire circumstances the town is facing—I know you wouldn't want to be seen as not providing value for the sizable amount you receive from us." Maggie held his gaze.

Stetson cleared his throat. "Of course not. We're always happy to help. I'll call Alex and see what I can take over."

"I'm not presuming that we need to impose on your time, Bill," Maggie said sweetly. "I was thinking that you could assign a senior associate to assist Alex—maybe thirty hours a week?"

Stetson opened his mouth to protest.

"Since the firm hasn't done anything for the town in the past six months, I think you should give us a little time to make up for that."

Stetson nodded slowly. "We'd be happy to assist," he said, sounding none too happy. "I've got just the person: Forest Smith. He's smart and aggressive and a hard worker. Let me talk to him in the morning."

"Good," Maggie said, rising. "Let me know, and I'll make the introduction to Alex." She headed to the door, then turned back. "I haven't spoken to Alex yet, so I'd appreciate it if you'd keep this quiet until I inform him of my decision."

"Absolutely, Mayor Martin."

Maggie was on her way to fetch a second cup of coffee the next morning when Alex bounded off the elevator, almost bowling her over.

"Good morning," she said. "You're in a hurry."

"I'm here to ask what the hell you're up to," he spat.

"If you're here to see me, you'd better ask for a mulligan and start over." Maggie looked him straight in the eye. "I'm the mayor of this town, and I deserve respect. You can be mad at me, Alex, and we can disagree, but you must be civil."

Alex stopped short and looked down. Maggie stood patiently and waited, her gaze never leaving his face.

He nodded, and she pointed down the hall. "You can wait in my office. I'm going to get a cup of coffee. May I get you one?"

Alex declined her offer, and she watched him stride down the hall. Sometimes being mayor was just like being a mother of recalcitrant teenagers. Still, she and Alex were supposed to be on the same side and his hostility was wearing on her last nerve. She took her time with her coffee, hoping he'd cool down.

"So, what's got you so riled up?" Maggie asked, motioning him to a chair and taking her seat.

"You're bringing in Bill Stetson to take over the investigation." His voice quivered in anger.

"I most certainly am not. How in the world did you get that idea?"

"My paralegal's cousin is a junior partner at the firm, and she heard about it last night. She told me first thing this morning."

"Oh, for heaven's sake! I'm going to kill Bill Stetson," Maggie replied.

"So it's true?" Alex surged out of his seat.

"Of course not! I'd never do that to you, and you know it. I went to Bill yesterday to ask him—tell him, really—to assign a senior associate to *assist* you. Help you with this blasted mountain of paperwork that's burying this investigation."

"Then why is Bill going to work on it?"

"He's not. I made that perfectly clear. The town isn't going to pay them one dime more than their retainer, so you can bet that Bill won't lift a finger."

"That's for sure."

"You should have seen him. I basically told him that since they've provided no services to earn their retainer for the last six months, I wanted thirty hours a week from the firm."

Alex smiled. "Good one. I'll bet he hated that."

Maggie nodded.

"But you're being fair."

"Thank you. He's assigning an attorney named Forest Smith. Do you know him? If you don't like him, we'll get someone else."

"We've been on opposite sides a couple of times. But he's a very capable lawyer."

"Good. Satisfied now?"

Alex looked at his hands folded in his lap. "Yes. I'm sorry I came in here, guns blazing."

"I didn't deserve that."

"No, you didn't. It won't happen again."

Chapter 28

Chuck Delgado tapped the end of his pencil against the top of the elevated, semi-circular bench in the council chambers. Councilmember Holmes was making a presentation about the citizens' forums, none of which he'd attended. Delgado raked his eyes over the crowd, trying to decide if he wanted to persuade any of the women in the audience to have a drink with him afterward. He was studying two women in the back row when Frank Haynes slipped in the side door and quietly made his way to his seat on the opposite side of the bench. Delgado tried to catch his eye, but Haynes never glanced up.

Maggie Martin surreptitiously watched the scene unfold.

Haynes removed his coat and placed it carefully around the back of his chair. He glanced in Delgado's direction as he opened the file folder containing the agenda and handouts supplied at every town council meeting. His head snapped back to the folder. There, on top of the agenda, was his long-lost cell phone.

Haynes hesitated, his hand resting on the phone before picking it up and turning it on. He studied the screen, then slipped the phone into his pocket.

He picked up the agenda and made a show of scrutinizing it. Maggie suppressed a smile. He must be wondering who found his phone and placed it in his folder. He'd have to suspect it was she. Anyone else would have turned it in directly to him to claim the hundred-dollar reward.

Haynes swiveled to look directly at Maggie who quickly cut her eyes to the front. Maggie leaned into her microphone and called Special Counsel Alex Scanlon to the podium.

"Thank you, Mayor Martin. As you know, our investigation is proceeding. We're aggressively pursuing the offshore banks. Gathering information from them has proven to be very difficult. We're dealing with complicated international law. We've recently secured the assistance of an attorney from Stetson & Graham," he said, and Chuck Delgado stiffened. "We're encouraged by our progress and hope to have more to report at the next council meeting."

Maggie rose. "Thank you. We all appreciate how hard you're working. Unless any of the councilmembers has something to add?" She paused while each member shook his or her head. "We are adjourned."

Delgado glanced longingly at one of the women in the back row but reluctantly abandoned his prey. He needed to find out which attorney from Stetson & Graham was now working with Scanlon. He pushed past Isaac and grabbed Scanlon's arm as he was making his way to the exit.

"So," Delgado began, "you couldn't handle this on your own. Needed to bring in the big guns."

Scanlon bristled. "You're the least qualified person in town to have an opinion on any of this," he shot back. "Despite all of your brushes with the law."

Delgado smirked, satisfied that he'd gotten under Scanlon's skin. "Bill takin' over for ya?"

"If you must know, they've assigned a senior associate to help. Not Bill Stetson."

"Who's that?" Delgado asked.

"A very capable young attorney named Forest Smith."

Delgado repressed the urge to grin from ear to ear.

Later that evening in his office above his liquor store, Delgado poured himself his third glass of Jameson's—neat—picked up his phone, and dialed a familiar number.

Frank Haynes cringed when he saw the name on his caller ID. He'd been pleased to escape after the council meeting without speaking to the fellow councilmember. "Chuck," he said curtly as he answered the call.

"Frankie boy," Delgado replied, trying not to slur his words.

Haynes checked his watch. It was after ten. Of course Delgado was well on his way to being intoxicated. He waited.

"You there, Frankie?"

"What do you want, Charles?"

"I've got good news, Frankie. Our esteemed mayor said that uppity professor from Chicago isn't working with the town anymore."

"Is that so? Why?"

"Said he's become too busy with other engagements. Probably tired of messing with us for no dough. Anyway, the other good news is that new lawyer investigating us—the one from Stetson & Graham—we own that kid."

"What do you mean, Charles? Bill Stetson is above reproach. The firm is clean."

"The firm, yes—but this Forest Smith kid is an addict. Prescription painkillers—got addicted after he broke his back in a skiing accident. Sad story, but good for business. We hoped Scanlon would go the same way after he survived his auto accident," Delgado paused to laugh. "But it isn't happening with him. This Smith kid is in deep. And his supplier is one of our friends."

"One of *your* friends, Charles, not mine. I don't have any involvement with drugs. And if you do, I don't want to hear about it."

"Don't go gettin' all high and mighty on me, Frankie. You're in this pension fund debacle up to your eyeballs, just like the rest of us."

Haynes remained silent, fervently hoping his Miami connection had cleaned up all of the records as he'd been paid to do.

"Anyway, I'll review the situation with Smith. Let him know what we expect of him."

"And what would that be?"

"He's our eyes and ears on the inside. Do what Scanlon tells him, but keep us informed. For now. And if he uncovers anything that incriminates us, we've got him in place to bury it." Delgado chuckled.

"Cover-ups generally backfire," Haynes said quietly.

"You'd better hope not," Delgado replied. Haynes hung up the receiver and leaned back in his chair, contemplating this new development. Maybe Delgado and his cronies would get away with embezzling from the town and the pension fund after all.

Chapter 29

Maggie bounded out of bed on Saturday morning. She was going ring shopping! She hurried Eve through her morning walk and managed to feed the kittens without them escaping and scrambling all over Rosemont. She was just stepping out of the shower when her phone rang. Her caller ID told her it was Susan. She quickly threw her hair in a towel and slung her robe around her shoulders.

"Hi, sweetheart," she said. "It's really early there. Is everything okay?"

"Fine, Mom. I know you're going to the jeweler today and wanted to make sure you saw the last few photos I pinned on our Pinterest board."

Maggie smiled. "I didn't, but I promise I'll check them before I leave. I'm not so sure they're all for me, anyway—some look more like you than me. How are things with the good doctor?"

"Beyond wonderful, Mom. Even though we're both busy, we see each other on the weekends and talk every day—even if it's just a quick goodnight ... Sometimes I worry things are going too well."

"Now that's just plain silly," Maggie chided her daughter. "A relationship shouldn't be a big struggle. You'll have challenges to face together, but dealing with each other shouldn't be one of them."

"I'm glad to hear you say that. I get scared when I'm too happy."

"That's nonsense," Maggie replied. "And I think we'll need to save that Pinterest board. I bet you'll be in the market for a ring soon, too."

"We'll see," Susan said, and Maggie heard the hope in her voice.

"I'll call you when we're done," Maggie said.

"You'll text me a photo of that ring before you leave the jeweler," Susan ordered.

———

John pulled up to Rosemont at ten fifteen, and Maggie was ready and waiting. They found a parking spot at the curb and were immediately buzzed in to the bright showroom of Burman Jewelers. Harriet Burman came around the glass case to hug John.

"We've been waiting for this day for a long time. And I'm so happy to meet you, Mayor Martin," she said, extending her hand.

"Maggie, please," Maggie said, shaking her hand. "And I'm thrilled to meet you—especially under these circumstances."

"Larry's got some diamonds that I think you're going to love. They're in a private room in the back. Let's get some settings you'd like, and we'll take them back to select the main stone."

"That's a great idea," Maggie agreed. She turned to John. "Did you have anything you wanted me to look at?"

John held up his hands. "Absolutely not. I'd have no idea. You pick it out, and I'll pay for it."

Harriet beamed. "He's perfect, isn't he?"

"Indeed he is," Maggie agreed.

"Do you have an idea of what you'd like?"

"Generally," Maggie replied. She wandered over to a case containing engagement rings and wedding bands. The two women spent the next thirty minutes discussing and evaluating a dozen settings, with Maggie returning each time to one with sweeping channels of baguettes circling a mounting for a princess-cut diamond.

"It looks nice on your hand," John ventured.

"Let's take it and a couple of the others back to see how they'll look with the central stone," Harriet suggested.

"Just this one," Maggie stated decisively. "This setting is the one I want."

"It's my favorite, too," Harriet said. "Very unusual. No one else will have one like it."

Harriet led John and Maggie to a private room with high spotlights focused on a small round table in the middle. A tray of six stones spread out on a black velvet cloth rested on the table.

Maggie gasped and turned to John. "I was assuming we'd get a two-carat stone."

"You said you wanted one big enough to see without reading glasses, so that's what I told Harriet to get."

"I was only kidding," Maggie laughed.

"Now she tells me." John winked at Harriet. "So which one do you like?"

Maggie turned back to Harriet. "How big are these?"

"They're all between 3.5 and 4.5 carats. And all very good diamonds. As I said, you've hit pay dirt with this guy."

"Good grief! Seriously?" She turned to John.

"Quit gawking and pick out your stone. Harriet's a busy woman," John replied.

"You're sure about this? I can pick any of these?"

John nodded. Maggie leaned over and kissed him. "You are the most generous man on the planet." She turned back to Harriet. "Okay, let's get busy!"

Picking the stone was easier than picking the setting; one spoke to her the minute she walked into the room.

"When can you have it set and sized?" she asked.

"We'll need at least a week. I'll give you a call when it's ready."

"Could you lay the stone in the setting so I can take a picture of it with my cell phone? My daughter will never let me hear the end of it if I don't send her a picture."

"Of course," Harriet said. "I was just going to suggest it."

It was almost noon by the time they'd said their goodbyes to Harriet and were back out on the sidewalk. "Let's head over to Pete's for lunch," John said.

"Perfect idea. And after what you've just done, I'm picking up the check."

"Give me a minute to clear that table by the window," Pete said, hailing a busboy.

"We're not in a tearing hurry," John replied.

"That's a first for the two of you," Pete remarked as Frank Haynes and David Wheeler approached.

"Hello, Frank, David," John said, shaking both their hands. "What're you two up to?"

"We just finished agility class," Haynes replied. "You should see David and Dodger. Head of the class."

David blushed. "I don't know about that. He was off today."

"Nonsense," Haynes said. "Seemed fine to me. Everyone—even dogs—are entitled to an 'off' day."

Maggie swiveled to look directly at Haynes. She never thought she'd hear the voice of moderation from him. Some people were full of surprises. "You're on your way out?" she asked.

"Yes," Haynes replied. "We usually stop in after class before I take David and Dodger home."

She turned to David. "Would you be available to swing by Rosemont this afternoon? I'd like to have some of the furniture in the attic moved around. I don't think it'll take more than an hour."

"Sure. That'd be fine."

Maggie didn't notice the hard gleam in Frank Haynes' eyes. "We're going to grab a quick bite and then John will drop me off at Rosemont. Can you come over in an hour?"

"I'll be there," David assured her.

———⁂———

Maggie had just hung up her coat when Frank Haynes' Mercedes sedan pulled up to her front door and he and David got out of the car.

"Frank," Maggie exclaimed. "I didn't expect to see you."

"I've been in that attic, remember?"

"Indeed I do," Maggie replied. "I'm still trying to forget that horrible day I got trapped up there. Thank God you came along, Frank. I'm still grateful."

Frank waved away the compliment. "Some of that furniture is fairly large. Since you said that John was dropping you off, I figured David might need a hand with it. So I offered to come with him to help."

Maggie stared, mouth agape. This was definitely not the Frank Haynes she experienced on a daily basis at Town Hall. "That's awfully nice, Frank," she replied.

The three of them were halfway up the first flight of stairs when Maggie's phone began to ring on the console table in the entryway.

"Just start moving the chairs by the windows into the center of the room," Maggie said, retracing her steps. "Let me get the phone, and then I'll be right up."

Frank Haynes smiled his Cheshire cat grin and took the stairs to the attic two at a time, with David on his heels.

Haynes switched on the overhead bulbs and gestured to the chairs. "Why don't you start sliding them over here?" he said, indicating a clearing in the center. "And I'll circle around to see what we've got."

David began tugging an oversized wing chair into place as Haynes proceeded slowly in the opposite direction. He might have missed the folder he was searching for if he hadn't stepped on it and started to slip. He looked down and there, under his right foot, was the folder he'd fantasized about since that fateful day just months ago when he'd forced the attic door open and rescued Maggie; the folder labeled *F.H./Rosemont*. He still didn't know why he hadn't taken it when he'd had the chance. But that chance was now presenting itself to him again.

Frank Haynes quickly bent and picked up the folder. He glanced at David, struggling with an unwieldy chaise. Haynes tucked the folder inside his jacket and tugged the zipper shut.

"Here, let me help you with that," he practically squealed with joy.

David gave him an odd look.

Haynes turned to the door. "And here's Mayor Martin. Tell us where you want all of this, and we'll be on our way."

Chapter 30

Frank Haynes turned left out of the long, winding driveway to Rosemont and headed his Mercedes sedan to David's house.

"Sorry it took so long," David said.

"I just need to check on something at one of my restaurants, that's all," Haynes replied, aware that he was becoming increasingly testy as time went on.

David nodded. "I really appreciate the ride home and the agility classes."

Haynes glanced at the boy. "The two of you have the knack for it. You remind me of me and my dog when I was your age."

"Did you do agility?"

"No. I didn't know about it back then."

David sighed. "I just hope Dodger is okay. He was definitely not himself today."

Haynes reached across and patted his arm. "Keep an eye on him. If you're still worried in a couple of days, we'll take him to Dr. Allen."

Frank Haynes pulled into David's driveway. "Let me know how Dodger is doing, one way or the other. Call me tomorrow, okay?"

David nodded and Haynes backed out of the driveway and headed for Haynes Enterprises. The allure of the folder hidden in his jacket was overpowering.

Frank Haynes sprinted up the steps to Haynes Enterprises. He was glad it was a Saturday and he'd be alone. He wanted to review the folder—the one he'd been fixated on since that day in the attic—in private.

The file was slim. On top was a genealogy of Paul Martin, obtained from an ancestry website. It showed that Silas Martin—the town's first millionaire and owner of the sawmill that once operated on the Shawnee River—died in 1937. Everyone in town now knew the property as The Mill, the fine-dining restaurant, inn, and spa that occupied the site. Silas left two sons, Hector and Joseph. It was well-known local folklore that Joseph, an attorney by trade, had moved away from his autocratic father to practice law in Cleveland, leaving Hector to run the sawmill with his father. Silas had disinherited Joseph and left his home, Rosemont, and his entire fortune to Hector. Hector was a bachelor who lived to the impressive old age of one hundred six. His brother, Joseph, predeceased him. According to the documents Haynes held, Hector left his estate to "his living heirs," which turned out to be Paul Martin. Nothing new there.

Next came a series of letters, paper-clipped together, from Paul to an attorney in Chicago. Haynes removed the clip, arranged the letters in chronological order and proceeded from the beginning. The attorney represented the estate of Hector Martin. He'd contacted Paul after Hector's death in 2000 to inform him of his inheritance. *What a sweet moment that must have been for that bastard Martin*, Haynes thought. The attorney continued that they were still searching for other potential heirs and would be in touch when that search was completed.

Paul wrote back to ask what the search entailed. The attorney replied that the public records of births and deaths could only be accessed in person at the Vital Records Office and that he wouldn't be able to make the trip to Westbury until sometime during the latter part of the following month.

The final letter in the sequence was from another lawyer in the firm, informing Paul that the attorney who had been handling the estate had retired and moved abroad. This attorney was now assigned to Hector's estate. No other heirs had been uncovered. He concluded by suggesting that Paul schedule a trip to Chicago to sign papers and accept the transfer of assets from the estate.

The final item in the file was a packet of bank statements and spreadsheets, detailing bank accounts, lists of stocks and bonds, and deeds to real property. Haynes almost missed the envelope stuck to the back of one of the bank statements.

He carefully removed it and drew out an old birth certificate that appeared to be an original. Haynes pulled a large magnifying glass out of his desk drawer and placed the document directly under the desk lamp. The certificate was dated June 6, 1938. His mother's birthday. It recorded the live birth of a female—the name, "Baby Girl"—born in Mercy Hospital.

Haynes gasped at what he read next. The mother was listed as Mary Rose Hawkins and the father as Hector Martin. The marital status box was checked: unmarried. His grandmother's name was Mary Rose and her maiden name had been Hawkins. And she'd worked at Rosemont as a parlor maid until she'd married his grandfather only a few weeks after his mother was born. He'd always assumed it had been a shotgun wedding.

Haynes slammed back into his chair. Was his mother the illegitimate child of Hector Martin? *Had she known?* He didn't think so—she would have told him. He swiveled his chair to look out the window. His mother had worked hard every day of her life, most of the time holding down two jobs, to make up for the profligate ways of his philandering father. A little bit of money might have made things much easier for her. For both of them, for that matter.

He turned his attention back to the papers on his desk. Was he Hector's grandson and the legitimate heir to his fortune? Was he— Frank Haynes—the rightful owner of Rosemont?

Haynes steepled his fingers and rested his chin on them, contemplating his next move. He needed to investigate his possible heirship, and he needed to do it as discretely as possible. Haynes smiled his mirthless smile. *What a delicious surprise to drop on the ever-charming Mayor Maggie Martin.* He could just picture the look on her face when she learned she'd have to pack up and move out of Rosemont. He'd be magnanimous, of course. Maybe even give her an entire weekend to vacate. He chuckled to himself.

Frank Haynes carefully gathered the papers on his desk and replaced them in the folder. He retrieved the key to his wall safe from under his desk, removed the painting that concealed it and opened the safe. The F.H./Rosemont folder would join the only other item in the safe—the jump drive with evidence incriminating Wheeler and Delgado. One day, he might need this evidence.

He pulled his jacket from the back of his chair, set the alarm, and locked the door to Haynes Enterprises. He'd contact the prominent New York City estate firm of Hirim & Wilkens first thing Monday morning.

Haynes frequently detoured to drive by Rosemont on his way home, and he followed the familiar practice this afternoon, slipping into the clearing along the berm of the road that ran below the back of the property. He'd spied on Maggie on previous occasions— watching figures moving in front of the windows, and always with a longing that was palpable. Whether it was for the house itself or the life being lived in it, he didn't know.

Tonight, however, was different. The house against the late afternoon sky stood dark and quiet and beautiful. Haynes turned off the engine and sat, staring at the home without seeing. What would his life have been like if he'd been raised there? If life had afforded his long-suffering mother a little comfort and security? Maybe she wouldn't have worked herself into an early grave. Maybe she would have been there to buffer the effects of his abusive father. Maybe she even would have divorced the bastard, and they could have lived a peaceful life in this glorious home.

Frank Haynes pounded his fist on his dashboard. "Damn all of you," he yelled, the words reverberating in the silent car. He rested his forehead against the steering wheel and tears coursed down his cheeks.

Chapter 31

Frank Haynes waved to David Wheeler when he arrived at the dog park late one Saturday afternoon. Despite his best efforts to work with Sally in the past three weeks, he and his border collie remained in the remedial group. *At the bottom of the remedial group,* he reminded himself wryly. Dodger loped along contentedly with David.

David handed Frank Haynes a Ziploc bag full of tiny pieces of cut-up hot dogs. "I've got training treats," Haynes said, pulling a bag of expensive tidbits from his jacket pocket.

"She'll like these better. Trust me," David replied.

Haynes looked at David. *He's in his element,* he thought. The shy boy—the one who mumbled, head down, contemplating his shoes— was nowhere to be found when he was talking about dogs. *I can relate to that.*

"Put a piece of hot dog in your hand and tell her to sit."

"Sit," Haynes commanded. Sally stood and wagged her tail. Dodger sat and Haynes gave him a treat.

"Okay. Give me your hand," David said. Frank stretched out his palm and David placed another piece of hot dog in it. "This time, when you tell her to sit, move this hand over her head and along her back. She'll try to follow the treat, and she'll sit automatically."

Haynes followed David's direction and, after squirming to try to follow his hand, Sally sat. "Good girl," Haynes praised as he gave her the piece of hot dog. Dodger thumped his tail from his seated position, and David laughed. Haynes reached over and gave him another treat.

"I think Dodger's milking the system. I'm going to run him on the course while you two work on this. Repeat until you're out of hot dogs," he said, signaling Dodger to follow him. "Holler when you're done, and we'll work on stay."

Haynes and Sally proceeded as instructed while Dodger flew around the agility course in perfect alignment with his master's commands. Things didn't go as smoothly when Haynes and Sally were on their own, but they were making progress in the right direction. Haynes was reaching into the bag for the last piece of hot dog when he heard David call to him from the agility course.

Haynes turned to see David running toward him. "Something's really wrong with Dodger," he said. "Can you come see?"

Haynes followed David on the run.

Something was, indeed, very wrong with Dodger. He lay motionless on the track on his right side, his one good eye moving wildly about. His breathing was short and shallow. Haynes bent on one knee, and Dodger turned his eye to him, keeping his head flat on the ground.

"That's a good boy," Haynes said softly. He touched Dodger's back and the dog yipped. "What happened?"

"He was weaving through those stakes," David said, gesturing in the direction of the track. "Going really fast, keeping close to them. It looked like he clipped one with his shoulder on his way out."

Haynes nodded. "His left leg's hanging here at an awkward angle. I'll bet he's torn something or dislocated it."

"Will he be all right?" David couldn't conceal the fear in his voice. "Can they fix it? They won't have to put him down, will they?" His voice quivered.

"No. Of course not. Don't even think that. We'll get him to Dr. Allen."

"But he's not moving. Is he paralyzed?"

"He's lying still because he's in pain. He's not paralyzed." And as if he could understand them, Dodger wagged his tail.

David stared at Dodger. "What do you think it'll cost?"

"Don't worry about that. I'm sure I can work something out with Dr. Allen."

"I'll pay it, but it might take some time."

Haynes nodded. "I'm sure you will." He looked at his watch. "Let's get him to Westbury Animal Hospital before they close for the day. I've got a sturdy blanket in my car. We'll make a stretcher and lay him in the back."

———

John Allen had a full schedule that afternoon, but told his assistant that he'd be happy to work Dodger in between patients.

"I won't ever turn away Frank Haynes, Juan. He's done more good for animals than anyone I know. I'll always make time for him."

"That's what I thought," Juan replied. "They're in Exam Room 3. Dodger is really uncomfortable."

John Allen opened the door to Exam Room 3 and was no more than a foot inside the door when he'd made a tentative diagnosis. He bent down and carefully approached the suffering animal. Dodger thumped his tail in greeting in spite of his obvious misery. "Do you know what happened to him?"

"We think he hurt his shoulder weaving through the stakes on the agility track."

John Allen nodded.

"Can you fix him?" David asked anxiously.

"Let me take some x-rays," he replied calmly. "We can wheel this table right back to our machine. That's a good boy, Dodger," he praised. "We'll be back."

The exam confirmed John's worst fears. Dodger had a messy shoulder dislocation, complicated by ligament tears and a hairline fracture. Dodger needed to be seen by a canine orthopedic surgeon. A specialist could perform the new surgical techniques that would be best. The nearest one was in Chicago and was extremely expensive. John sighed. He felt sorry for this boy, still grieving the death of his father. He'd treat Dodger for free, but knew that the specialist would not.

John returned to the room where David and Frank Haynes waited. "Dodger's suffered a very serious injury to his shoulder. I can treat his pain—we've already given him a shot, and he's happily asleep—and we can immobilize the shoulder until it heals, but he needs orthopedic surgery to really repair the damage."

"So do the surgery," Haynes said.

"I don't have the necessary equipment here, Frank," John replied. "You'd have to take him to a specialist in Chicago."

"Then that's what we'll do. Can you refer someone?"

"I can't afford that," David said quietly.

"I'm going to pay for it, David. You don't have to worry about that." John clapped Haynes on the back and squeezed his shoulder. David beamed. Frank Haynes turned aside. "Can you set it up for us, John?"

"Yes, but you'll need to get him there tomorrow. And I'm guessing you'll have to leave Dodger there for a few days. The surgery will probably cost four or five thousand dollars."

Frank Haynes waved his hand in dismissal. "Just let me know when and where. We'll have to leave very early tomorrow morning," he said to David. "Can you miss school? Your mother will have to approve."

"She will," he said, turning grateful eyes to Haynes.

"Good," John said. "This is the best thing for him. And I'll talk to the surgeon—I should be able to handle all of the follow-up care. I'll keep him sedated here tonight." He turned to Haynes. "You can pick him up as early as you want tomorrow. I'll help you get him loaded into your car. If you can drive him in a van or an SUV, that would be best. We'll lay him down in the back."

"I'll rent one," Haynes replied.

"Can I see him before we go?" David asked and his voice cracked.

"Sure," John said. "Juan can take you back." He summoned Juan on the intercom.

"That's a really kind thing you're doing for that boy, Frank," John said after David and Juan departed from the exam room.

Haynes flushed. "Thanks for seeing us without an appointment. I'll let you know how it goes in Chicago."

———

While John Allen was busy that afternoon at Westbury Animal Hospital, Maggie Martin found a thirty-minute break in her schedule to attend to a personal errand of her own. She was buzzed in to Burman Jewelers clutching a full-page ad she'd torn out of a magazine. The ad was for a classic Rolex watch that John had admired one Sunday afternoon when she'd been snuggled next to him, reading her magazine, while he watched a football game on television.

Harriet greeted her warmly. "Are you here to visit your ring? It's not quite ready yet."

Maggie laughed. "I hadn't even thought of visiting it. Does anyone do that?"

"You bet they do. Would you like to see it?"

Maggie shook her head. "No. Not until John's with me and it's time to put it on."

"It'll only be a few more days," Harriet assured her. "What have you got there?"

Maggie held out the Rolex advertisement. "John admired this watch, and I'd like to give it to him. As a surprise for him when I get the ring."

"This is stunning. And we carry Rolex."

"Do you have it?"

Harriet shook her head. "No. But we can order it. I'll have our distributor overnight it to us." She looked at Maggie over the top of her glasses. "This costs almost as much as your diamond. You know that, don't you?"

Maggie beamed. "That's the plan. I'm a modern woman, after all."

Harriet laughed. "I sure hope you're starting a trend. We'd double our revenue."

"When you get the watch, will you wrap it for me?"

"Of course. I'll put the two of you in that private viewing room in back when you come in to get your ring. I'll have it sitting on the bottom shelf of the case that sits right inside the door. It'll be all set."

"Perfect," Maggie said, handing Harriet her credit card. "And don't breathe a word about this. I want it to be a surprise."

"No worries there," Harriet replied. "Jewelers keep more secrets than you can imagine."

Chapter 32

"No, don't interrupt him if he's in surgery," Maggie sighed. "But ask him to call me as soon as he gets out, okay? Before he starts seeing patients. It's vitally important that I talk to him." She hung up the receiver after Juan promised to do as she requested. She'd declined to tell him why she was calling. Juan might think that her ring being ready to be picked up was not "vitally important."

Maggie pulled up her calendar for the day on her computer screen. Her morning was uncharacteristically free, but she had a Transit Department meeting. Tonya Holmes would be at that meeting. Maggie hoped that John could get away for a few minutes to meet her at the jewelers this morning. Tonya was one of the first people she'd like to see her ring.

Maggie forced her attention on the report they'd be discussing at the transit meeting. The prospect of curtailing bus service was unappealing. It disproportionately affected low-income earners. Wasn't this the group that needed their assistance the most? The method the department used to set the schedule was archaic, to say the least. She rifled through the papers and found the table she was seeking. Surely there was a computer program that municipalities used to match bus routes with rider usage.

Maggie became engrossed in a detailed Internet search of the subject and almost let an incoming call go to voice mail. She caught herself at the last minute and answered in a breathless rush. "Maggie Martin."

"Hey there, good lookin'," John said. "Juan insisted that I call you as soon as I finished surgery. Is everything okay?"

"Yes. Sorry. I didn't mean to alarm you." Maggie paused. "The ring is ready," she continued sheepishly.

John laughed. "Well, I guess that qualifies as 'vitally important.' Do you want to pick it up tonight after work?"

"No. I'd like to pick it up now," Maggie said, unable to keep the note of pleading out of her voice.

"What's the rush?"

"You have to ask? There's a four-carat diamond sitting in a box less than a mile from me, and it's got my name on it. That's the rush! Plus, I have a meeting this afternoon, and Tonya Holmes will be there."

"And you'd like to show off your ring."

"I'm not sure I'd put it that way, but ... yes." She heard John typing on a keyboard.

"I've had a cancellation, so if you can leave right now, I'll meet you over there."

Maggie squealed. "On my way. Thank you, John."

"You look frozen," Harriet said, ushering Maggie into the private room in the back.

"It wasn't too bad. When John said he could meet me here, I was so excited I tore out of Town Hall like the place was on fire and made a beeline for the shop. I didn't even stop to get my car."

"Jewelry can do that to a gal," Harriet observed. "Do you want to see it?"

"Yes, but John should be here when I do. Is the watch ready?"

Harriet nodded. "Can I get you a cup of coffee while you wait?"

"No, thanks. John's on his way. He won't be long."

John, however, was not "on his way," and it was a full thirty minutes before the buzzer sounded again.

Maggie turned to the door with relief. She knew she should have returned to Town Hall and picked her ring up after work, but she also knew that she'd sit there all morning, waiting for John, if that's what it took.

"I got snagged on the way out the door. Sorry, honey," John said, giving her a quick kiss.

Harriet was right behind him, a beautiful purple velvet box in her hand. "I'm going to hand this to John and leave you two alone in here. If it doesn't fit or there's anything you don't like, just let me know. We close at six. You can stay in here until then, or as long as you like, and we won't disturb you," she said, closing the door with a mischievous wink.

Maggie and John smiled into each other's eyes. He took her hand and led her to the chair on the other side of the small table in the room. He moved the table aside and got down on one knee. "I know we've already had this conversation—and you've said yes. I'm not giving you the chance to change your mind," he added hastily. "But a proper proposal should include a ring, and I didn't have one last time. So I want to do this again—for the record books, as they say." He took both of her hands in his. "Margaret Martin, will you make me the happiest man on earth and do me the great honor of marrying me? I will devote the rest of my life to believing in you, supporting your hopes and dreams, and loving you."

Maggie looked into the face of this dear man that she loved so completely. "Yes. There's nothing I want more." They kissed long and hard.

When they finally drew apart, she said, "Now let's get that ring on my finger!"

Harriet had sized it properly; everything was perfect. Under the bright overhead lighting, Maggie turned her hand this way and that, admiring the remarkable ring. John beamed.

"I hate to break this up, but I've got to get back to my patients," John sighed.

"Not so fast. There's one more thing we need to do while we're here," Maggie said.

John raised his eyebrows. "I have something for you." She leapt from her chair. "Sit right here," she said, moving him into the seat she had just vacated.

She picked up a square box, wrapped in gold paper and tied with a maroon ribbon. She got down on one knee and took both of his hands in her own. "I love you with every fiber of my being. You are the kindest person I've ever met. And the most honest. I trust you completely. I'll devote myself to your happiness." She picked up the box and handed it to him. "I wanted you to have something really special to mark our engagement, too."

John looked at her, flabbergasted. "What in the world is this?"

"Open it and find out," she said, wiggling like a five-year-old at a birthday party.

John tore open the paper to reveal a Rolex box containing the classic watch. He removed the watch from its holder and turned it over in his hands.

Maggie watched him anxiously. "I think it's the one you liked; it was in that magazine ad you commented on. But if it's not—if you don't like it—Harriet can order you whatever you want. My feelings won't be hurt or anything."

John cleared his throat. "It's not that. It's perfect and I love it. I never in a million years thought I'd own a Rolex, and I certainly never thought I'd receive one as a gift from my fiancée."

Maggie beamed. "There you are then. We've both received lovely gifts today. Put it on," she encouraged. "I want to see how it looks.

145

And Harriet can size it." John slid the watch on his wrist and secured the clasp. He locked Maggie into a fierce embrace. "Thank you, darling. You are a most surprising woman, Maggie Martin. There's no one else like you on the planet. I'm one lucky guy."

Chapter 33

Glenn Vaughn rushed to answer the phone before it woke his sleeping wife. Gloria was fighting a cold, and he wanted her to get as much rest as possible. At their ages, these things could turn into pneumonia fast. He looked at the kitchen clock. If this were a phone solicitor calling before nine in the morning, they'd get a piece of his mind.

"Vaughn residence," he answered sternly.

"Glenn, it's Frank Haynes."

Glenn brightened. He'd be forever grateful to the councilman for his help in obtaining the zoning variance that allowed Fairview Terraces to conduct profit-making ventures on their campus—activities that provided the income to bring the mortgage on the senior center current and stop the foreclosure on their community. "How are you, Frank?"

"Sorry to call so early. I hope you were up."

"Already on my second cup of coffee. What can I do for you?"

"I need your help, Glenn. Are you still working with David Wheeler? You're his court-appointed mentor, aren't you?"

"I was. David finished his program months ago. The court expunged the theft from his record. I've talked to him a couple of times since, and he seems fine. Very busy with school and that dog of his. Why? Is he in trouble again?"

"He's fine," Haynes quickly replied. "Great kid. It's his dog I'm calling about."

"I heard you two were taking agility classes together. And that David and Dodger were at the head of the class."

"They were, until Dodger tore up his shoulder. It was so bad that John Allen couldn't perform the necessary surgery. We had to take him to a canine orthopedic surgeon in Chicago. The operation was last week and went very well. Dodger will recover, but he may never be able to run an agility track again."

"I'm assuming David has you to thank for that expensive surgeon, Frank." Haynes remained silent. "I'm glad to hear he'll recover. I'm sure David is disappointed to give up agility training for a while. The last time we spoke, that was all he talked about."

"That's why I'm calling, Glenn. David has gone into a tailspin over this. I've been checking on him and Dodger every few days, but I think it'd help if you called him. He likes you, and I think he'd listen to you. He needs to understand that healing takes time before things can return to normal. I guess he just needs some hope," Haynes concluded.

"I'd be delighted to help. He was doing a good job of getting back to normal at school and recovering from his dad's suicide. Thanks for letting me know, Frank. I'll see him after school today."

———

Glenn Vaughn waited for David Wheeler outside the entrance to the high school, much as he had the first time he met the boy after being appointed his mentor. This time, David came through the doors with a group of boys, jostling and joking. David wasn't contributing, but at least he wasn't a loner anymore.

David spotted the older man as Glenn raised his hand and waved to him. "Mr. Vaughn," he called, running over to him. "Is something wrong with the courts?"

"No. Everything's fine. I've missed seeing you and thought I'd pull in to find out how you're doing."

David shrugged. "Okay, I guess."

"How's school?" Glenn asked, turning to walk to his car along the curb, drawing David with him.

"It's school. Fine"

"Are you doing well in your classes?"

"All A's and one B."

"That's terrific, David. You're a smart kid. Those are the marks you should be getting."

David shrugged again.

"You don't seem too pleased with them."

"It's not that, Mr. Vaughn."

"Why don't we go get something to eat?" Glenn asked when they reached his car. "Spoil my dinner and make Gloria mad at me. What do you say?"

"Yeah. Okay."

They got in Glenn's sleek old Cadillac, and he headed to Tomascino's. "Pizza sound good?"

"Sure."

Glenn let the boy recede into silence until they were tucked in a booth near the kitchen and had placed their order. He looked at the boy steadily until he returned his gaze. "So—what's got you so down in the dumps?"

"I dunno. It's Dodger, I guess."

Glenn nodded. "I understand he had surgery. How's he doing?"

"Okay. Healing well. But it'll be a long time before he's fully recovered—if ever."

"I hear that you're doing a great job taking care of him."

David replied with his characteristic shrug.

"If he's recovering, why are you upset?"

"It's just that we were doing that agility stuff together and it was really fun. We were good at it. He may never be the same. I just miss it, that's all."

"I understand how disappointing it is to be forced to give up things that you love. At my age, it happens all the time." Glenn silently contemplated the situation. "There are other activities you can do together, as a team. I think that's what you're really missing."

"Like what?" David asked.

"You could train him to be a therapy dog."

"Like for blind people? And give him up?" David asked. "I'm not doing that."

"No. Not a companion animal. I'm talking about dogs that go into hospitals and nursing homes to see sick people. Visits from dogs can reduce blood pressure and help healing. I've seen it. These dogs bring people lots of joy. They even go to children's hospitals. Is Dodger good with people? Do you think he'd like that?"

"He's the friendliest dog in the world. He loves to get petted."

"Does he sit and stay? He can't jump on anyone."

"You should see him," David replied. "He's really well trained, because of the agility courses." David drew in a breath. "How do we start?"

"You need to be certified to go into hospitals. You'll have to take a training class and pass a test."

"Is it expensive?"

"Nope. Free. I'll pick up the paperwork tomorrow and leave it in your mailbox at home."

"Awesome," David replied as their server placed an extra-large, extra-cheese, five-meat pizza on their table. David dug in with gusto.

"In the meantime, why don't you bring him over to Fairview Terraces this weekend? You can check out how he behaves and see if it's something you'd like to do. We have lots of residents in wheelchairs. It would make their day to see him."

David brightened. "We can do that. How about Saturday morning? That's when we had agility class, but we can't do that anymore."

"Perfect. Here's the address," he said, writing it on a scrap of paper and sliding it across the table. "Come over at nine thirty, and I'll take you to the nursing wing."

"Thanks, Mr. Vaughn. I'll see you Saturday."

David was anxious to get going again and was certain Dodger, cooped up inside the house since he came home from Chicago, was suffering from cabin fever. An outing to Fairview Terraces would be just the thing for Dodger.

"Come on, boy," he called as he clipped the leash on his collar. It was cold this Saturday morning but at least it was dry, and they would only be outside for the walk from the parking lot to the entrance. "We get to park in employee parking because of you." He gently lifted Dodger into his mother's car. "How 'bout that? And your job is to walk around and let people pet you if they want to. No licking anybody," he admonished. "Does that sound good?"

Dodger thumped his tail.

Glenn Vaughn was waiting inside the nursing wing of Fairview Terraces when David Wheeler pulled into the employee parking space near the entrance. He opened the door and hurried down the steps in case David needed help, but he and Dodger were out of the car and turning toward him before Glenn reached the parking lot.

"You made it," Glenn said, reaching for David's hand and grasping it firmly. David smiled and shook the older man's hand. "How's Dodger today? He looks good. Is he up for this?"

"He's great. I think he doesn't know he's still recovering. I'll bet he'd try to run an agility course if he had the chance."

"I guess dogs don't have any better sense than people," Glenn observed. "Let's get you inside."

"So, we just walk up and down the halls and see if anyone wants to pet him?" David asked. "What if no one's interested? Do we leave?"

"They'll be interested, all right. The nursing staff posted a notice and they've been telling the residents. There's already a dozen people in the lounge waiting for him, and the nurses on duty made me promise that you'd go see them. The head nurse told me that studies show animals reduce the stress that nurses experience and allow them to be better caregivers. There are hospitals back east that make rescue animals available in the staff lounge. The staff loves it and a lot of the animals get adopted, so everybody wins."

Glenn held the door open for David and Dodger to pass through. "Dodger's still recovering, so don't get carried away. Let him stay as long as you're both having fun. If he gets tired or bored, take him home. This is just a trial to see if the two of you enjoy it."

David nodded. "Thanks, Mr. Vaughn."

Glenn pointed to a line of six wheelchairs along the wall. The woman in the wheelchair at the end smiled broadly and beckoned to them. "Looks like you've got your first customer."

Dodger greeted the woman with polite restraint, sitting patiently by her chair and allowing her to pat his head and rub his ears. When she was done, Dodger didn't try to paw at her hand or nudge her with his head for more attention. He waited patiently for his master's direction.

"What a nice doggy you are. So well behaved. Thank you so much for bringing him, young man," she said to David. "I don't think we've ever had a young person bring their pet to see us. In fact, we don't get animals in here very often. I always had dogs and cats of my own. One of the things I miss most living in this wing of Fairview Terraces is that we can't have pets."

David looked at the woman. "I'd hate that. It must be really hard."

"It is," she agreed. "Maybe you can come back on a regular basis. We'd all love it, and by the looks of Dodger, he'd love it, too."

David nodded. "We're just trying it out today. We want to be sure Dodger behaves himself."

The woman laughed. "I'd say he's passing with flying colors. You ought to see about going to the children's wing at the hospital as well."

David looked at the gentle, noble animal sitting so peacefully at his side. If it weren't for Dodger's warm body in the bed next to him every night, snoring lightly, David was certain he wouldn't be able to put aside his sorrow and fall asleep. And now Dodger was spreading his magic to others. David's heart swelled with pride.

"I'll look into it," David said, moving to the man in the next wheelchair, patiently waiting his turn.

The scene was repeated over and over, and by the time David and Dodger were ready to leave Fairview Terraces an hour and a half later, David's mind was made up. He found Glenn Vaughn reading the newspaper in one of the reception chairs at the entrance.

"Mr. Vaughn," he stated solemnly. "We'd like to come back here. Next week, if that's okay. And we'd like to get tested so Dodger can go to the hospital."

Glenn folded his paper and set it on an end table. "I was hoping you'd say that. I was watching the two of you for a while. Then I talked to some of the staff and the residents. Everyone enjoyed your visit immensely."

"Dodger's a wonder. He makes people feel better."

Glenn stood. "It's not just Dodger, son. You have an easy, genuine way of interacting with people. You put them at ease. You may not know this, David, but that's a rare and helpful quality to have."

David blushed and turned his head to stare out the door.

"People will be talking about this visit all week. I'm proud of Dodger, but I'm more proud of you. Let's get the two of you certified as soon as possible. You may not want to go back to agility after this."

Chapter 34

Forest Smith turned up the collar on his coat against the icy wind as he headed to his car in the deserted parking lot of Stetson & Graham. He hadn't left work earlier than eleven o'clock any night since he'd been assigned to assist Special Counsel Scanlon with the town's fraud investigation. Tonight was no exception. He was unlocking his SUV when he saw headlights approaching in the window's reflection. Turning, Smith shielded his eyes noticing the car was headed straight toward him.

A black sedan pulled up next to him. The darkly tinted front-passenger window came down and the driver leaned toward him. "Forest Smith," came a gravelly voice. "I'm Chuck Delgado. Get in. We gotta get to know each other."

Smith hesitated. He knew who Chuck Delgado was, of course, and had heard the rumors of his ties to organized crime.

"I'm not gonna do nuthin' to you," Delgado said. "I just wanna talk."

Smith bent and spoke through the open window. "Then we can talk in my car."

"Have it your way, kid," he said, putting his car in park. Delgado climbed out from behind the steering wheel, leaving the engine running.

Smith unlocked his SUV, and both men settled themselves in the front seats.

"See?" Delgado said. "No trouble. And there won't be any trouble if you take care of your friends."

"You're not a friend," Smith stated firmly.

"Maybe not, but your dealer is."

Smith's eyebrows shot up.

"We know about your fondness for painkillers. Our boy supplies you. And any customer of his is a friend of ours. Particularly if he's a hotshot young attorney trying to make a name for himself."

Smith stared at Delgado in stony silence.

"I thought you'd warm up to me." Delgado smiled, pleased with himself. "Here's what we need you to do. Simple, really. Just keep us informed of what's going on with the investigation. Hell—I'm a councilmember—I'm entitled to be informed."

"I don't know anything. I'm just helping Scanlon push paper."

"I think we both know that's not true. Or won't be for long."

"What exactly are you looking for?"

"You tell us everything you know, and we'll decide what's important to us." Delgado stretched his arms and cracked his knuckles. "Here's how we'll do this. We'll meet once a week, just like we're doing now. Isn't this cozy?"

Smith turned away from Delgado. "You cooperate, and we can help with your career, too."

Smith finally nodded.

"Smart boy. Good decision. How's about we celebrate our new relationship?" He pulled a flask out of his breast pocket.

"I don't drink and drive," Smith answered icily.

Delgado shrugged. "Gotta have some fun once in a while, buddy boy." He reached for the door handle. "I'll see you here next week, same time." He turned back to the younger man. "And don't go doin' nuthin' stupid. You don't wanna mess up that bright future of yours," he said as he heaved himself out of the passenger seat and stumbled to his car.

Chapter 35

Maggie was in her seat in the council chamber as the department head and managers of the Transit Department filed into the room. The other members of the council who sat on the Transit Committee were Tonya Holmes and Russell Isaac. Tonya hurried to her seat as Maggie was calling the meeting to order. Russell Isaac was nowhere to be seen.

"Ladies and gentlemen, thank you for your very thorough report," she said, resting her hand on a thick stack of papers, "and your recommendations for budget cuts." She turned to Tonya. "Have you had a chance to review these in detail?"

Tonya looked at Maggie and opened her mouth to reply, but her words froze on her lips. She stared, wide-eyed, at the flashing orb on Maggie's left hand.

Maggie smiled and shook her head. *Later,* she mouthed.

Tonya cleared her throat and began. "I've reviewed them. The cuts to bus routes will yield the budget savings the council requested of the department, but we were hoping that the department could come up with other ways of saving money besides discontinuing essential services for a significant portion of our citizens."

The department head smiled smugly and shrugged. "There really isn't anything else we can do," he stated. "If you want to save money, that's the only way."

"Really?" Tonya shot back. "You haven't gone out to bid on your maintenance contract in over five years; you've made no effort to avail yourself of federal funds to defray the cost of newer, more energy-efficient vehicles; and you set the bus schedules using paper and pencil. It looks to me like you've made no effort whatsoever to modernize your department."

"What are you suggesting?" he demanded.

"Maybe we should cut costs by replacing you with someone that's interested in making improvements and running the department efficiently."

The temperature in the room seemed to drop precipitously while the Transit Department head and Councilwoman Holmes glared at each other.

Maggie broke the silence. "I had some of the same questions this morning when I reviewed your report. Why don't you use a computer program to generate your routes? I researched the issue. There are a number of programs available to municipalities."

"They cost money. And aren't we supposed to be saving money?" he retorted.

"They're not that expensive. Have you investigated any of them?"

A manager seated in the row behind the department head raised her hand.

Maggie nodded to her. "Yes. Do you have something to add?"

"Thank you, Mayor Martin. I've been looking into this very issue for the past several years. I've put together recommendations."

The department head swiveled stiffly in his chair to face her.

Maggie and Tonya exchanged glances as the woman flushed and looked down at her hands.

"Do you have them with you? We'd like to review the issue in detail. What's the bottom line?"

The woman cast a sidelong glance at the department head and cleared her throat. "I believe we can revamp our bus routes, adjust our fee schedule, provide expanded bus service, and almost double our ridership revenue. We won't need to cut our routes, and we can contribute more money to the general fund," she concluded proudly.

"Now that's the kind of thinking we need on Westbury's staff," Tonya declared.

Maggie cut in. "That would be an outstanding improvement." She turned to the department head. "I'm glad to see that your department is filled with such competent, creative people."

"I was just getting to this," he lied.

"Let's review this proposal in depth and reach a decision on it before we leave here today," Maggie said. "We don't have the luxury of sitting on our hands."

She turned to the manager. "If this will do what you say it will, we need to act on it now."

———

The transit meeting finally concluded at seven o'clock. The department head shook hands unenthusiastically with Maggie and bolted for the exit before he had to speak to Tonya.

"You won't be sorry, Mayor Martin," the manager who put forth the winning proposal said, pumping Maggie's hand. "I'm positive this will work. It'll be even better than projected."

"We appreciate your speaking up," Tonya interjected. "I know that wasn't easy. And if you get any backlash from your boss, you let me know."

"He won't be any trouble," she said. "I've worked for him for years. He just hates change. I think he's scared of his computer. Now that you've made the decision, he'll let me implement it."

Tonya nodded. "We won't forget whose idea it was."

"Thank you," the woman said happily as she made her way to the door.

"We're finally alone," Tonya said, turning to Maggie. "Let me see that ring you're sporting. You practically blinded me during the meeting. I almost pulled my sunglasses out of my purse."

Maggie grinned and held out her hand, waving her ring finger up and down.

"Holy cow, girlfriend," Tonya exclaimed. "Is this what I think it is?"

Maggie nodded.

"When did this happen? Did he propose properly, down on one knee and everything?"

"He sure did. It was so romantic. On New Year's Eve."

"New Year's Eve? That was ages ago. Why didn't you tell me?"

"We got so busy with Roman getting lost and the new kittens and everything, it just didn't seem like the right time. And John let me pick out my own ring, so we decided to wait until I had it."

Tonya stared at her pointedly. "You certainly picked out a gorgeous ring for yourself. Forgive me for being nosy, but I've got to ask. How big is that diamond?"

"It's four carats."

Tonya gasped.

"Can you believe it? I told him I wanted a stone large enough that I wouldn't need my reading glasses to see."

"Good move. You certainly won't need any help to see this." Tonya hugged her. "I'm so happy for both of you, Maggie. George will be thrilled to hear this. I can't wait to give him the good news. We were heartbroken when the two of you broke up last year. You belong together."

"Thanks. You and George are very special to both John and me."

"When's the big day?"

"We haven't gotten that far, yet. We need to coordinate the date with my kids and my granddaughters' school holidays. But one thing is certain—the wedding will be at Rosemont."

Chapter 36

Loretta knocked on the closed door to Frank Haynes' office and cringed in anticipation of his response. She knew she was on thin ice because of her frequent absences to take care of her sick daughter, and she didn't want to do anything to further annoy him.

Loretta poked her head into the office. "Sorry to disturb you. You've got a visitor."

"Delgado?" Haynes looked up from his computer screen. "I told him not to come here anymore—since he upsets you so much."

Loretta looked sharply at her boss; she didn't know if he was being sarcastic or if he was trying to be nice. She'd bet on his being sarcastic. "It's David Wheeler, sir."

"David?" Haynes rose from his chair and walked swiftly past her to the reception area.

"What can I do for you?" he asked, motioning the boy to follow him to his office. He turned to Loretta. "Can you get David something to drink? What do we have?"

"We've got sodas in the refrigerator." She turned to David and gave him an appraising glance. She'd never known Frank Haynes to offer anything to anybody when they visited his office. "Would you like something?"

"A Coke would be great," he replied, twisting his cap in his hands.

"Would you like something, Mr. Haynes?" she asked, and he shook his head.

She placed the soda can on a coaster in front of David Wheeler and exited the office, leaving the door open. Loretta was curious about this boy who had intruded upon Frank Haynes, uninvited, yet received such a warm reception from him.

"How's Dodger? Dr. Allen tells me he's making a remarkable recovery."

"He's doing great. But Dr. Allen doesn't think he'll be able to return to the agility class anytime soon. Maybe not ever."

"You don't know that for certain. You have to give these things time," Haynes said. "Don't be discouraged."

"That's the thing. I'm not discouraged. Mr. Vaughn suggested that Dodger would make a good therapy dog. You know—for old people and sick children. We've gone to Fairview Terraces three times, and Dodger is a natural. You should see the way people react to him." David leaned forward in his chair and quit fidgeting with his cap. "It's incredible. I think Dodger knows what these people need and that he's helping them. I'm convinced of it."

Frank Haynes smiled. "I'll bet he does. I've never seen a therapy dog in action, but I've heard about them. There's definitely something to it."

"We're going to get certified to go to the hospital. I've read all about it, and I've been working with Dodger. He knows all that stuff anyway. We take the test this Saturday."

Frank Haynes nodded. "That's terrific, David. Good luck to you both. Thanks for stopping by to tell me," he said, starting to rise from his chair.

"That's not why I came, Mr. Haynes," David said.

"Frank, remember?"

David dug into his pocket and produced a ten-dollar bill, which he slid across the desk toward Haynes. "I want to start paying you back for all you've done for Dodger and me. Now that we can't represent Forever Friends in the agility trials."

Frank Haynes picked up the bill and came around his desk to sit next to David. "I don't want any of the money back that I gave you. It was a gift. And instead of representing Forever Friends at the agility trials, why don't you represent us at the hospital and nursing homes? I think that'll be even better public relations for us."

Loretta restrained herself from falling out of her chair. *Maybe Frank Haynes does have a decent bone in his body.* But why didn't he ever show that to her?

Glenn Vaughn was pushing back in his recliner on Saturday afternoon, preparing for a nap in front of the television when Frank Haynes called again.

"I wanted to thank you, Glenn. I just had a visit from David. The kid's spirits are high as a kite. He couldn't stop talking about taking Dodger to Fairview Terraces."

"You should have seen them, Frank. Dodger is a terrific dog, friendly and calm. David's done a terrific job of training him. But the remarkable transformation was in David."

"Really?"

"David has a warm, charming bedside manner, and it's genuine. I'm telling you what—he should pursue a career in medicine. He'd make a great doctor. Or maybe a vet."

Frank Haynes paused and realized he was smiling ear to ear. He sure was proud of that boy. "Good to hear, Glenn. Thank you for setting this up for him. He told me all about it. He's fired up to work with the children."

"It's your interest in this kid that got the ball rolling, Frank. I'm glad you called me."

"Thanks, Glenn. Let's keep in touch." Haynes ended the call with the unaccustomed feeling of being genuinely happy for someone else.

Chapter 37

Frank Haynes tossed the copy of *The New York Times* onto the Lucite coffee table in the sleek lobby of Hirim & Wilkens, attorneys-at-law. He pursed his lips as he checked the time on his Rolex; he'd been waiting almost an hour. The New York City skyline outside the floor-to-ceiling windows was shrouded in a foggy mist generated by a weather front that was in no hurry to move up the coast. He turned as a middle-aged woman in a severe black suit, hair swept into a tight bun at the nape of her neck, called his name.

"Mr. Wilkens will see you now."

Haynes glared at her.

"I'm sorry you had to wait, Mr. Haynes. This way, please. Can I get you something to drink?" she asked as she started down the long interior corridor lined with modern paintings done in shades of gray, black, and brown.

Haynes swallowed his indignation and followed in her wake. He'd chosen Hirim & Wilkens for their reputation—creative, confidential, and ruthless. He'd made the long trip here; he wasn't going to turn back now.

The woman ushered him into a corner office overlooking Central Park and quietly shut the door. The man behind the steel and glass desk was on the phone but motioned Haynes to a stiff leather chair on the other side of the desk.

Haynes sat and looked pointedly at the attorney.

"Keep at it. Good work. Call me as soon as you've got something." He replaced the receiver on the handset and rose, extending his hand. "You must be Frank Haynes. Simon Wilkens," he said.

Haynes shook his hand but maintained his icy stare.

"Sorry about the wait. I've been on the phone talking to some of my sources. That's who I was just talking to," he supplied.

"So you've reviewed the paperwork I sent you?"

"Indeed I have, Mr. Haynes. Very intriguing."

"And? Have you drawn any conclusions?"

"If the baby born to Mary Rose Hawkins was your mother, then you would have inherited an interest in Rosemont. Hector Martin's will was poorly drafted. My guess is that he wrote it himself. Normally, the closest living heir would inherit. That would be you, as grandson, over Paul Martin, a great-nephew. But the will bequeathed his property to 'my living *heirs*.' That would be both you *and* Paul."

"So I own a half-interest in Rosemont? Is that what you're saying? Is there any way to interpret that clause differently?"

Simon Wilkens raised a hand. "Let me finish. Hector's been dead for more than ten years. The estate was administered and closed. The law provides for something called a statute of limitations."

Haynes nodded. "I know what that is. You have to sue within a certain amount of time or you lose your right to do so."

"Exactly. Well put. There has to be certainty and finality to things. If the personal representative of Hector's estate simply overlooked your possible inheritance, then the statute of limitations to pursue him or the estate has expired."

Haynes slumped back into the uncomfortable chair. "So—I'm screwed. A day late and a dollar short. Is that what you're saying?"

"Not quite. We need to do some more digging."

Haynes head came up. "What do you mean?"

"If evidence of your relationship to Hector Martin was purposely concealed by someone, so that the personal representative couldn't

have found out about you even if he tried, then the statute of limitations is tolled. That means it doesn't begin to run until the
information about your relationship to Hector could have been discovered."

Haynes sat and quietly considered this.

"Did anyone know that Hector Martin was your mother's father?
Did you know he was your grandfather?"

Haynes shook his head. "No. I had no idea until I found that old
birth certificate last week. My grandmother died when my mother
was a teenager. I don't think my mother had any idea. Surely the man
that raised her as his daughter would have known. He would have
seen the birth certificate."

"Not necessarily. In those days, the fathers weren't in the room
when the baby was born. He might not have seen your grandmother
that entire day, or longer. By that time, the birth certificate could
have been safely placed with the Vital Records Office. Your grandmother signed it, but she probably never had a copy."

"I have the original," Haynes said, reaching into his briefcase and
handing the envelope he'd found in the folder to the lawyer.

Simon Wilkens carefully withdrew the pivotal document and examined it. "It does appear to be the original. And you say you found
it in a folder in the attic at Rosemont?"

Haynes nodded.

"Do I need to know how you came into possession of that folder?"

Haynes ignored the question. "Where do we go from here?"

"As you know, the personal representative of the estate retired
and moved abroad while it was in administration and another attorney in his firm took over. We need to contact the firm to find out
what investigation they undertook to find Hector Martin's living
heirs. It's possible that this task fell through the cracks during the
transition to the new attorney, and you'd be left with a negligence or

malpractice action against the attorney, which would be barred by the statute of limitations."

"And if they conducted a thorough search but didn't find any-thing—like this original birth certificate—because someone had removed it from the Office of Vital Records to conceal my relation-ship to Hector?"

Simon Wilkens smiled. "Then we can sue the estate of Paul Martin to recover what's rightfully yours. You might be celebrating next Christmas at your new home—Rosemont."

Chapter 38

Loretta arrived at work thirty minutes late. Nicole had been feverish all night, and Loretta had no choice but to drop her off at the babysitter that morning. Thank goodness the woman would take her children when they were sick. She didn't know what she would do otherwise.

She considered letting Mr. Haynes know she was there, but thought better of it. If he were concentrating behind closed doors, he might not realize she had been late at all. No point in drawing attention to it.

She logged onto her computer and had just begun inputting data when her cell phone rang. She pulled it out of her purse, and her heart sank when she saw that the babysitter was calling.

"Loretta," the woman said before she could even say hello. "Nicole's burning up. Her fever is over one hundred five."

Loretta slid out of her desk chair and grabbed her purse from her drawer. "Can you give her Tylenol?"

"Already have. It's not working. I've put a cold compress on her head."

"I'm leaving right now."

"Drive safely. We'll be waiting outside. The cold air will help."

Loretta opened Frank Haynes' door without knocking. He looked up, and she ignored the anger flashing in his eyes.

"Nicole's got a very high fever, and I need to take her to the emergency room."

She was halfway to the front door when she heard, "Will you be back?" She didn't turn around to answer him.

———

Frank Haynes saved his calculations on his financial statements and heaved himself from his chair. He'd better take a look at Loretta's desk after she'd left so abruptly. He'd need to make the bank deposit. He was up to his eyeballs in work and resented the fact that he was now completing the tasks he hired Loretta to do. He wouldn't hire a temporary worker to ease the load—the less people poking around in his business affairs, the better.

Loretta's absenteeism was becoming a problem.

He added up the deposit, banded the bills together, and searched for the bank bag. Loretta was an efficient and accurate bookkeeper. If her attendance weren't so poor, she'd be a very competent employee. Those three kids of hers posed a problem, especially that sickly one.

He sat back in her chair. He'd hired her because his sources confirmed that she had been Paul Martin's mistress. Haynes sighed. He'd tried to pump Loretta for any dirt she had on Paul or Maggie Martin. So far, she hadn't given him even one speck. And now, for all his trouble, he was stuck grossly overpaying a bookkeeper that didn't show up for work most of the time. He pushed the chair back from her desk. He'd been a fool to let the situation continue. He knew what he had to do.

———

Frank Haynes pulled into the lot at Mercy Hospital in the late afternoon. He had termination papers and a generous check for Loretta Nash. She'd texted him that her daughter had been admitted for tests and that she didn't know when she would be able to return to work. Did she really think he could run his business that way?

He stopped at the reception desk inside the tall automatic doors and was told that the children's wing was on the third floor. He emerged from the elevator and almost ran into Loretta as she was escorting two children onto the elevator.

"Mr. Haynes," she said, brushing the hair out of her eyes. She looked terrible and, although he was no expert on women, he thought she had been crying. "I'd like you to meet my children. This is Sean and Marissa."

The boy stuck out his hand and said, "Nice to meet you, sir." He shook the boy's hand and turned to the girl as she said, "We're so glad you hired Mommy. We like it here."

Haynes didn't know what to say.

"I was just taking them down to the cafeteria to eat. They're hungry, and we may be here a while."

"Why don't I take them to get something to eat?" he heard himself say.

"Would you?" she asked. "I really don't want to leave Nicole."

"What's the matter with her?" he asked.

She shook her head in warning, and he could see that she was fighting back tears. "Could you drop them at their babysitter? I'll text you the address." Loretta dropped to one knee and drew her children close. "Mommy's got to stay with Nicole tonight. I want you to go with Mr. Haynes, eat a good dinner, do your homework, and go to bed on time."

"We want to stay with you," they both cried. "We want to help," Marissa protested.

"You can't help me by staying here. Being good for Mr. Haynes and doing what I ask is how you can help me." She hugged them hard and kissed them, then stood and turned to Frank Haynes.

"Why are you here?" she asked.

"We can talk about it later. I'll come back after I've dropped these two off."

"Thank you, Mr. Haynes," she said as the elevator arrived and Frank Haynes took charge of the two children.

With the two strapped into the backseat of his Mercedes sedan, Haynes headed for one of his fast-food franchises. At least he knew what kids liked to eat. He wanted to get them fed and deposited at their babysitter's so he could finish what he started.

They were waiting for Sean to finish his shake when Marissa turned to him. "Mommy says that you're mean a lot because you're lonely."

Haynes stopped with his coffee cup halfway to his mouth.

"She says that we should be very grateful to you because Nicole would die without issurence from Mommy's job."

"Insurance," Sean corrected.

"If you're saving Nicole, I don't want you to be unhappy and lonely," Marissa said, looking at him with large, solemn eyes. "So I made you a valentine for Mommy to give you on Valentine's Day. But I want to give it to you now." She reached into her backpack. "I made it after school, and it took me a whole week." She straightened and held it out to him.

Haynes took the construction-paper heart, stiff with glue and heavy with sequins, doilies, and lace, and opened the card with shaky hands. How many years had it been since someone had given him a valentine card? Had anyone ever made one for him? He reached in his pocket for his glasses to read the inscription. In a curly, childish hand, it read:

To Mr. Haynes Our Hero Thank You for Helping Nicole XXXXOOOOO Marissa Nash.

"Those mean hugs and kisses," she said, pointing.

Haynes stared at the card. He was on his way to fire their mother and take away her "issurence." He was going to wipe his conscience clean with a check to her that made absolutely no difference to his net worth. He looked over their heads into the dark night outside the long windows. How in the hell had he become this person?

"Don't you like it?" Marissa asked, peering at him.

Haynes cleared his throat. "I like it very much, Marissa. Very much."

─────

Frank Haynes stepped off the elevator on the third floor of Mercy Hospital later that night. The corridor lights had been dimmed and most of the patient rooms were dark, save for the fluorescent lights of monitors and the occasional television. He slipped quietly along the corridor until he came to the room marked "Nash, Nicole."

The door was ajar, and he knocked quietly in case Nicole was asleep. No one answered, but he could see Loretta's purse on the floor in the corner, and he knew she was there. He cautiously pushed the door open and entered the room.

Nicole was hooked up to an IV and a host of monitors, but appeared to be sleeping peacefully. Loretta, also asleep, was slouched in an uncomfortable-looking armchair, her head leaning against the wall. He stood and surveyed the scene before him. To think that he had been prepared, only a few short hours ago, to take away the poor woman's job and the benefits that this child so obviously needed. He'd made a lot of mistakes in the last few years—getting involved with Delgado and his cronies to make a few bucks off the town's pension fund being the biggest one—but he wasn't going to make this mistake.

Haynes reached into his pocket and pulled out the envelope that he'd prepared earlier that day. He removed the termination notice and reinserted the check once intended to be a severance payment.

He took a pen from his pocket and scribbled her name on the envelope. On one of his business cards, he wrote:

Was going to give this bonus to you next payday, but thought you could use it now. F.H.

He dropped the card into the envelope, sealed it, and stuck it into her open purse. Frank Haynes sighed and took one last look at mother and daughter. If he believed in God, now would be the time to pray. He turned and slipped silently from the room.

———

Loretta shifted in her chair and turned her head to the door. Had someone just left the room, or was she imagining things? She rose stiffly and tiptoed to the doorway. She looked down the hall in time to see a tall man in a long overcoat step into the elevator. Although she hadn't seen his face, she was certain it was Frank Haynes. Loretta shivered involuntarily and wrapped her arms around herself as she turned and retraced her steps to the chair in the corner of her daughter's room.

She checked her watch. The cafeteria would close in thirty minutes. If she wanted something for dinner other than vending machine snacks, she'd better get down there. Loretta picked up her purse and noticed the envelope protruding from the center pocket. She turned it over in her hands, noting her name written on one side in the familiar hand. *So Frank Haynes was in this room.* Loretta leaned back into her chair and opened the envelope with shaking hands. She pulled out the business card and read the brief message, then turned her attention to the check.

Loretta gasped and held the check directly in the circle of illumination from the can light in the ceiling. She had read the amount correctly. She collapsed back into the chair, pressing the check to her chest. Ten thousand dollars would make all the difference in the world to her and her kids right now.

She looked up, past the ceiling, and mouthed a silent prayer, blessing Frank Haynes.

Chapter 39

Loretta held a spoonful of scrambled egg to Nicole's lips. "Come on, honey, you have to eat. Food helps you grow big and strong," she said, coaxing her to take a bite.

Nicole wrinkled her nose and shook her head. "Tastes yucky," she said.

Loretta took a small bit of the egg. She had to agree, it was rubbery and far too salty. "Let me see if they've got anything else at the nurse's station. Maybe some vanilla pudding?"

Nicole nodded and lay back on her pillows.

As she made her way to the nurse's station, Loretta kept looking back at the door to her daughter's room. She wanted to catch Nicole's doctor on his morning rounds.

She was just heading back to the room with cartons of pudding and fruit cocktail when Nicole's doctor stepped off the elevator. "Ms. Nash," he called. "I'm glad you're here. Nicole's my first stop this morning."

"How is she?"

"Let me look at her this morning, and then we can talk. I have some of the test results back."

"Is she okay?"

"We'll get to all that," he said as he walked into her room and greeted Nicole.

"How are we today, Miss Nicole?" he asked. "Do you mind if I have a look at your hands and feet today?"

Nicole squirmed when he touched her.

"Am I tickling?"

Nicole nodded.

"Okay—I'll do my best not to," he said as he carefully examined her feet.

He listened to her heart, then examined the area around her eyes.

"Have you been eating?" he asked, looking at her untouched breakfast tray. "Are you hungry?"

Nicole nodded. "Not that," she said, pointing to her tray. "Ick."

The doctor smiled. "I'd have to agree with you." He turned to Loretta. "I see your mom's got the good stuff from the nurse's station for you. Will you eat that for us?"

Nicole nodded as Loretta opened the pudding, inserted the spoon, and handed it to her daughter.

"You work on that while your mother and I go outside to talk, okay? Can you finish it for us?"

Nicole nodded happily, digging into the pudding.

The doctor swept his arm toward the door and followed Loretta into the corridor. "Let's go into this quiet room off of the reception area," he said.

Loretta swallowed the lump in her throat and followed him into the small room. When they were seated, Loretta said, "You're making me very nervous with all this." She gestured to the room. "Something must be seriously wrong with her."

The doctor nodded. "Nicole has a very rare kidney disease that we sometimes see in children. It's called nephrosis. That's why her hands and feet are swelling and she's puffy around the eyes."

Loretta froze and turned terrified eyes to the doctor.

"The disease is idiopathic, which means that we don't know what's caused it. It's more common in boys, but girls can get it, too.

176

Her kidneys are letting a protein known as albumin leak into her urine, and the albumin level in her blood is low. Her blood cholesterol is also high. It generally strikes children between the ages of two and six."

"So what do we do about it?" Loretta asked, forcing herself to calm down and listen to what the doctor was saying.

"We'll treat her with a course of steroids called prednisone. Are you familiar with it?"

Loretta shook her head.

"It's a powerful and effective drug, but it can have very serious side effects. You should see improvements right away, and we'll monitor her with blood and urine tests, and then start a gradual decrease of the drug. You'll need to follow our dosage instructions exactly. Can you do that?"

"Yes, of course I can. Will this fix her condition? Will it ever come back?"

"It might. We just don't know."

"If this drug doesn't work, or if it keeps coming back—then what?"

"There are other drug therapies we can try. And eventually dialysis."

Loretta gasped. "Would she need to be on dialysis for the rest of her life?"

"I wouldn't worry about that. It's very rare that a child needs dialysis. The prednisone should work beautifully. We just have to wait and see."

"And if drugs and dialysis don't work? Then what?" Loretta realized that her voice was becoming shrill, but she couldn't contain herself. "She can't live a long life on regular dialysis."

"I know this is extremely distressing, but we're nowhere near that point." He waited for her breathing to return to normal. "If dialysis stops working for a patient, they are a candidate for a kidney transplant."

Loretta's hands flew to her face. "A transplant? Aren't those touch and go? Isn't it really hard to get on the list?" she asked and her voice cracked.

"We've been successfully doing kidney transplants for many years. There can be complications, but we know how to manage them. And unlike other transplants, the donor doesn't have to be dead. A healthy person can live a normal life with only one kidney. A relative might be a very good match." He leaned toward her and rested his hands over hers. "We're a very long way from considering a transplant. I don't want you to worry about that."

Loretta forced herself to nod. "What about my other kids? Is it contagious?"

"Absolutely not. Don't worry about your other children getting this." He allowed her to absorb this bit of good news. "I reviewed her lab results this morning, and I think she can go home. Give her the prednisone as directed. The nurse will go over all of it with you. Send her back to school tomorrow. Return to your normal routine as much as you can."

"Then what?"

"You'll need to bring her in for tests in about eight weeks. Or if she gets worse, of course. Ms. Nash," he said, looking her squarely in the eye. "I'm not going to tell you this isn't serious, but we're going to treat her and I expect her to be fine."

Chapter 40

Maggie returned to her desk after her second meeting with the head of the Transit Department. *That man can bore the paint off a barn,* she thought as she slipped into her chair and pulled her lunch out of her desk drawer. She'd taken him to task for being so slow in implementing the changes approved by the committee. *Tonya is probably right—it's time to replace him.* She opened the foil packet containing celery and carrot sticks and began to nibble. She hated firing people. Even if she eased him gently into a cushy retirement, it would still be hard. She was scowling when she reached over to answer her phone.

"Mayor Martin? Gordon Mortimer here. I hope I'm not getting you at a bad time."

"Not at all. And, please, call me Maggie. How are you?"

"Fine, thank you. I'll get to the point. I've done considerable research on your silver collection—consulted my colleagues in London. I trust you got most of it secured in safes?"

"It's either in my attic or a bank safe deposit box."

"I was low on my estimate of the lot excluding the Martin-Guillaume Biennais. I told you I thought it was worth at least five hundred thousand. I think we're realistically looking at six hundred to six fifty. The value of silver in such excellent condition has soared in recent years. But the Martin-Guillaume Biennais is the real pièce de résistance. There are several active collectors of his work on the scene right now, with very little available for them to buy. Two of his silver sauceboats recently went at auction for over one hundred thousand dollars. You've got nine matching pieces in your tea set. And it's in pristine condition. My contacts in London think it would bring at least eight hundred thousand dollars at auction."

Maggie choked on a piece of carrot. "Are you serious?" she sputtered.

"Indeed I am. I'll finish my appraisal report this afternoon and email it to you and the insurer. I wanted to give you the good news myself and make sure you had everything safely tucked away."

"The Martin-Guillaume Biennais is at the bank, thank goodness. A lot of it is still in the attic."

"I wouldn't leave it there for long. Get yourself a cabinet safe."

"I was planning to do that. I'll order one this afternoon."

"Yes," he answered, and she could detect a note of disapproval in his voice that she hadn't done so already.

"One more thing before I let you go. How much is that chocolate pot worth?" Maggie asked.

"Comparatively speaking, it's not terribly valuable. It's a lovely piece, but shows a lot of wear. They must have used it quite a bit in their daily lives. I'd say it would bring twenty-five hundred on its best day."

"Good. I'd like to give that to the lady who helped me sort it all out."

"That would make a very nice thank you," he replied. "Have you decided what you want to do with the collection?"

"Anything of great value—especially the Martin-Guillaume Biennais—I'll sell. I'll keep some of the pieces, and I'd like to let my son and daughter pick out a few items for themselves. Can you help me place the rest with an auction house?"

"I most certainly can. You can maximize what you get for them by carefully choosing the auction. That's one of the services I provide."

"Good. I'd have no idea."

"When will you be ready to sell them?"

"My kids are both in California. I'm hosting an Easter carnival at Rosemont again this year, and I'm hoping that they'll both attend. I'll have them look at the silver then, and we can put what's left up for auction after that."

"If I might suggest, madam, leave the Martin-Guillaume Biennais and the other really valuable pieces at the bank and take your children to see them there. No sense taking any chances."

"You're right. Good idea."

"I'll email you the appraisal. Please call me when you're ready to proceed. And if you have any questions in the meantime, don't hesitate to call on me."

Maggie hung up the receiver, her earlier gloom obliterated. She looked at her meager selection of string cheese and veggies and swept them into the trash. She picked up her purse and coat and checked the time. She'd be able to retrieve the chocolate pot from her attic before her conference call.

Maggie reached the door of Celebrations just as Judy Young was turning the sign from Open to Closed. She saw Maggie hesitate on the other side of the glass, opened the door, and said, "This never applies to our busy mayor. I've got a few minutes before I need to get home. What do you need?"

"I actually stopped by to give you something. To thank you for all the help and support you've given me since my first days in Westbury. Here," she said, sliding a silver bag sprouting mounds of white tissue paper across the counter to her friend.

"Wait a minute," Judy said sharply. "Let me see that left hand of yours. What do we have there?" She seized Maggie's hand and pulled it toward one of the overhead lights, and whistled softly. "Is this what I think it is?"

Maggie nodded, and Judy swept her into a warm embrace. "I'm so happy for you," she said.

"Best news I've had all week," she added, then turned back to Maggie suddenly. "Who knows? Can I tell people?"

"So far, just Harriet at Burman's ..."

"Of course," Judy agreed.

"My daughter and Tonya Holmes." She watched as Judy clapped her hands in glee. *Nobody relishes having the scoop on town news more than Judy Young,* she thought wryly.

"When will you get married and where? Were you stopping in to look at invitations? Because if you were, I can stay late."

"The where is Rosemont, of course. We haven't decided when yet. And we may just have a small, family wedding."

Judy clucked her tongue. "You can't do that. You're the mayor, and everyone in town adores John Allen. We all consider ourselves your family, and we'll want to be there."

Maggie held up her hands in protest. "John and I will discuss it. We've got plenty of time, whatever we decide to do. And I'll get my invitations at Celebrations. But I didn't come here for that. I came here to give you this," she said, gesturing to the package that Judy had abandoned on the counter when she spied Maggie's ring.

"I love presents," Judy said, spinning around. "I sell tons of them here in the shop, but it's pretty rare when someone brings one to me." She began carefully removing the wadded-up sheaves of tissue paper. "It's heavy," she observed as she carefully removed the item from the bag.

"You didn't," she squealed as the final piece of tissue fell to the floor. "It's that chocolate pot from your attic. I love it!" She looked at Maggie with gleaming eyes. "But I can't take this. It's got to be far too valuable, and it belongs to Rosemont, not to me."

"It doesn't belong to Rosemont any longer. It's yours. I'm thrilled to be able to give you something that you really like." She cast her eyes around the shop. "And something that you can't buy for your-self."

Judy paused, one hand on the object she admired so much. "It's too much," she began, and Maggie put up a hand to silence her. "The appraiser said that it's too worn to carry any premium at auction. I'm probably giving you the least valuable item in the lot." She looked directly into Judy's eyes. "It would mean the world to me if you would accept it."

Judy pulled the item toward her and hugged it to her chest. "If you really mean it, I'd be thrilled to accept it."

"I do," Maggie said, beaming.

"About that wedding," Judy began.

Maggie turned to the door. "That's a discussion for another day. Come lock up after me."

Maggie settled into a wing chair by the fire after supper that evening and checked the time on the mantel clock. Mike should be on his way home from work, which was always a good time to talk to him. She had her son's undivided attention in the car.

"Hey, Mama Mia," he said brightly. "Or should I refer to you as Your Honor?"

"Mom fits the bill," Maggie replied. "You're in a good mood."

"Amy's getting over her morning sickness. Everything is so much better when she's up and at 'em."

"Glad to hear it. She was so dreadfully sick with the twins. And how are my adorable granddaughters?"

"Fine. Slogging through the daily grind of school, piano lessons, and sports. Life is good. We'll all be glad for a break in the routine over spring vacation, though."

"That's why I'm calling. If you do come out here, I'll schedule the Easter carnival during your visit. The girls will love it, and I think you'll have a lot of fun, too. Plus, I have something I want you to see."

"What would that be?"

"Did Susan tell you about the silver we found in the attic?"

"Maybe. Yeah, I guess so. You know how she rambles. I really wasn't paying attention."

Maggie laughed. "You should have listened to this story." She proceeded to summarize her earlier conversation with the appraiser.

"I'm speechless, Mom. It's like something out of a novel. This kind of thing doesn't happen in real life."

"It's happened to me. And I'm going to sell most of it. It's far too valuable for me to use, and I see no point in storing it and insuring it. That alone will cost a pretty penny. I want you and Susan to come home during the week of the Easter carnival and select a few items for yourselves and your kids so I can put the rest up for auction."

"Let me talk with Amy tonight. Have you spoken to Susan?"

"Not yet. She's been hard to reach lately."

"I know. She's in trial. I'm seeing her tomorrow for breakfast. Why don't I talk to her about it then?"

"Perfect. Get me the dates you'll be here, as soon as possible. I need to get started on the carnival."

Chapter 41

Irritated by the interruption, Special Counsel Alex Scanlon shifted his eyes from his computer screen to the paralegal standing in his doorway. "Yes?" he snapped.

"Sorry to bother you, but you've got to see this."

"What?"

"Just come. To the reception desk," she said over her shoulder as she turned away.

Alex sighed and pushed his glasses onto his forehead. He needed to stretch his legs, anyway. He followed her to the lobby and was greeted with the sight of two tall stacks of cardboard boxes. The deliveryman was wheeling in another load.

Alex rubbed his hands together as he gleefully inspected the shipping label on top of the nearest box. It was from a bank in the Caribbean. The courts had granted their motions to compel document production weeks ago and now, finally, the banks were complying.

"You know what this means?" he asked the paralegal.

She nodded. "I'll spearhead the effort to unpack, catalog, and organize all of this. It may take us a week or more, especially since we can't work overtime."

"You get started and work as much as you need. I'll get the overtime approved. The good citizens of Westbury are clamoring for answers, and we finally have what we need to get them. Forest and I will start our detailed review this weekend."

"I'll do my best," she replied.

"You always do. Sorry I was so testy when you knocked on my door."

She smiled. "No worries. I knew you'd want to see this."

Alex nodded and turned back to his office. It was time to launch this investigation into high gear. He'd tell Forest Smith to clear his schedule for the next month.

Forest Smith hung up on the call from Alex Scanlon. He understood what he needed to do next, and it made his gut churn. How in the hell had he allowed himself to get into this predicament? He knew painkillers could be habit forming, knew he was falling down the slippery slope of addiction with each pill he took. And now Delgado—someone with mob connections—was blackmailing him.

Smith pulled the crumpled scrap of paper from his pocket and stared at the 800 number of the twelve-step program. It was time. He picked up his cell phone and walked out into the parking garage to place the call in private. With any luck, they'd have a meeting in town that evening.

Forest Smith tucked his car into an opening between the trash dumpsters behind the Episcopal church and turned off the ignition. He leaned back against the headrest. He'd graduated at the top of his law school class and landed a prestigious job. He was an excellent lawyer who always exceeded his quota of billable hours and was on track to make partner at Stetson & Graham. And then he'd had his accident and become an addict. He'd been lying to himself for months, telling himself he could quit at any time. But he hadn't quit. And now he was being blackmailed by the mob. He'd heard that people needed to hit bottom before they were willing to admit to an addiction. He'd hit rock bottom.

He rubbed his hand across his eyes. There had to be a way out of this. Facing his problem was the first step. Forest got out of the car and entered the church by the rear door. He followed the hallway, heading toward a room at the end where light from an open door spilled into the corridor.

He wasn't prepared for the sight that greeted him when he tentatively stepped into the room. Forest was acquainted with everyone in the room, including the leader of the meeting, Special Counsel Alex Scanlon.

Forest froze. Alex came over to him and held out his hand. "You're welcome here, Forest, and everything is confidential. Have a seat, and we'll talk after the meeting. It's time to start."

An hour and a half later, when the room had cleared, Alex and Forest sat facing each other. "I had no idea so many of us are in the same boat," Forest said.

Alex nodded. "I remember my first meeting. I came away feeling less alone and much more hopeful about my situation."

"You've been clean for a while. How hard has it been?" Forest asked.

"It's been a whole lot easier since I've been part of this group. And my sponsor has been extremely helpful." Alex looked directly into Forest's eyes and held his gaze. "Would you like me to be your sponsor?"

"Will it be awkward, since we work together?"

"I think it'll be helpful. I understand the pressures of your life."

Forest nodded. "If you'd be willing to do it, I'd be grateful."

Alex took out a business card and wrote a phone number on the back. "The only people who have this number are my brother and Marc. And now you. Feel free to call me any time, day or night. And there will be many times when you'll need to call. Do you understand?"

Forest nodded. He added the number to the contacts in his cell phone and tucked the card into his wallet.

He exited the church through the rear door. He'd known he could rely on the confidentiality of the other attendees in the meeting, but he didn't want his car to be seen by anyone driving by, particularly Delgado.

He felt more hope than he had in months and approached his car with a spring in his step. He was reaching for his seat belt when a hand reached over the seatback and clamped onto his right shoulder.

"Gettin' ourself straight, are we, Smithy?" came the familiar voice.

"What the hell do you think you're doing?" Smith retorted, locking Delgado's gaze in the rearview mirror.

"Scared ya, didn't I?" Delgado laughed. "I'll bet you pissed your pants."

Smith remained silent.

Delgado released his grasp on Smith's shoulder and leaned forward, the whiskey strong on his hot breath. "I came lookin' for ya tonight 'cause we heard that fag Scanlon got a bunch of those documents you've been tryin' so hard to get."

"So?"

"So," Delgado thundered. "We should have heard it from you, first. That's exactly the kind of thing we need to know. Since you didn't call, the boys thought you needed a reminder. They was gonna do it themselves, but I said, 'No. Smith's a good kid. Let me do it this time.' Lucky for you, Smithy, they agreed." Delgado leaned in, and Smith could smell the whiskey on his breath. "This'll be the only time. You understand? Next time the boys'll come, and you won't like that."

"How did you know where to find me?"

Delgado sat back. "We always know. Don't forget that."

"We received documents. That's all there is to tell."

"And do you remember what you're gonna do with those documents? You're gonna get your hands on every scrap of paper that came in and tell us everything that's on all of them. We decide what's important and what's not."

Smith's shoulders sagged and he nodded.

"You report only to me."

"That's it?"

"For now. We'll have more for you to do, you can be sure of it." Delgado reached into his pocket and tossed a bag of painkillers onto the front passenger seat. "I brought you a little present. Just to show how much we care," he said. "Pity you're trying to give 'em up. I guess you can always throw them away." He reached for the door handle and heaved himself out of the car.

Chapter 42

Maggie was answering email when her phone chirped to alert her to a text message from Susan:

All coming to carnival except Aaron. Need to plan wedding. Talk tonight at 7?

Maggie quickly typed back

YES!!

and returned to her inbox with renewed vigor. If she knew her daughter, she already had a boatload of ideas to discuss.

Maggie popped a low-calorie frozen entree into the microwave and fed Eve and the kittens as soon as she stepped through her kitchen door. She raced upstairs to shed her business suit and heels, and was back downstairs in her favorite sweats by the time the bell on the microwave pinged to signal her dinner was ready. She ate standing at the counter while sorting through the day's mail, ignoring her grandmother's voice in the back of her head saying a lady always sat down to eat. *Not today's ladies,* she thought.

Maggie ensconced herself in her favorite overstuffed chair in the library by the French doors, with Buttercup curled up on her lap and Eve snoozing on the hearthrug. Blossom and Bubbles chased each other in and out of the room. Maggie relaxed in the silence and was just starting to nod off when her phone rang.

"Okay, Mom," Susan said. "Do you have something to write with?"

"How about 'Hello. How are you?' first?" Maggie replied.

Susan laughed. "Sorry, Mom. I guess I get a bit hyper-focused at times, don't I?"

"You most certainly do. And it's generally a good trait. But sometimes you need to stop and smell the roses."

"We're on such a tight deadline for the wedding."

"We are on no such thing. We've got plenty of time. John and I aren't kids anymore. We'll just do something small and simple."

"That's ridiculous. The whole town will want to attend. Since you've decided to marry at Rosemont, you have a venue with plenty of room. And you said you want to have it outside—on the back lawn? So the weather needs to be good. No winter wedding, although those are so pretty. Fur wraps over our dresses and snow-dusted trees ..." she trailed off wistfully.

"We're still aiming for June. Right after school is out. What's on your schedule?"

"It's open the entire month. Aaron has boards at the end of May, so that should work for him, too. We were talking about coming out to visit Alex and Marc this summer. Aaron hasn't spent much time with Marc, and since he's Alex's partner, he'd like to get to know him."

"Then you can kill two birds with one stone. I'm thinking a late morning wedding, followed by a buffet luncheon. That should cut down on the cost," Maggie said. "I'll get the invitations from Judy Young; Pete can cater the luncheon; Laura will do the cake; Marc can play his keyboard; and we'll make bouquets and boutonnieres and centerpieces out of the roses that bloom all over the back garden. So that takes care of it all."

"That most certainly does not 'take care of it all.' You've got to decide on your dress, your hair, and your makeup. Who's going to stand up with you? Will you have a wedding party? I assume you'll have Sophie and Sarah as junior bridesmaids?"

"Of course I want the girls to be in the wedding. Everything's so much more involved now than when I married your father. I wore a nice dress I already had. I did my own makeup, fixed my own hair. I didn't dream of doing anything else." She paused. "I guess I'll need your guidance—will you be my maid of honor?" she asked. If her daughter was this excited about her wedding, she wasn't going to throw cold water on her ideas. Why not let Susan have some fun with it?

"Oh, Mom, of course! I know I've been busy, but I want to help any way I can. I've started Pinterest boards for everything—your gown, John's tux, the decorations, the girls' dresses. And I'll get one set up for me now, too. It takes at least eight weeks to order a dress, so we need to decide on them fast."

"You've been busy on this."

"I've been working on them since we talked on New Year's Day. I pin things while I'm talking to Aaron on the phone—he's working and studying for his boards and this trial's been eating up a lot of my time, so we're both too exhausted to do much of anything. And I usually pin a few before I fall asleep in bed. I've got about two thousand images already."

"Holy cow. You have been busy, honey. I'm not sure I have time to look through all of them."

"That's okay, Mom. I'm doing this mainly because it's fun. I'll send you any that I really want you to see."

"Perfect."

"I also have some makeup ideas for you. You'll need to have a couple of trial sessions with makeup artists before you pick one. Expect to pay about two hundred fifty dollars for each trial."

"What? That's crazy. There's not much anyone can do with this old mug of mine. I'm not sure that Westbury has anyone who claims to be a makeup artist, anyway."

"Westbury has to have a makeup counter. We'll find it when I'm there for the carnival this spring. Maybe I should start a Pinterest page for the carnival. How's that coming along?"

"Other than the date and that it's being held at Rosemont, I have no idea. The same people are working on it again this year. Tim Knudsen's been soliciting donations, and George Holmes has added some new games. It was so successful last year that I'm not worrying about it."

"That's a first, Mom. Good for you. You've got your hands full as mayor."

"I'm so glad that you're all coming for it. Why don't we carve out a day while you're here and devote it to wedding planning? We'll pick out our dresses, and you can drag me to the makeup counter."

"Genius plan. Let's do it. And set up a cake tasting at Laura's, too."

"The twins will love that. We'll let them choose. I'll get it all arranged. I can hardly wait to have you here again. Are things still good between you and Aaron?"

"Sure. I just didn't know being in a relationship could be so lonely—we barely see each other. But I'm fine. I've got Pinterest and your wedding to help me cope."

"You can call me anytime. You know that."

Chapter 43

Maggie Martin dabbed at her nose with a wad of tissues and juggled a large plaque as she waited for the elevator to take her to the first floor of Town Hall and the large employee break room where a retirement reception was in full swing for the Vital Records clerk. The eighty-two-year-old woman was retiring after sixty years of service—a record for the town, as far as anyone knew. Maggie should have made her way downstairs an hour ago, but this cold had settled upon her like shrink wrap and she didn't have the energy or inclination to be social.

Maggie scanned the row of offices on the executive floor. All doors were firmly shut except the third from the end. Could Frank Haynes be at Town Hall this afternoon?

Maggie made her way down the hall, and a coughing spell announced her presence before she could knock. Haynes swiveled in his chair and looked up.

"Good grief, Maggie. You should be home in bed. What are you doing here?"

"I agree. I feel terrible. I think I've got a fever," she managed between coughs. "I stayed to present this plaque to the Vital Records clerk. She's retiring after sixty years. And all the town is doing for her is giving her a plaque and a little punch-and-cookies reception in the break room."

Haynes became suddenly attentive. "Would you like me to deliver it to her?"

"Would you, Frank? I'd really appreciate it. I need to get out of here. And I don't want to give her this nasty cold. Some sendoff that would be."

"I'd be delighted to. Just leave it there at the end of my desk," he said, pointing and reaching for his package of sanitizing wipes.

"Good idea, that," Maggie said, eyeing the wipes.

"What time is the reception?"

"Now, I'm afraid. They're waiting for you."

Haynes looked at his watch. "It's almost five. If no one else is doing anything for her, I'll take her to dinner. How would that be?"

"Very thoughtful, Frank. I'm sure she'd love that," she said, eyeing him curiously. She wished she knew what caused the nice Frank Haynes to come out of hiding.

Haynes finished sterilizing the plaque, grabbed his coat from the hanger on the back of his door, and turned out his light. "I'll make your excuses for you. Why don't you duck out the back?"

<hr />

Frank Haynes strode into the break room as the crowd began to thin, leaving the remaining two employees of the Vital Records Office and a handful of other senior staff to witness his presentation to the clerk. Haynes rose to the occasion and made flattering, if generic, comments about her exemplary dedication to duty and leadership of her office. The woman flushed and seemed genuinely pleased with the recognition.

Haynes stepped aside to allow her to receive the well wishes of her coworkers. When they were alone, he asked if she would like help carrying the plaque and her small box of personal items to her car.

"I don't drive anymore, Mr. Haynes," she said. "I'm going to wrangle this home on the bus."

"Nonsense. I won't hear of it. Let me give you a ride home, please. In fact, I'd like to take you to dinner, on behalf of the council," he added, "to thank you for your service."

"Well," she hesitated. "That would be very nice."

"That'll give me a chance to hear all about the department that you've run so well for over half a century. Imagine that," he said. And to probe what she might know about the possible theft of his mother's birth certificate from the Vital Records Office. Fate might have delivered into his hands the perfect person to answer his questions about the Vital Records Office at the time of Hector Martin's death.

Frank Haynes asked Pete to show them to a quiet booth where they could talk. He held the clerk's chair and insisted that she have a glass of wine to celebrate her retirement. Alcohol always oiled the tongue. He ordered a seafood appetizer to share, and the clerk gasped. "We can't eat all of that. And it's so expensive."

"Don't worry about the cost. Pete can box up anything that's left over, and you can take it home. What are the most unusual things you can remember happening in your department?" he asked.

"The change over from typed index cards to the computer system was traumatic, to say the least. It was wonderful, though. I always thought it would be, you know. I wasn't one of those who feared change. Oh, no. Not me. Why ..."

Haynes stifled a yawn and refilled her glass. He'd let her ramble, then steer her to the time period around Hector Martin's death. He finally found his opening as the waiters placed their entrees in front of them.

"What about the months after Hector Martin died? I heard there were some real issues then," he said, baiting his hook.

"Well," she paused, leaning over the table toward him and lowering her voice. "I should say so. That lawyer from Chicago came in as we were closing. I told him he'd have to come back the next day. I always closed the department on time. You could set your watch by the hours we kept," she said proudly.

Haynes nodded.

"He pleaded with me to let him get in. Said it would only take a moment. That his wife was pregnant and about to deliver. He needed to drive home that night." She dabbed her mouth with her napkin. "Why'd he come in the first place if his wife was about to give birth any moment?—that's what I want to know," she said. "Anyway, I let him in—for just a few minutes, mind you. And he was quick about his business. Thanked me profusely, and he was gone. I locked up and went home."

"That's all?" Haynes asked, stifling his disappointment.

"No—that's not all. Don't you remember? That's the night that the fire broke out and destroyed all of our paper records. The fire examiner said it smoldered for hours before the alarm came in. Most of our records had been put onto the computer by then, and we backed up our systems, so the damage wasn't great. But the real old stuff hadn't been scanned and it was all lost."

"I don't remember hearing about this."

The woman shrugged. "It didn't get much attention. They blamed it on faulty wiring and figured we lost a bunch of old stuff that we didn't need anyway. The council at the time was delighted to save the money it would have taken to get all of those old records onto the computer."

"So what was lost?"

"Everything before 1951." She shook her head. "To this day, I think something fishy went on that night."

"Is that so?"

"I'll bet dollars to doughnuts that attorney took something out of the records and set that fire to cover his tracks. I tried to tell the fire chief that, but he wouldn't listen to me."

Haynes nodded. "You might be right," he said. He needed time to think this through. He signaled to Pete to bring him the check. "I've imposed on you long enough, but I've really enjoyed our conversation. May I call you again sometime to hear more?"

She raised an eyebrow. "Of course you can. You'll know where to find me when you drop me off."

———

"I'm glad you called, Mr. Haynes. I was just finishing a letter to you," Simon Wilkens said. "Your grandfather's law firm cooperated with us—after a bit of gentle persuasion," he chuckled mirthlessly. "They sent an attorney to the Vital Records Office in Westbury before they closed the estate. He didn't find the birth certificate that you provided to me. It wasn't part of the official records."

"So that means they weren't negligent in handling the estate?"

"Precisely."

"Unless the attorney stole the birth certificate."

"That seems very far-fetched, Mr. Haynes," Simon Wilkens said. "Malpractice is one thing; malfeasance is quite another."

"I called you, Simon, to report a very interesting conversation I had with Westbury's Vital Records clerk. Former Vital Records clerk, actually. She just retired after sixty years in that office. I took her to dinner last night to celebrate her last day and a few glasses of wine loosened her up nicely."

"What did she say to convince you that this lawyer expunged the birth certificate from the public record?"

"She remembers an attorney from Chicago who begged her to let him have access to the records at closing time. He used some sob story about his wife being about to give birth and he couldn't spend the night in Westbury—he had to get home. She remembers that he was only there for a few minutes and that a fire broke out later that night. They were in the process of scanning records into the computer but hadn't gotten to any of them dated before 1951. All of the records prior to that year were destroyed."

"That's quite a story. Did they conclude it was arson?"

"She says that the town council was relieved they didn't need to spend any more money scanning old records and dropped the matter. The fire marshal wasn't interested in her mystery man from Chicago."

"There's nothing to connect this to your case," Wilkens added.

"Except the timing. She remembers that it was shortly after Hector Martin died."

Wilkens was silent, digesting the information. "If we could prove that the estate's attorney was paid off by Paul Martin, we'd have a case to bring against the firm and Paul's heirs. It seems like a very long shot."

"I'll work on getting the evidence," Haynes said. "I'll use my connections here in Westbury. Sit tight and I'll get back to you."

"Remember to stay on the right side of the law, Mr. Haynes," he admonished. "Even smart people do stupid things when a lot of money is involved."

"You don't have to worry about me getting caught on the wrong side of the law," Haynes assured him as he hung up the phone.

He wouldn't step across that line again.

Westbury was a small town, and people in small towns talked. Secrets that had been buried for decades could be uncovered. Or so he hoped.

Chapter 44

"Come on, sweetie, it's time to get up now. I've already let you sleep an extra half hour. You'll make everybody late if you don't get moving," Loretta said as she brushed the hair from Nicole's damp brow.

She turned on the bedside lamp and carefully regarded her daughter's upturned face. She wasn't seeing miraculous effects from prednisone. If anything, her eyes seemed puffier. She reached under the covers for one of Nicole's hands and recoiled in alarm. It was swollen to almost double its size.

Loretta stood quickly. "You're not going to school today, honey. I think we need to see the doctor again."

Nicole nodded.

"We'll drop the big kids off at school first." Loretta slid Nicole's feet to the side of the bed and inserted them into her fuzzy pink slippers. "You can stay in your jammies. We'll put your coat over them."

Marissa and Sean were waiting quietly by the door when Loretta came slowly down the stairs, Nicole leaning heavily against her.

Marissa turned scared eyes on her sister. "Again?" she asked.

"It'll be okay," Loretta said with a confidence she didn't feel. "She just needs a change in medication. It's a very common thing."

Marissa nodded, but Loretta could tell that she didn't believe her.

Traffic was light, and she dropped her older children at school just before the first bell. She placed a call to Nicole's doctor and detailed her condition for the nurse. "We're double-booked this morning, Ms.

Nash. Based upon what you've described, I think you should take her to the emergency room at Mercy Hospital."

Loretta clamped down on the panic rising inside her. "We're on our way," she said.

"One of our doctors is making rounds there now. I'll tell him you'll be there soon."

Loretta and Nicole were once more in a private room on the third floor. The staff needed to perform some tests and would probably change her medication. The doctor expected to discharge her that afternoon or the next morning, at the latest.

Nicole endured all the poking and prodding without complaint and was now napping in front of the television. Loretta realized she'd forgotten to call Mr. Haynes to tell him she wouldn't be at work. She grabbed her purse and tiptoed out of the room to find Nicole's nurse. "I have to go to work for a few minutes. Would that be okay?"

"Parents have to do it all the time around here. Don't you worry about a thing. We'll take good care of Nicole, and we'll call you if we need you."

"I've been absent so much—I can't afford to lose my job."

The nurse squeezed her hand. "You're fine. Don't feel guilty about it, either. Just drive safely. And if you're not back by the time I leave, I'll tell my replacement."

Loretta smiled, squeezing the woman's hand back and thinking, *Sometimes an ounce of kindness is all we need to sustain us.*

Loretta walked into Haynes Enterprises to find her boss seated at her desk, preparing the previous day's bank deposit. The sight pulled her up short. She knew he hated covering for her.

"I'm so sorry, Mr. Haynes," she blurted out. "Nicole got worse, and she's in the hospital again. I just came from there."

Frank Haynes took in her disheveled appearance and the heavy bags under her eyes and swallowed the retort that had been on his lips. He cleared his throat. "I'm sorry to hear that," he replied.

Loretta cocked her head. Had she heard him correctly?

"I can do that," she said, stepping behind her desk and gesturing to him to get up. "She's had all her tests and is napping. The nurse will call me when I need to go back." She looked at Frank Haynes, who now stood awkwardly on the other side of her desk. "This job is very important to me and my family, Mr. Haynes. I don't know what I'd do without it. And I'm truly sorry that I've been absent so much. With just the two of us here, I know it makes things hard. I'll be here whenever I can."

Haynes remained where he was and fiddled with the jar of pens on her desk. "I know that, Loretta. You've done a very good job since you've been here." He lifted his eyes to hers. "I hope your little girl gets better soon. Stay as long as you like today, and let me know when the deposit is ready. I'll run it over to the bank." He retreated to his office and closed the door. If he had turned around, he would have seen Loretta staring at him, eyes wide, as if she'd witnessed a miracle.

Loretta worked at a blistering pace for the next several hours. After Frank Haynes had shown her such compassion, she wanted to do her best for him. It was almost four when she poked her head around his door to tell him she was leaving. "The hospital called. They said that they think the doctor will discharge her by dinnertime."

Haynes nodded. "You'd better go."

Loretta walked into Nicole's room twenty minutes later. The bed was empty, and there was no sign of Nicole. She raced to the nurse's station where a woman she didn't recognize rose to meet her. "Are you Nicole's mama?" she asked. Loretta nodded, her eyes wide with fear. "Don't worry—she's fine. We've got a visit from a therapy dog goin' on in the children's lounge. The kids love it. She was well enough, so I took her down there." The woman pointed to a room at the end of the wing. "Go take a look."

Loretta released the breath she had been holding and smiled at the nurse. "I guess I let my imagination run away with me," she said sheepishly.

"Everybody does that in this place, honey," the nurse replied. "Now go have some fun with your child."

Loretta nodded and proceeded down the hall. She paused in the doorway to the children's lounge and watched the scene unfolding before her. The young man who'd come to Haynes Enterprises— *What was his name again? David something*—had charge of a midsized dog who was patiently fielding all of the hugs, petting, and even tail-pulling that a passel of sick children could dish out. He moved his head to one side to gently nuzzle an older boy, and Loretta saw that the dog had only one eye. Nicole was crouched next to the dog, with her arm slung across his back, rubbing his left haunch and murmuring, "Nice doggy, good doggy." Loretta's heart caught in her throat. Nicole leaned over and ran a line of kisses down the dog's back.

Loretta approached the dog's master. "I'm Loretta Nash. We met at Haynes Enterprises. Nicole is my daughter," she said, touching Nicole's shoulder.

The boy nodded. "I remember. I'm David Wheeler. And this is Dodger."

"Hello, Dodger. Aren't you a wonderful dog?" She turned to David. "How long have you been doing this?"

"We just got certified last week," he answered. "Dodger started out as an agility dog, but he was injured and can't compete for a while. Maybe not ever again. So he became a therapy dog. I think he's really good at it."

"He certainly is. It's nice for these children to have something fun to break up their day. Television and books can only go so far."

David nodded. "I know. I've read studies that show that petting an animal relieves stress and promotes healing. We learned about it when we were studying to become a therapy team."

Loretta smiled at him.

"Speaking of fun things for kids, do you know about the Easter carnival at Rosemont next weekend?"

Loretta narrowed her eyes and shook her head.

"They had one last year, and this year will be even better. The hospital is putting together a section of games for sick or disabled kids. They've asked Dodger and me to come, too. Why don't you bring Nicole? She'd have a blast."

Loretta hesitated an instant too long.

"Can we, Mommy? I want to," Nicole lifted bright eyes to her mother.

"I don't think we would be welcome there," Loretta stammered. "Ms. Martin and I aren't friends."

"You don't have to be friends," David replied. "It's for the community. And it's free, too. They just collect a voluntary donation for the town pension fund."

Loretta looked at her daughter's shining face.

"How can you refuse?" David asked.

Loretta nodded. If her kids would have fun, she needed to let them go.

Loretta turned as the nurse called her name. "The doctor has discharged Nicole. I've got her new prescription here to go over with you."

Loretta extended her hand to her daughter. "Come on, sweetheart, we're going home."

Nicole shook her head and hugged Dodger around his neck.

"You can see him at the carnival," Loretta said.

"Dodger's getting tired. We should be leaving soon, anyway," David broke in and helped Loretta peel Nicole off of Dodger. "We'll see you next week, at Rosemont."

Chapter 45

Maggie stepped into Celebrations at six o'clock the Saturday morning before Palm Sunday. "Thank you for meeting me so early," she told Judy Young. "I want to sign off on the wedding invitations and get them ordered before this crazy week starts."

"And rightly so. You're cutting it pretty close for a wedding at the beginning of June."

Maggie sighed heavily and signed the form Judy put in front of her.

"But don't worry," Judy assured her. "I'll get them for you." She placed the order on the counter behind her. "I'll have time to send this in before the shop opens at nine. Where are you headed this early on a Saturday morning?"

"I'm off to the airport. My family's coming in on the red eye. I've borrowed John's Suburban, with the extra seat, to haul them all to Westbury. I just hope I have enough room for their luggage."

"Will they be here through Easter?"

"Yes. My granddaughters are on their school break and they wanted to come to the Easter carnival—which I have you and the others to thank for organizing and promoting. I haven't lifted a finger."

"I think running this town and planning a wedding is enough, don't you? You're hosting the carnival at Rosemont; that's plenty. We've got everything covered. All you need to do is show up."

"Good, because that's all I have time for this week. The girls and I are going to pick out our dresses, attend a cake tasting, finalize the food for the reception, and something else that I'm forgetting ... oh ... we're testing makeup for the wedding."

"That is a lot," Judy agreed.

"I'm not sure I require all of this, but everyone else seems to think so. It's easier to just go along with it all."

"This will be the most talked-about wedding in these parts in more than a decade." She looked wistfully over Maggie's shoulder. "A June wedding at Rosemont. It needs to be perfect."

"Argh ... Don't you start on me, too." She checked her watch. "I'd better scoot. If I run into any traffic, I'll be late."

<hr />

Forest Smith slowed his pace to a walk, then leaned forward and grabbed his knees to stretch out his back. He'd set out to start running again and his back was protesting mightily. After the accident, he missed this morning routine the most. It cleared his mind, and he always slept well when he ran. He was determined to resume the practice. He patted his jacket pocket and felt the baggie of painkillers that Delgado had given him. Just one tablet would allow him to continue his run.

Smith wandered to a small stand of trees at the side of the path where he would be hidden in deep shade. He removed one tablet from the baggie and held it between his thumb and forefinger, poised to pop it into his mouth.

Smith didn't know how long he remained like this before he dropped the tablet and crushed it beneath the heel of his running shoe. He opened the baggie and did the same with the other pills, then pulled out his cell phone and punched the number for Alex Scanlon.

Alex answered on the second ring. "Good morning. What's up?"

"Sorry to call so early."

"Don't be. I expect you to call anytime you need me, day or night. That's what my sponsor does for me and what I'm committed to doing for you. What's going on?"

"I just got rid of my stash of pills."

"Good for you, Forest. What happened?"

"I went for a run this morning—first time in months. Running is the best stress reliever for me. But I couldn't make it for more than a quarter mile before my back pain made me stop. I had some pills with me, and I knew one would give me the relief I needed to continue my run. I almost took it. I had it in my hand. But I stopped."

"I understand how frustrating it is when your recovery from an injury takes so long that you feel like you'll never get better, like you'll never get your life back. I self-medicated myself for months until I realized I was doing more damage to myself."

"I know that, intellectually, but it's hard to put into practice."

"That's why I go to the meetings." Alex paused. "I thought you said at the meeting that you'd gotten rid of your stash?"

"I did." Forest Smith took a deep breath. "That's the other reason for this call. Chuck Delgado gave me some pills. On the night of the meeting. He was waiting for me when I left that night."

The line was silent. "You'd better tell me everything."

"Delgado knows I'm an addict; I was buying from his people. He also knows I'm assisting on the investigation. He's attempting to blackmail me. He'll keep quiet about my addiction and illegal purchases if I destroy anything that would incriminate him or his cronies."

"I see," Alex replied stiffly.

"He wants to see anything I find that implicates him. I was never going to do it, of course," he added hastily. "You believe me, don't you?"

Alex remained silent.

"What I planned to do was see what the documents showed and then decide what to do."

"Hoping that there wouldn't be anything, so you wouldn't have to face this dilemma?"

"I guess so, yeah."

"How likely do you think it is that there won't be anything in those documents? He's all but confessed. And what about his attempted blackmail? That's a crime, too."

"I know it is, Alex. Believe me, I know. I've been tortured by this whole situation. My first step was to go to the meeting, to get myself clean."

"That's a good first step, Forest. In your shoes, I would have done the same. I'm not trying to come down hard on you. Just thinking about how we should handle this now that Delgado's made a move."

"I have an idea on that, actually. I think we can turn this to our advantage."

"Meet me at the office in an hour, and we'll talk about it there," Alex replied. "And Forest—you've done the right thing."

Chapter 46

Sophie and Sarah bounded onto Maggie's bed at dawn on Monday morning. She opened one eye as Eve circled in her basket and snuggled back into her blanket. "What are you doing up so early? Are your Mom and Dad awake?"

"No. Mommy sleeps a lot now that there's a baby in her tummy," Sophie said. "And Daddy's not up yet. But we're awake so we went to see the kittens."

"You did?" she said, brushing the sleep from her eyes.

Sophie took a deep breath. "We did. But we let them out of the kitchen. We're sorry, Gramma. We know they're supposed to stay in there at night. But we opened the door a teensy crack, and they zoomed out of there."

"Don't be mad at us," Sarah pleaded.

Maggie smiled and drew them into a hug. "I'm not mad. They move pretty quickly, don't they? Where are they now?"

Both girls shook their heads in unison. "We don't know," Sarah said. "They went all over the place."

"I know how we'll get them back. We'll put their food out. Those three are chow hounds." She threw the covers back and found her robe and slippers. "Come on, Eve—if I'm up, you're up," she said to her faithful companion.

"We've got a busy day today," she said to her twin granddaughters. "Did your parents tell you? We're going to pick out pretty dresses for all of us to wear at the wedding, and we're going to choose the flavor of my wedding cake. Will you help pick it out?"

The girls nodded vigorously. "Go wake your aunt, and let's get started on our day."

Their first stop was Archer's Bridal, the only bridal shop in Westbury. Anita Archer sprang from her chair behind the counter when Maggie came through the door. "Mayor Martin. It's a pleasure to meet you," she said, pumping Maggie's hand.

"This is my daughter, Susan Martin; my daughter-in-law, Amy; and my granddaughters, Sophie and Sarah." She turned to Anita. "I'm afraid we're here on short notice. You may have heard that I'm getting married in June." Anita Archer nodded vigorously. "I need a wedding gown, and Susan and the girls need dresses. They're in the wedding party."

Anita Archer had to restrain herself from clapping her hands in glee.

"Can you help us with this, or are we cutting things too close? Should we go buy something off the rack?" Maggie asked.

"Good heavens, no!" the woman replied, indignantly. "You don't want to do that. I can help you with all of it right here. I've got designers that can get your dresses here in time. Do you know what you'd like?"

Susan pulled a folder out of her large shoulder bag. "We do," she said, producing a series of photos of brides and bridesmaids.

"Oh ... these are lovely," the woman replied. "We've got things like this in our couture line. They're a bit pricey. Do you have a budget in mind?"

The woman held her breath as Maggie uttered Anita Archer's favorite words in the English language. "Cost doesn't matter. We'll go with whatever we like best."

This gloomy Monday morning suddenly turned brilliantly sunny for Anita Archer.

With gowns and dresses selected and ordered, the group moved on to Laura's Bakery for the scheduled cake tasting at eleven o'clock.

"I don't know what I was thinking. Now we'll never get the twins to eat a decent lunch," she said to her health-conscious daughter-in-law.

"Who cares?" Amy replied. "It's a special day when you can help your grandmother plan her wedding. Besides, my sweet tooth has been on overdrive this entire pregnancy. I want a piece of cake!"

"Let's see what Laura has lined up for us," Maggie said. "Her cakes are all glorious. The hard part will be settling on just one flavor." Half an hour later, they all agreed—it would be impossible to pick just one. Maggie ordered alternating layers of pink champagne and chocolate-almond, encased in cream-colored fondant decorated with white roses. With the decision made, they stepped across the threshold to Pete's to grab a quick lunch before venturing to the makeup counter at the trendy salon on the square.

—⁂—

Maggie led the expedition to the attic after breakfast Tuesday morning. Susan insisted that "the viewing," as her family called it, could wait until after they'd ordered their dresses for the wedding. With that detail sewn up, the time had come.

"Gosh, Gramma," Sophie said, scanning the attic. "This is huge."

"And creepy," Sarah chimed in, biting her lip. "Do you keep the door locked?"

"I most certainly do. But there's nothing to worry about up here except perhaps your overactive imagination," she reassured her granddaughter. "This is a very friendly attic. I spent an entire day up here, remember? There's nothing but treasures. And dust." She looked at Sarah, who shrugged and hid behind her father.

"The silver's over there," Maggie said, pointing to two long tables along the back wall.

"All of that?" Susan said, pushing a threadbare ottoman out of her way as she surged toward the tables. "Holy cow, Mom. I had no idea." She surveyed the tables. "This is all so beautiful. There are some very interesting pieces here. I've never seen anything like them."

"And there's more in the bank vaults. All the really valuable stuff is there. We're driving to Ferndale as soon as we finish here. You're not going to weasel out of going," Maggie stated in her sternest Mom voice.

Susan looked over her shoulder at her mother. "I wouldn't want to 'weasel out of going.' Not after seeing all this."

Mike stepped forward and took Amy's hand to help his pregnant wife traverse the littered attic.

"I'd pictured this in my mind," Amy said, "but nothing like this."

"I want you to take as much of this as you'd like," Maggie directed.

"Don't you want it?" Amy asked.

"I've already removed what I want. I'm going to sell everything you don't take." Maggie turned to her granddaughters. "That includes the two of you. I want you to have pieces from Rosemont's attic, so that you can hand them down to your children one day. And if there's nothing here you like, you may find something in the bank vault."

Susan and Mike stopped culling through the items on the table and looked at each other. Susan nodded at her brother, and he turned to Maggie. "There's more than enough here, Mom. We want to see the stuff in the bank vault—especially the tea set by that guy whose name I can never remember—but we want you to sell all the really valuable stuff."

Maggie nodded. "That's the most practical approach." She turned toward the stairs. "Take your time. I'm going to check in with my office, and we'll set out for Ferndale when you're done. I've labeled boxes with each of your names," she said, pointing to a stack at the end of one of the tables. "Put anything you want in your box. I can send it to you or keep it here. If you divide up everything on these tables, that's fine with me. We've got a small fortune to sell in the bank vaults."

Chapter 47

Chaos engulfed Rosemont in the days leading up to the carnival, the Saturday before Easter. Maggie couldn't tell who took more delight in running up and down the stairs—the twins or her new kittens. The weather was sunny and warm. They hiked on the trails by the Shawnee River and went for ice cream in town. Eve and Roman were included in everything.

Joe Appleby and his crew mowed and trimmed the lawn. Deliveries of supplies for the carnival arrived with increasing frequency and were stored on the back patio. Maggie marveled at the efficiency with which everything was coming together.

She had scheduled the entire week as vacation, but needed to go into Town Hall on Thursday afternoon. She packed off her family for a day at the nearby science museum and set out for Town Hall on foot.

The trees surrounding the square were in bud, circling the gray stone courthouse in a band of vibrant green. Spring bulbs of hyacinth, tulip, and daffodil made their joyous presence known in scattered clusters on the lawn. Maggie breathed deeply and paused to survey the scene in front of her: the businesses lining the square, their bright awnings and inviting signs; a hulking man walking a trio of miniature Yorkshire terriers; and an older couple sitting close on a park bench, pointing to something in the newspaper they held between them. To think she'd almost thrown in the towel on helping this wonderful town and these kind and gentle people restore their financial safety and security. She glanced at the sky. *Help me get this right*, she implored before resuming her walk to her office.

Maggie intended to spend only a couple of hours at her office. Her desk was covered with messages and mail, which she carefully moved to one side so she could concentrate on signing checks. She was sliding the stack back into place when her eye fell on the message from Alex Scanlon marked urgent.

Maggie hesitated, then picked up the phone and placed a call to him.

"I thought you were on vacation," he said. "You shouldn't be calling me from Town Hall."

"Your message is marked urgent, and I was here for a few minutes anyway, so I thought I should return your call. What's up?"

"We got the documents from the offshore banks. They finally complied with the court's orders. Boxes and boxes of documents."

"Thank goodness," Maggie replied. "I'm so glad to hear it. What have you found so far?"

"We've only started to go through them," Alex said. "Forest Smith and the paralegal team are making the first pass through them. I'll review anything that they think might be significant. So far, we've only found items that put the finger on William Wheeler."

"That's disappointing. We both know he wasn't smart enough to pull this off by himself."

"We've just begun. Don't despair. We're going through every inch of paper with a fine-toothed comb."

"Good," Maggie said. "I was going to call you today, anyway. Would you and Marc join us for brunch on Easter Sunday?"

"Thanks, Maggie. We'd love to. I'm sorry that Aaron was too wrapped up preparing for his boards to make the trip, but we'd love to see Susan and Mike and his family." Alex hesitated. "I know that I've been short with you lately, and I'm sorry. I've never worked so hard in my life. I've been testy with everybody, which is no excuse. I just want you to know that Marc and I both miss you. We became very close when we stayed with you all those months and neither of us want to lose that."

"This past year has turned all of us inside out," Maggie replied. "None of us has been at our best. I miss both of you, too. I think of you as part of my family. It'll be good to have you there on Sunday."

"What do you want us to bring?"

"How about some good champagne? Let's celebrate the progress we *have* made this year."

Once she returned that first phone call, the stack got the best of Maggie and she spent the rest of the day in her office, feverishly returning calls and emails. She knew it was time to quit when she saw the text from Mike telling her that they were on their way home. She forced herself to sweep the unanswered mail into the box at the edge of her desk, log off her computer, and head for the door.

Frank Haynes stepped out of his office as she approached the elevator.

"Mayor Martin," he called. "I thought you were off this week, preparing for the extravaganza at Rosemont on Saturday."

"Will we see you there, Frank? Will you be courting the press again, like you did last year?"

Haynes bristled. Maybe he had misled that reporter and taken too much credit for last year's successful carnival. He'd also donated prizes worth more than a thousand dollars. Didn't that entitle him to some recognition? "I'll be there to present the prizes I'm donating again this year," he answered stiffly. "If the press deems that newsworthy, who am I to complain?"

Maggie eyed him steadily but held her tongue. She didn't want to stir up trouble with him. They stepped onto the elevator together.

"What are you donating this year?" she asked.

Haynes hesitated a split second. In truth, he hadn't given it a moment's thought and didn't know what he'd be bringing. "The usual fare—tablets, e-readers, a television. And I think I'll add a bike this year. What do you think?"

"Bikes are always popular in the spring."

"And Forever Friends will donate coupons for a free dog or cat."

The elevator stopped on the ground floor and they exited into the lobby.

"You can drop everything off at Rosemont tomorrow night. We're having pizza for everybody who's helping. You didn't come last year, but why don't you join us tomorrow?"

"I'll see what I can do," Haynes replied, knowing he'd like nothing less.

———

Maggie slept fitfully the night before the Easter carnival, waking almost every hour. Her lack of involvement in the planning process was driving her crazy. *Once a control freak, always a control freak,* she told herself. She looked at her bedside clock at four fifty-five and decided it was time to get up.

Maggie padded noiselessly down the stairs, leaving Eve snoring in her basket, and started a pot of coffee. Her kitchen looked like a foreign land, every surface covered with boxes and bags, filled with who-knew-what. She spotted a row of pink bakery boxes and pulled one down from the top of the stack. She carefully lifted one corner of the box and was greeted with the sight she'd been hoping for—an entire box of Laura's banana muffins—half plain and half with chocolate chips.

Maggie told herself she shouldn't as she carefully loosened the tape and extracted one of the muffins—with chocolate (*eureka!*). She shook the box to re-distribute the remaining muffins and cover her tracks, feeling sheepish as she did so. *Surely one muffin for breakfast was allowed?*

Maggie bundled herself into a shawl that hung by her kitchen door and took her coffee and muffin to the back lawn. She walked to the end and perched on the top of the low stone wall that marked the end of the lawn and the beginning of the woods. The rising sun hit the dew and set it sparkling like a net of diamonds. She pulled off a chunk of the muffin and popped it into her mouth, savoring the heady aroma of her coffee and feeling the contentment borne of the knowledge that she was exactly where she was meant to be, doing what she was meant to do.

By the time Maggie fed the kittens and made her way upstairs to collect Eve, the light was on under Susan's door, and she heard the low tenor of Mike's voice, admonishing his girls to be quiet and let their mother sleep. She knocked softly and opened the door. "I need some help. Can I steal these two?" she asked, pointing to Sophie and Sarah. Mike gave her a silent thumbs-up and herded the girls out the door.

"Let's feed Eve, and then we can all come back upstairs and get ready in my room. How does that sound?" she asked, and they both nodded vigorously. "We can feed the kittens," Sophie offered.

"Not this morning," Maggie responded quickly. "I've already done that. They're tucked away in the laundry room for the day, and I don't want you letting them out. With all the commotion around here today, they could easily get lost. We don't want that, do we?" She fixed them with a stern glance.

"We won't, Gramma," Sarah answered seriously.

Getting ready with her two granddaughters underfoot took almost twice as long, but Maggie finally managed to pull herself together and stepped onto the back lawn as Sam Torres pulled up in his pickup truck, followed closely by George Holmes and Tim Knudsen. Within thirty minutes, everyone who had any part in planning the carnival was on site and setting up whatever was needed. Maggie was prepared to lend a hand, but every offer of help was declined with the assertion that they were "all set."

Maggie wandered to her perch at the bottom of the lawn and surveyed the scene. The gables and peaks of Rosemont were silhouetted against an azure sky. A light breeze fluttered the streamers and skirted tables that now dotted the lawn. John, Alex, Marc, and Susan were hiding eggs. She waved to John, and he made his way toward her.

"You've done it again, my dear," he said as he gathered her in his arms.

"I haven't done one single solitary thing." Maggie declared. "The others deserve all the credit this time." She swept her hand to indicate the group scurrying to and fro on the lawn, finalizing preparations for the opening of the carnival, a matter of minutes away.

"Isn't that the definition of true success? To leave a legacy that lives on after you?" John surveyed the scene.

Maggie turned her face to his. "Dr. Allen—you are the kindest, wisest man on earth." She stood on her tiptoes and kissed him. "I hope you're right."

"I know I am." He pointed to the twins. "Sophie and Sarah are having a blast. They'll remember this—and be telling their grandchildren about it—when they're your age."

"I don't know about that. But I hope so."

John cocked his head to the woods behind them. "Want to hide out in there and neck while all this is going on? Nobody'd ever notice we're gone."

Maggie laughed. "It's tempting, but you'll just have to wait until Monday when everyone's gone home. We'd better get going. The gates open in ten minutes."

—— ∞ ——

Sophie and Sarah were, indeed, having the time of their lives. They won the three-legged race easily, taking advantage of the special teamwork that comes so naturally to twins. They were headed to the lemonade stand when they noticed a cluster of children gathered around a boy and a one-eyed dog under a banner that read "Mercy Hospital: A Child's Place."

They hung back and watched as children waited in line for their turn to spend time with the dog. The last child in line, younger than most, was accompanied by a girl close to Sophie and Sarah's age.

Sarah caught the older girl's eye and smiled. "Are you going to see the dog?" she asked.

Marissa Nash nodded. "My sister met him when she was in the hospital, and that boy told her that Dodger would be here. My mom wasn't going to let us come until my sister wanted to pet the therapy dog."

"Where's your mom?" Sophie asked, looking around.

"She's not here," Marissa replied. "She started to come with us, then changed her mind. She said we could stay if my brother and I watched Nicole the whole time. Sean took off the minute our mom left, and now I'm stuck with her."

"That's not fair," Sophie stated flatly. "Have you played any of the games?"

Marissa shook her head.

"What's wrong with your sister?" Sarah asked.

"I'm not sure, but she's been sick a lot, and she's been in the hospital twice. Mommy told us that the doctor can fix it, but they haven't found the right pill yet."

Sarah and Sophie nodded, absorbing the information. "Why don't we all go around together?" Sarah proposed. "One of us can always be with Nicole, and we can take turns doing stuff."

Marissa beamed. The instant bond that children so easily form was made, and the girls were inseparable for the remainder of the carnival. Sophie even helped Nicole collect enough eggs to finish sixth in the egg hunt. Susan was manning the prize table when the four girls ventured over to select Nicole's trinket.

"I wondered where the two of you had gotten off to. I see you've made some new friends," she said, smiling at Marissa and Nicole.

"This is my aunt Susan," Sophie said proudly.

"And who are you two lovely ladies?" Susan asked.

"I'm Marissa Nash, and this is my sister Nicole."

Susan looked at Nicole carefully and asked, "Did you come to see that doggy today?" Nicole nodded. "He's really special, isn't he? So calm and gentle." Nicole nodded again and sat down on the grass.

"Have you had fun today?" she asked, directing the question to Marissa.

"Loads of fun," she said, turning to Sophie and Sarah, and the three girls giggled.

"And we're going to get together again when we come back for the wedding. We already asked Mommy if we could have a sleep over at Rosemont with Marissa. She said, 'We'll see.'" Sarah supplied in a tone that indicated she thought the plan was set in stone.

"Sounds like a perfect idea to me," Susan said, awash with the fond remembrance of those special "vacation friends" she'd made when she was their age. "Are you going to the egg toss? It's about to start."

The three older girls set out across the lawn, but Nicole stayed put. Marissa turned back and pulled her sister's hand. "Don't feel good," Nicole protested.

"Oh, come on, Nicole. You can do it. Just one more game?"

Susan walked around the table and crouched down to where Nicole was sitting. "Do you need a rest, sweetie? Do you want to stay with me and help with the prizes while your sister goes with my nieces?" Susan turned to Marissa. "Would that be all right with you? She'll be safe with me, and I'll be right here the whole time."

Marissa looked at her sister. "Will you stay with the nice lady?" Nicole nodded almost imperceptibly. Marissa needed no further confirmation. She planted a quick kiss on her sister's head and tore after Sophie and Sarah.

———

Frank Haynes pulled his Mercedes sedan into the familiar berm of the road that ran below Rosemont. He rolled his windows down to let the breeze blow through the car as he sat and spied on the sea of activity on the back lawn. The jumbled voices of the crowd were pierced by an occasional cheer and round of applause. He could almost make out the words that George Holmes was delivering through that megaphone. Would he allow this carnival to continue if he were the owner of Rosemont? He didn't think so.

Haynes checked his Rolex. Time to make his entrance.

Parking by the front door, he looked up to examine the façade of Rosemont. All of this should be his. He fought the bile rising in his throat and skirted the house to enter the back lawn. He paused at the edge of the house and forced his features into a pleasant expression.

Haynes shook hands as he made his way to George Holmes, the carnival's de facto master of ceremonies. Holmes handed the megaphone to Haynes and said, "Try not to take all the credit this year, will you, Frank?"

Haynes glared at him as he grabbed the megaphone. "Citizens of Westbury," Haynes intoned, "we've had a beautiful day again at Rosemont, haven't we? Have you all had fun?" He was greeted with whistles and cheers in response. Haynes scanned the crowd and stopped when he spied the reporter from the *Westbury Gazette*.

"Mayor Martin," he called. "Where are you, Maggie? Let's get her up here to show our appreciation, shall we?" An enthusiastic round of applause spread through the crowd.

Joan Torres went to the admission table where Maggie was tallying the gate receipts with Tim Knudsen and snagged her by the arm. "You're being summoned," she leaned in to whisper in Maggie's ear. "Looks like he's taking the high road this year and giving you the recognition you deserve."

"Don't believe it for a minute," Maggie whispered back. "He's up to something." She joined Frank Haynes as he yelled, "Another round of applause for our own Mayor Maggie Martin," and posed with her for the newspaper's photographer.

Maggie extricated herself as soon as the picture was taken and moved off to the side.

"I now have the distinct pleasure of doing one of my favorite duties on behalf of Haynes Enterprises," he continued. "Giving things away! This year has been another banner year for my company. To thank all of you for your support, we're giving away more prizes than ever." He paused and motioned for applause. "We've got a flat screen television, a tablet, an e-reader, and both a boy's and a girl's bike." He pointed to the table behind him where the prizes were displayed.

"Does everyone have their raffle tickets out? Who wants to draw the winners for us?" He scanned the crowd and his eyes fell on David Wheeler. "How about David Wheeler, everyone? He was kind enough to come out today with his therapy dog, Dodger. They're right over there," he said pointing to the boy who was now trying to make himself invisible.

"Come on, David," John Allen called and escorted the boy to the fish bowl on the prize table. He took Dodger from David and went to stand with Maggie.

"Haynes knows how to work a crowd when he wants to, doesn't he?" he said softly.

"That's an understatement. I can't tell when he's being genuine. I'm firmly convinced he's a snake—like when he called me up there for applause. He just wanted our picture in the paper together. But then he's nice to David, and I believe he really means it." She sighed. "You never know with Frank."

They turned back to the scene unfolding in front of them as David Wheeler drew the winning tickets and Frank Haynes read the numbers. After all the winners had been announced, the crowd began to disperse.

"Looks like another successful fundraiser at Rosemont," John said. "I'm going to help the winners carry that television to their car."

Maggie nodded. She weaved through the crowd, searching for Frank Haynes, and found him peering into the French doors to the library.

"Looking for something, Frank?" she said as he started and turned to her with an unsettling expression of longing.

He cleared his throat. "I was remembering that time I rescued you from the attic." He turned to the door and pointed. "I was wondering if this was the door I unlocked to get in."

Maggie frowned. "This door doesn't have an exterior lock. You came in through the kitchen door—on the other side of the house. Don't you remember?"

"Now that you mention it, yes." He slapped his hand on his pants pocket and withdrew the keys to his car. "I'd better be going. I have another engagement," he lied.

Maggie intended to mention the odd encounter to John but the scene slipped from her mind as Rosemont was once more engrossed in the kind of controlled chaos that marks a circus breaking camp. She and Tim Knudsen totaled the day's donations while the others restored order to the back lawn. It was suppertime when everything was back in place, and Tim Knudsen announced that they'd almost doubled the prior year's take, raising twenty thousand dollars for the pension fund.

Alex Scanlon went into the kitchen and returned with three bottles of champagne and a stack of plastic glasses. "I think we deserve to toast ourselves, don't you?"

Mike uncorked the bottles, and Marc and Susan passed the glasses to the assembled workers. "To another successful Rosemont Easter carnival, to our beloved Westbury and our esteemed Mayor Martin," Alex declared. Maggie flushed as the group raised their glasses to a chorus of "Here, here."

It wasn't until she laid her exhausted head on her pillow at midnight that she remembered the strange encounter with Frank Haynes. She'd tell John about it the next day at brunch, she thought as sleep overtook her.

Easter was a lazy day at Rosemont. Maggie had invited Alex and Marc, the Torreses, Judy Young, the Holmes, the Knudsens, and the Vaughns to drop by in the afternoon. The picture-perfect weather of the preceding week was replaced by a cold front bringing with it a misty drizzle. Even the girls were still worn out from the day before and were content to lay on the rug and listen to the adults chat while Marc played the piano in the conservatory.

The Torreses were the last to leave in the late afternoon. Amy declared that it was time for them to pack up and get ready for their flight in the morning. Susan offered to pick up a pizza from Tomascino's for dinner. Alex and Marc followed her to the door. "The next time we'll see you, it'll be at the wedding," Alex said. "You'd better bring that brother of mine with you. I know he's studying for his medical boards, but enough's enough."

Susan smiled. "You can be sure of it. I called him last night to tell him how much fun he missed. He really is sorry that he couldn't make it."

"I know," Alex replied. "Give him my best. Tell him I'm proud of him."

Maggie leaned into John. "There's something I've been dying to tell you, but I can't for the life of me remember what it is."

John laughed. "These last few days would do that to anybody. You know where to find me when you remember. I'm going to head home now. I've got an early surgery in the morning."

"Aren't you going to stay for dinner? Don't you want to say goodbye to the kids?"

"I've been eating all afternoon, if you hadn't noticed, and I've already said goodbye. You should have a few minutes alone with them."

Maggie reached up and kissed him firmly on the lips. "I'll see you tomorrow night, mister," she said with a gleam in her eye.

Chapter 48

Alex Scanlon and the mayor were on their way. Forest Smith opened another energy drink and returned to the "war room" where the boxes of documents from the offshore banks lined the walls. The meeting with the mayor was to take place in secret, and the paralegals working on the case were exhausted and relieved when he told them that they could go home an hour ago.

Forest peered into the hallway, then locked the door from the inside. It was time to go through the culled documents he had stashed at the back of a box labeled Completed/Nothing.

He carefully loosened the tape holding the box shut and drew out a sheaf of documents an inch thick. He brought them to the workstation at the end of the room, switched on the desk lamp, and examined each document carefully. Satisfied that he had everything he needed, he settled in to wait.

Forest roused himself from his chair when he heard footsteps in the hallway. He checked his watch. It was ten fifteen. Alex knocked softly and called his name.

Forest opened the door, then locked it after Alex and the mayor entered the room. Alex made the introduction.

"Alex's told me you've done an incredibly thorough job of dissecting these documents. I've been involved in a number of large fraud cases in my former career as a forensic accountant. Believe me, I know how tedious and taxing that task is."

"Thank you, Mayor Martin," Forest replied.

"Call me Maggie, please. Alex said you've got documents you want me to see?"

Forest nodded. "Over here," he said, leading her to the papers laid out for her review.

"We haven't found much," Alex interjected. "But what we have implicates Chuck Delgado and, of course, William Wheeler."

"That's not a surprise," Maggie said. "We knew about Wheeler, and we all think Delgado is a crook. But I would have expected others to be involved. What about Ron Delgado? Or Frank Haynes?"

"Nothing." Alex shook his head. "That's why we wanted you to look at what we've found. As a forensic accountant, you may be able to see things we've overlooked."

Maggie shook her head. "I don't know about that, but I'd like to see what you've got." She took a seat and pulled a stack of papers toward her.

An hour and forty-five minutes later, she leaned back in her chair and summoned the two men to look at a series of documents she had spread out before her.

"The paper trails established by these documents don't add up. The amounts on the transfers don't make sense. I'll need more time to go through the rest of these documents, and they'll have to be examined under magnification, but I'm convinced that some of these have been altered and redacted," she said. "Others have been created for the purpose of implicating Delgado. Only about a third of them look legitimate."

Alex nodded slowly and raked his fingers through his hair. "That's what we were afraid of. Somebody wants us to nail Delgado. Wheeler's dead. I want Chuck Delgado, but I also want whoever is setting him up." He turned to Maggie. "How difficult will it be confirm your suspicions? Will you have to go through all of this?" He swept his arm around the room.

Maggie nodded. "I'm afraid so. You know how high the standard of proof is for criminal convictions. It will take months of work. And that's if I tackled the project full time. Which I can't do."

Alex cursed. "We can't let them get away with this. We'll just have to work harder. The paralegals are really talented; maybe you can work with them—show them what to look for? Supervise their efforts. They can go through all of this again."

"Or maybe one of the bad guys will do something stupid and show their hand? Give us the evidence we need," Forest said.

Both of them turned to him, and he laid out his plan.

Forest Smith shivered in his dark car while he waited for Chuck Delgado to arrive for their rendezvous. He checked the clock on the dashboard. Delgado was fifteen minutes late. Smith was about to start his engine when he saw a set of headlights turn the corner and slowly approach. Delgado parked and waddled to the passenger side of Smith's car. He pressed the unlock button, and Delgado slid into the seat beside him.

"Whatcha got for me?" he asked.

"A room full of evidence, all pointing to William Wheeler."

"That's good. Just what we expected. Wheeler acted alone," Delgado began.

Smith raised his hand. "Save it," he said. "That's all there is now. We've been through everything. I found evidence that implicated you." He paused and turned to Delgado, taking malicious pleasure in watching the color drain from Delgado's florid complexion.

Delgado licked his lips, "Like what?"

"Papers signed by you to open bank accounts. Wire transfer forms signed by you. There isn't much—just a handful of items—but enough to put you away."

Delgado took a well-used handkerchief from his pocket and wiped his forehead. "You find anything on anybody else?" he asked.

"Nope. Just William Wheeler and you."

"Nothing on Frank Haynes?"

"Nothing."

Delgado leaned back in his seat. "That bastard," he mumbled. He turned to Forest Smith. "You need to get anything with my name on it outta there, you understand? Do that, and there'll be a nice payday for you. Money or pills. You choose."

"I don't want either one." He reached into the backseat and picked up the plain brown envelope containing the incriminating documents and handed it to Delgado. "Here you are. They're all there."

Delgado opened the envelope and began examining the contents. "Shit," he said. "This is my signature, but I don't remember signing these. Somebody must have slipped them in with something else I was signing."

"Or maybe you're drunk so often that you don't know what you're signing," Smith said.

"What the—who the hell do you think you are talking to me like that? You work for us now, remember? I own you, you rat-bastard lawyer."

"Not anymore, you don't. Our association is now done."

"What're you talking about? We're done when I say we're done."

"On the contrary, Mr. Delgado. That envelope contains copies. The originals are in my safe deposit box. And I've left letters detailing all of this if anything happens to me."

He reached across Delgado and opened the passenger door.

"I felt it prudent to insure my personal safety. If you make any further move to contact me, I'll make sure that evidence finds its way into Alex Scanlon's hands. And you'll be spending a lot of time in William Wheeler's old jail cell."

"You think you're so high and mighty, don't you? We control all of the oxy in the tri-state region. Where ya gonna go for your fix now? None of my boys will sell to you."

"I'm doing quite well in my twelve-step program, thank you for asking. Now get the hell out of my car," he said, giving Delgado a shove.

Delgado stumbled and sprawled on the frozen ground. Forest Smith turned on his engine and spun away, pelting Delgado with a spray of gravel. He punched the familiar number into his speed dial when he was a mile down the highway.

"Mission accomplished. He bought it hook, line, and sinker."

"Well done," Alex replied. "Do you think he's worried?"

"Big time. Now all we have to do is wait for him to do something stupid."

"Watch your back, okay? Don't take any chances. Letting him think that incriminating evidence will come out if something happens to you may not protect you. Don't forget, somebody out there wants Delgado to go down for this. They might be more than happy to orchestrate your death so the evidence comes out."

"Understood," Smith said, glancing nervously in his rearview mirror.

Chapter 49

Maggie slid into the booth next to John Allen. "Stuart's Steakhouse is pretty fancy for a Monday night, isn't it?"

"I'm considering this a long-overdue date night. We haven't had a moment alone since before the kids came to visit."

Maggie leaned into him and sighed. "You're such a romantic. I'm a lucky gal."

John kissed the top of her head. "I'm assuming they all got home safe and sound. No delayed planes or missed connections?"

Maggie nodded. "Mike texted when they landed, thanking me and telling me what a good time they had. They're excited for the wedding." She turned to him. "Did you know that the girls made fast friends with another little girl at the carnival? They're planning a sleepover at Rosemont when they're back in June."

"Won't you be too busy with the wedding?"

"It'll be fine," Maggie relaxed into his arm resting along the back of the booth. "By that time, everything that needs to get done had better *be* done."

The waiter approached their table. "I don't want to interrupt. Do you need a few minutes?" They shook their heads and placed their usual orders.

"So where do we stand on the wedding?" John asked. "I know you girls worked on it like mad last week."

"It's all done—as long as the dresses and invitations come in on time. You've got your tux, right?"

"Altered and hanging in my closet. Do you want to see it?"

Maggie shook her head. "If you can't see my dress before the wedding, I shouldn't see your tux."

The waiter placed their entrees on the table, and they began to eat in companionable silence. When Maggie was almost done with her filet, she cut the remaining chunk in half and motioned to the waiter. "May I get a doggie bag for these, please?" she asked.

John looked at her askance. "I hope I'm the doggie that you're thinking of. That's at least ten dollars' worth of steak."

"You know that these are for Eve and Roman. They're such good doggies. They deserve a treat."

"You know that people food isn't good for them. And that I'm the local veterinarian? It won't be good for business if my own dogs get sick from poor nutrition," he admonished.

Maggie rolled her eyes.

"And where would my sweetheart like to go for our honeymoon? Can you still get away for two weeks, like we talked about?"

"I'm taking two weeks, come hell or high water," Maggie replied firmly. "As for where—I haven't given it any thought."

"The beach? The mountains? City or country? Domestic or abroad?"

Maggie began to rub her temples with her fingertips. "Ahhhhh … I don't think I can cope with planning one more thing; this wedding is already bigger than what I wanted. All I know is that I want to be with you and I want us to do something relaxing—something very different from our daily lives here. I need to immerse myself in a new environment."

John searched the face of the woman he cherished. "Why don't I plan the whole thing? I'll tell you what I've got in mind and you can approve or veto, but I'll do all the work. Seems only fair since you've taken on the wedding."

Maggie turned to him, her eyes bright. "I'd love that. But don't tell me a thing about it. Let it be a wonderful surprise—like our first date at The Mill. Remember how well that turned out?"

A smile spread across John's face. "If you really mean it, I'd love to. I've got something in mind already."

"Don't give me any hints. No matter how much I beg."

John laughed. "You've got it. My lips are sealed. But what about your wardrobe? I'll have to tell you what to pack."

Maggie shook her head. "Nope. Not even that. Susan will be here the week before the wedding. You can tell her, and she can pack for me."

"I hope I don't disappoint you," John said seriously.

"You never could," Maggie assured him.

"Let's get the check and head back to Rosemont," John replied huskily.

The month of May was filled with fittings, consultations, and endless emails and phone calls. If Maggie were honest, she spent at least half of her workday attending to the details of her wedding. Despite the fact that the first batch of invitations arrived with a typo, Judy Young was able to expedite the corrected order and Maggie deposited them in the mail only a few days later than planned. Everyone on the guest list already had the date circled on their calendars, anyway. The RSVPs were streaming in, and the latest count showed that they could expect two hundred and eighty guests.

Frank Haynes had received his invitation at his home address, the address he called home because someone (almost certainly Paul Martin) had destroyed the evidence that would have assured that he—Frank Haynes—inherited Rosemont. He'd be damned if he'd attend and celebrate Maggie's good fortune at his expense.

Haynes was tossing the invitation in the trash when an idea occurred to him. He smiled broadly. *What a delicious idea.*

He returned the invitation to its envelope and placed it carefully inside his briefcase. He'd speak to Loretta in the morning.

Loretta Nash looked up as Frank Haynes approached her desk. She relaxed. He was smiling. Maybe she wasn't in trouble.

"When you were interviewing for this job, you mentioned that you knew about Rosemont."

Loretta eyed him warily and nodded.

"As you may have heard, Mayor Martin and John Allen are getting married there in June. I received my invitation this morning," he said, pulling the invitation from its envelope, "and was wondering if you'd like to join me."

Loretta stared at him.

"Not as a date, mind you. Nothing of the sort. We still have a professional relationship to maintain." He searched her face as he said the next words. "Since your friend Paul owned Rosemont, I thought you'd be curious about it. This is your chance to see it up close."

Loretta's head was spinning. What in the hell was Frank Haynes doing? Had he figured out about her and Paul, or was he really trying to be nice? One thing was sure, she wasn't going anywhere near Maggie Martin's Rosemont wedding.

"I can't take time away from my kids on a Saturday. Sean's in softball, and we have a game," she lied. "Thank you for asking me, but I won't be able to make it."

Haynes stood the open invitation on her desk. "I've already RSVP'd for two, so if you change your mind, let me know. It'll be something that people around here will talk about for the rest of their lives. You'd be sorry you missed it."

Chapter 50

Loretta tried to ignore the invitation that had been sitting on her desk for weeks, but found herself picking it up and reading the engraving over and over again—the wedding was a week from Saturday. If things had turned out differently, maybe she and Paul Martin would have gotten married at Rosemont. She was daydreaming about her own Rosemont wedding when the shrill ring of the phone on her desk brought her back to reality.

"Loretta," came the school nurse's brisk voice. "Nicole's real bad again. I'm so sorry, honey, but I think she needs to go back to the hospital. Now."

Loretta was already picking up her purse. "I'm on my way. I'll call the doctor from my car."

Loretta threw Frank Haynes' office door open. "The school just called. I have to get Nicole to the hospital." She turned on her heel and ran to the door. She never heard Frank Haynes tell her to take whatever time she needed and to let him know if he could help.

Loretta and Nicole walked through the doors of the emergency room of Mercy Hospital and were admitted directly to a room. *One of the advantages of being well known to the hospital staff,* Loretta thought sadly. A nurse took Nicole's vital signs and drew three vials of blood. Her doctor entered the room less than thirty minutes later, accompanied by a team of pediatricians and nephrologists that he said would be performing a thorough review of Nicole's condition. Loretta nodded, as fear settled its vice-like grip on her heart. Why couldn't they figure out how to help her daughter?

After the team left, Loretta stood over the hospital bed looking at her daughter's small, swollen face reposed in sleep. The new medicine wasn't working. She fished her cell phone from her purse, called her babysitter to make arrangements for Marissa and Sean, and then collapsed into the familiar bedside chair, waiting for the doctors to return.

Almost an hour later, a nurse motioned to Loretta to join her in the hallway. "They're ready to see you," she said. Loretta turned eyes wide with fear to the woman. "It'll be okay," she said. "You've got the best team in the state looking after your little girl. They'll know what to do." The nurse put her arm around Loretta's shoulders and walked her into the consultation room where the doctors were assembled.

The doctor held out a chair for her, and she sank into it before her knees buckled under her.

"The medications we've used so far haven't performed as expected," he said. "There are others we can try, but her condition is getting worse. We're all in agreement," he motioned to the doctors seated at the table. "We should start Nicole on dialysis as soon as possible."

Loretta clutched the edge of the table with white knuckles. Tears formed in the corner of her eyes. "Will she ever get better? Will she need dialysis for the rest of her life?"

"We still believe we'll be able to control this with medication," he stated, and the other doctors nodded in agreement. "And that she will grow out of this condition. But for right now, she needs dialysis."

"Okay," Loretta croaked. "When will you do it? And where?"

"We've scheduled it for six o'clock tomorrow morning. Right here at the hospital."

Loretta nodded.

"There are other places she can go in the future, but for now, we'd like to monitor her. Would that be all right with you, Ms. Nash?"

Loretta found her voice. "Of course. If that's what she needs," she said, searching the faces around the table and seeing agreement in each one.

"She'll rest comfortably here tonight. Go home and get some sleep. You can be with her during the procedure. Be back at five thirty."

Loretta stopped at the babysitter's home to pick up Sean and Marissa. The kindly woman took one look at Loretta and insisted that they spend the night with her. "They've already had dinner and are hard at work on their homework. Go home, eat something, and go to bed. The last thing your family needs is for you to get sick."

"Thank you, I'll take you up on that—but let me put them to bed and kiss them goodnight," she said, turning grateful eyes to the woman.

"Don't worry about paying me, either. I know how expensive hospital care is. I'll help by keeping your big kids whenever you need. They're no trouble at all."

Loretta turned on the television to distract herself from the dark fears that intruded the quiet apartment. She warmed up a can of soup, kicked off her shoes, and sank into the sofa to eat her meager dinner, forcing spoonfuls into her mouth until she was certain she'd be sick if she took another bite. The remainder went down the disposal. She wrapped herself in an afghan and lay down, willing herself to get some sleep.

Loretta opened her eyes to the flickering light of the television and checked her cell phone—almost four thirty. Somehow she'd managed to get a few hours' sleep and felt slightly better. She showered, put on a clean pair of jeans and shirt, gathered her long hair into a ponytail, and skipped putting on makeup. If she went to work today, this would have to do.

When she arrived at the hospital, Loretta found Nicole awake and staring miserably at the ceiling of her room. "Not feel good," her daughter mumbled as Loretta rushed to her side, taking her hand and holding it to her cheek.

"I know, sweetie. The doctors have a plan to help you. They're going to clean your blood with a very special machine. And then you'll feel better."

Nicole blinked. "It'll be real soon now," she continued, "and Mommy will be with you the whole time." Loretta turned as a young man pushing a wheelchair tapped softly on the door.

"I hear a very pretty little girl named Nicole Nash needs a ride downstairs. Is that you?" he asked, looking at Nicole. She attempted a smile. The man checked the chart at the foot of her bed and made notes on his clipboard.

"How about your mother and I help you sit up and get in this wheelchair?" he asked as Loretta lifted Nicole's shoulders and he swung her feet off the bed. Nicole offered no resistance, and they guided her into the seat. Loretta held her daughter's hand tightly in her own as they proceeded to the elevator and down two floors to the large room labeled Dialysis Center.

"This'll make you feel better real soon," one of the nurses reassured softly as she positioned Nicole in an oversized reclining chair that all but enveloped the little girl. Nicole turned her face into her mother's arm while the nurse hooked Nicole up to the life-saving equipment. Nicole never uttered a sound, but Loretta felt her child's body tense with each poke and prod. *If only I could spare her this—all of this,* Loretta thought.

"You're all set now, honey," the nurse said, brushing a strand of hair from Nicole's damp forehead. "You're tired, aren't you? Why don't you take a nap while the machine does its work? Would you like that?"

Nicole nodded and soon she was asleep. Loretta attempted to read a magazine she pulled from a rack by the door.

The nurse checked on Nicole shortly after seven and turned to Loretta. "This takes quite a while. Why don't you go downstairs and get some breakfast? She won't know you're gone," she said, looking at the sleeping child.

Loretta nodded, realizing that she was famished. She stretched and headed to the cafeteria. The line wound out the door. She finally got her food and found a seat in the crowded room. She'd been gone longer than she'd anticipated and ate her eggs and toast quickly. She groaned when she saw the swarm of people waiting by the elevator and took the stairs instead. Whether propelled by paranoia or mother's instinct, she didn't know. She just knew that she needed to get back to Nicole.

Loretta pushed through the doors of the Dialysis Center and headed toward the spot where she'd left Nicole not more than forty-five minutes earlier. Nicole's nurse intercepted her halfway across the room.

"Nicole's been moved down the hall," she said. "We needed to discontinue the procedure early."

"Why?" Loretta's voice sounded shrill even to her own ears.

The nurse took her arm and led her to the room where Nicole lay, pale and still, swaddled in blankets.

Loretta put her hand to her mouth to stifle a sob. "What happened?"

"We're not sure. This happens sometimes," the nurse said. "People can be sensitive to some of the things we use."

"So what do you do about that?"

"We can make adjustments. We have lots of options. This'll get worked out just fine," she said reassuringly.

"And if it doesn't 'get worked out,'" Loretta choked out the words. "What then? She can't live with this disease."

"There's a lot of ground to cover before you get to that point. Don't worry about that now."

Loretta reached under the blankets and took Nicole's hand. "Mommy's here now, sweetie. I won't leave you ever again. You're gonna feel better soon, and we'll go home."

The nurse nodded from the doorway. "Yes, you will," she said. "We're going to figure this out."

Chapter 51

Susan and the twins were waiting by the front door when Anita Archer unlocked Archer's Bridal on the first Monday of June. "We're all set for you," she said. "Your dresses are hanging in the fitting room. We'll mark the hems and get you on your way in no time."

Sophie and Sarah raced ahead, anxious to try on the ankle-length dresses swathed in layers of pink organza. Anita turned to Susan. "Everything you selected is so pretty. Your mother's been in for her fitting and has picked up her gown. This'll be a lovely wedding. I'm so proud that Archer's is supplying the bridal wear. When we heard the mayor was getting married, we were afraid that she'd go back to California to some fancy shop there to buy her dress."

"No way," Susan said. "My mom would never do that. She supports Westbury all the way."

"We know that now," Anita said. "Why don't you get into your dress while I see to the girls?"

"I'm sure it's fine. The sample was the right length. Besides, isn't it a little too late for alterations?"

"It most certainly is not," Anita replied sternly. "If I have to sew around the clock between now and the wedding, I'm going to make sure these dresses fit perfectly. There will be pictures in the paper and all over social media. I want the world to know that Archer's Bridal does top-quality work."

Susan held up her hands. "Say no more. I'll be right out."

"I plan to have everything ready for you on Wednesday," Anita called to Susan as she picked up her pincushion and headed to the dressing room where the twins were twirling in their new pink dress-es.

———

"We need to be on our best behavior this week," Susan said as they left Archer's Bridal and turned toward Rosemont. It was a glorious summer morning and the walk would do them good. "You got to come on the plane early with me so that we could help Gramma," she reminded them. "When your parents and Aaron arrive on Thursday, I want to hear Gramma tell them that she couldn't have done it without you."

The girls nodded in unison. "We know, Aunt Susan. We're not going to get in the way or do anything bad."

"And we promise not to chase Eve or scare the cats," Sarah added.

"The only thing we get to do is have Marissa over for a sleepover," Sophie said, looking at Susan.

"I've already talked to Gramma about that, and she said it's all right if Marissa comes over tomorrow or Wednesday. Do you know how to get in touch with her?"

Sophie nodded. "I've got her number up here," she said, tapping her head.

Susan laughed at the mannerism that her brother used so often. "Why don't you call her now and see if we can pick her up tomorrow morning?" she said, fishing her cell phone out of her purse and handing it to Sophie. "We could go for a hike along the Shawnee River in the morning, have lunch at The Mill, and get manicures and pedicures in the afternoon. My treat for all of us. Make it a real girls' day. How does that sound?" Susan knew it would be most helpful to keep the girls out of her mother's hair this week.

Sarah's eyes got big. "That would be wonderful. We've never had our nails done before."

"You'll need it for the wedding," Susan said. "Be sure to ask Marissa if that would be fun for her. And we'll pick up pizza for dinner and eat it watching movies in my room. You can all sleep there, if you want," she said looking directly at Sarah, who had crawled into bed with Susan during the wee hours the previous night.

Sarah flushed. "Our room is scary without Mommy and Daddy," she said.

Susan ruffled her hair. "I was the same way when I was your age—always sneaking into Gramma's bed. You won't be scared to be alone when you're grown up," she said softly.

Sophie placed the call, and it was apparent, from listening to Sophie's side of the conversation, that all of Susan's plans were enthusiastically received.

They rounded the corner and started up the long, sloping driveway to Rosemont. "Race you," Susan said, pushing off and sprinting up the hill.

———

Maggie was delighted to have Susan and her granddaughters to herself for a few days, but was even more thankful the girls had the long-awaited sleepover with Marissa to keep them occupied. She had a lot of loose ends to tie up at Town Hall before she took time off for the wedding and their two-week honeymoon. Once everyone arrived on Thursday, she planned to set an out-of-office message on her work email and deal with everything when she got back.

Tuesday promised to be clear and mild, a perfect day for a hike. Susan pulled into the parking lot of Haynes Enterprises and shut off the engine. "Why're we picking Marissa up here?" she asked.

"Their babysitter is sick so Marissa and her brother had to go to work with their mom. Nicole's here, too. She has to go to the hospital today."

Susan shook her head. "I remember that sweet little sister of hers. What's wrong with her, do you know?"

Sophie shrugged. "Something with blood."

Susan paused on the bottom step. "Why don't we invite her brother to go with us? He'd love the hike. And lunch. I'll think of something else for him to do while we're at the salon."

"We don't want some stupid boy with us," Sophie said, rolling her eyes.

"Aunt Susan's right. It'd be awful to spend all day at your mom's work and then the hospital. We can't do that to him," Sarah said to her twin.

"Okay," Sophie fumed. "But don't blame me if he spoils it all."

"We'll make sure that doesn't happen," Susan said, opening the door to Haynes Enterprises.

———

Loretta Nash looked up as the two girls, close in age to her older daughter, came through the door followed by a tall, striking blonde with the vibrant blue eyes and solid self-assurance that epitomized Paul Martin. She swallowed and took a deep breath. She'd been fighting off an anxiety attack ever since Marissa informed her that her friends' aunt—the daughter of her former lover—would pick Marissa up from Haynes Enterprises. Worn to a frazzle by the constant demands of Nicole's illness, Loretta had merely nodded and steeled herself to get through the encounter as quickly as possible. She hoped Maggie Martin's children didn't know about their father's mistress.

"Hello, Ms. Nash," Susan said, holding out her hand. "Thank you so much for letting us have Marissa for the day. Sophie and Sarah talked about nothing else on the plane out here." She bent to talk to

Nicole, who was slumped in a chair. "Hi, sweetie. Do you remember me? We met at the carnival at Rosemont." Susan turned to Loretta. "I understand you're taking Nicole to the hospital later today."

Loretta took a deep breath and found her voice. "Yes. She's having dialysis."

Susan stepped back, then turned to Sean as she tried to conceal her alarm. Sean was playing a game on a cell phone. "We're going hiking by the Shawnee this morning, then having lunch at The Mill. Would you like to go with us? It's going to be a beautiful day."

Sean's fingers stopped flying over the keys and he shifted his gaze to his mother. "Could I, Mom?"

Loretta hesitated. She hadn't been prepared for Susan to be so nice. Was she making a mistake, letting her kids get involved with Paul's family? Her older children needed a break from the tension and uncertainty that engulfed them right now. If they had an offer to do something fun, she wasn't going to let her own sticky past spoil things for them now. "Of course you can," she replied. "If you're sure?" she said to Susan. Loretta reached into her purse and pulled out her wallet.

Susan touched Loretta's arm. "No. Please. This is my treat." Susan turned to the kids. "Come on. Let's get out of here so your mom can go back to work." She tore a Post-It note from a pad on Loretta's desk and wrote her cell phone number on it. "If you need anything, please call me. We'll be out and about all day, so we can easily pick up anything you need."

Loretta nodded and swallowed the lump in her throat. "Be good, you guys," she said, waving to Sean and Marissa.

"Call me when you want me to bring Sean home. And good luck today," Susan said to Loretta and Nicole as she pushed out the door.

—◦◦◦◦◦—

Sean turned out to be a great asset on the hike, clearing branches and brambles from the trail and steering them away from poison ivy. They were famished by the time they sat down at The Mill for lunch. Even Sarah found something she liked on the menu and cleaned her plate.

Susan turned to Sean as they climbed into the car to head back to the town square for their salon appointments. "I'm sure you don't want to hang out in the waiting area while we're getting our nails done," she said.

Sean shrugged. "I don't mind."

"Actually, I was wondering if you'd do an errand for me."

"Sure," he said tentatively.

"I was thinking we should get something for Nicole. Maybe a new stuffed animal she'd enjoy? And something for your mom. Since we've had such a fun day, and they haven't."

Marissa turned to her brother. "Nicole wants that doll in the window of Toys on the Square. The one that has the old-fashioned prairie dress. They have dresses for girls that match the doll. She's been begging for it, but we don't have the money. Mommy says that Nicole's medicine costs more than she makes in a month."

"Then it's settled. Let's get her that doll and the dress to match. What about your mom? What does she need?"

"She left her sweater at the hospital the last time they were there, and she never got it back. So I think we should get that."

"Or she needs new slippers," Marissa supplied

"Perfect idea. We'll get both. Pick them out while we're busy at the salon, and we'll run in to pay for them after we're done. When will your mom and Nicole be home from the hospital?

"We don't know," Sean said. "She may have to spend the night."

Susan drew a deep breath. "Then we'll take them to the hospital. And you can come with us to Rosemont, if you want."

Susan and the four children entered Mercy Hospital late that afternoon, excited to deliver their newly purchased gifts. They were shown to the waiting room outside the Dialysis Center and settled in. They didn't have long to wait. Loretta approached them with a smile on her face.

"Hey, guys," she said. "Did you have a fun day?"

Marissa stuck out her hands and rippled her fingers. "Look, Mommy."

"Beautiful!"

"And we got you something," Sean said, handing her two bags bearing the names of shops on the square.

"What's all this?" Loretta asked, turning to Susan in surprise, tears beginning to prick the back of her eyes. "You shouldn't have done this."

"We had so much fun today, we didn't think it was fair," Susan said. "They picked everything out themselves. Go on. Open them."

Loretta pulled the tissue out of the first bag and withdrew an ivory fisherman's knit cardigan, long and belted. "It was on sale," Sean said proudly. "And it's just like the one you lost."

"It's much nicer than the one I lost," Loretta replied.

"Look at this," Marissa urged.

Loretta unwrapped a pair of sheepskin slippers. "Exactly what I've been wanting." She slipped off a shoe and inserted her foot. "They're the right size, too." She gathered her two older children into her arms and looked up at Susan. "Thank you."

"My pleasure. I thought you deserved something nice. All of this can't be easy. How's it going in there?" she asked, gesturing to the closed door of the procedure room.

"Much better this time," Loretta replied. "They had to discontinue dialysis before they were done last time. I was so afraid it would happen again."

"I could tell that you were really worried," Susan replied.

"We've got stuff for Nicole, too," Sophie interjected.

"She's all done, and they're observing her for a little while. Let's go in, and you can give them to her yourselves."

Nicole lay in her bed, propped on a mountain of pillows, watching cartoons on television. She smiled and leaned forward as the group approached. Sean placed the first of two large gift bags on the bed. Nicole squealed with delight as Sean helped her take the doll out of its wrappings. She cradled the doll in her arms, placing the doll's long curly hair behind its shoulders and straightening the skirt of its dress. Nicole looked up and beamed.

Susan laughed and caught Loretta's eye. "Marissa and Sean knew what their sister wanted, didn't they? They're great kids. You should be very proud of them."

Loretta quickly turned away and swallowed hard.

"There's more," Sarah said. Marissa placed the other bag on the bed, next to her sister. Nicole kept her new doll clamped to her side with one hand and reached into the bag with the other. She withdrew the dress that was identical to the one her doll was wearing and held it out to her mother. "On," she said.

"I'm not sure we can get you out of that hospital gown, yet," Loretta replied, folding the dress. Storm clouds gathered on Nicole's face, and she was about to let out a wail when the nurse, who had been watching the happy scene unfold, rose from her chair.

"I think it's time we got you out of here," she said to Nicole. "Are you ready to go home, sweetheart?"

Nicole nodded vigorously.

"What have you got there?" the nurse asked. Nicole turned the doll in her arms so that the nurse could see her. "She's beautiful, isn't she? Looks just like you. And what's this here?" she said, reaching for the dress in Loretta's arms. "A matching dress? Isn't that pretty. I'll bet people will think you're twins when you wear this. Would you like to put it on? I want to see the two of you."

Nicole continued to nod. "Will you let me hold your doll while your mommy helps you with your dress? I'll stand right here, and I'll take real good care of her."

Nicole shook her head, turned, and handed her precious new doll to Susan, and then stuck her arms in the air. Her mother slipped the new garment over Nicole's head and got the hospital gown off of her and the new dress neatly in place with a speed resembling that of a practiced Broadway dresser. Susan returned the doll to Nicole's out-stretched arms.

"Can we take pictures for Facebook?" Sophie asked Susan.

"Let me take one of all of you," Susan said. "Loretta—you get in the picture, too."

Chapter 52

The rain predicted for the middle of the week was stuck in the Dakotas, and perfect weather graced all of the preparations. Anita Archer had the alterations ready by Tuesday, and Joe Appleby and his crew finished the landscaping Wednesday. Amy, Mike, and Aaron arrived on Thursday night as planned, and Pete orchestrated the setup on Friday morning.

Three hundred chairs now sat in rows along the bottom of the lawn for tomorrow's ceremony and thirty-eight round tables waited to be dressed for the luncheon reception at the top of the lawn. "We'll have the food set up buffet-style on the covered patio, and we'll have three bars around the perimeter," he told Maggie. "The flowers will be here first thing in the morning, and we'll have all the tables ready by nine o'clock. An eleven o'clock ceremony on a Saturday is perfect. Don't worry about a thing. Nothing can go wrong now."

Maggie smiled and squeezed his shoulder. "You said you'd take care of everything and you have."

"All you have to do is practice the ceremony then come over to the Bistro for the rehearsal dinner."

Maggie nodded, surveying the scene when a familiar furry shape escaped through the kitchen door and sped across the lawn skidding to a halt at her feet. Pete reached down to pat Eve, who was now nipping at his heels.

"Which reminds me of one more thing I need to do—" she said, scooping Eve up in her arms. "Get this one and those three cats, Bubbles, Blossom, and Buttercup, corralled and off to Westbury Animal Hospital for boarding while we're gone. I think it's high time we got them out of our hair." She nuzzled Eve's neck and started up the lawn. "See you after the rehearsal."

The pastor arrived fifteen minutes late, but otherwise the rehearsal went off without a hitch. The sound system worked well in the outdoor space, and the twins took their instruction seriously, walking at the pace their mother instructed. "It'll be a beautiful day for a wedding, and I promise not to be late tomorrow," the pastor said after they finished as the wedding party was heading around the side of the house.

Aaron and Susan, inseparable since he'd arrived, were strolling hand in hand down the driveway. "We're going to walk over to Pete's," she called over her shoulder.

"There's room with us," Maggie began, then stopped. How long had it been since she and John had any time to themselves? A few minutes alone with him was exactly what she needed.

Maggie took John's hand as they slowly climbed the stone steps to the massive front door of Rosemont. "My life has been so blessed since I moved to Westbury. And I wouldn't have moved if it hadn't been for this grand old house." John put his arm around her shoulders and drew her close. "I'm marrying the best man I've ever met here. And I might never have met you if Eve hadn't found her way to Rosemont on that first, fateful night when I got snowed in." She kissed her fingertip and pressed it to the inside of the doorframe.

John laughed. "I have to admit, I'm looking forward to moving in with you after the wedding. We've barely had a chance to talk, much less spend time together, for weeks."

"Are you ready for this wedding to be over with?"

"Would you be mad if I said I was?"

"No. I'd say I'm feeling the same way. Shall we ditch them all and just stay here?"

"Be a no-show at our own rehearsal dinner? Mayor Martin, I'm surprised at you. Certainly not. They'd all think I'd put you up to it. I'm not taking the blame."

"Okay, spoil sport. Let me run upstairs and get a sweater. The breeze has really picked up. It's got a bite in it, don't you think?"

The sun rose in a brilliant blue sky that Saturday morning, scattering light like diamonds across a two-inch blanket of snow that fell over-night, covering Westbury and the surrounding counties in the latest snowfall of the season since the 1930s.

Maggie realized something was amiss as soon as she awoke. The light peeking through her heavy bedroom drapes was far too bright for the hour displayed on her bedside clock. She padded to her win-dow and drew the curtain aside. An unbroken layer of snow rose and fell between every chair, table, and trellis on the lawn below. It was a beautiful sight, to be sure, but definitely not one she wanted to see on the day of her outdoor wedding in June.

Maggie stood, rooted to the spot, staring at the scene below and blinking. She was about to drop the drape back into place and call John when two men came around the side of the house. Sam Torres and Tim Knudsen. And they were carrying brooms and shovels. She watched as they set to work brushing the light snow from the chairs.

Maggie tugged at the crank on the casement window, finally suc-ceeding in getting it open. "Good morning," she yelled, leaning out the window.

Sam looked up, searching for the source of the sound. She waved and he saluted in return. "Don't worry," he called, cupping his mouth with his hands. "Joe Appleby and his crew are on their way. We've got it covered."

Maggie made an exaggerated thumbs-up and cranked the window shut. She was halfway to her nightstand to retrieve her phone when it rang. Maggie answered and Judy Young jumped right in. "Maggie. Don't worry about a thing. We're on it. You just get ready. Leave the rest to us."

Maggie laughed. "You are the most incredible people in the entire world. Tim and Sam are out on the back lawn, dealing with the snow right now. I guess we'll have to pull something out of the closet to wear. We'll freeze, otherwise."

"No," Judy said sternly. "Wear the dresses you bought. Anita says they're gorgeous. Joan Torres and I have something planned for that, too."

"You do, do you?" Maggie said, bemused by her friend's take-charge attitude.

"Yes. And I'm too busy to talk about it right now. The wedding's at eleven. Joan and I will be over there at ten. Your job is to enjoy getting ready for your wedding!"

Judy Young and Joan Torres arrived at nine forty-five with two vintage white mink stoles and two pink faux fur capes in hand. One stole had belonged to Judy's mother, and Sam had given the other to Joan on their tenth wedding anniversary.

"The capes were in my grandchildren's dress-up box," Joan said. "It's been years since anybody's been in that box. I've been tempted to get rid of it many times."

"These are beyond perfect," Susan gushed. "Look at them, Mom. Just stunning."

"It's actually getting warm out. You may not need them," Judy said.

"No way. We're wearing them," Susan turned to her mother, "Don't you think, Mom? It's your wedding. You should have the say."

"I agree. They're lovely, and it means the world to me that you're letting us borrow them." She turned to Susan and pointed to Judy's stole. "That one will look beautiful with your dress." Susan draped the silvery mink around her shoulders over the long, slim column of blush-colored silk that drifted gracefully to the floor.

"I love it," Susan replied. "Are you sure?"

Maggie nodded. "Why don't you and Judy take the capes to the girls?" When they were alone, Maggie turned to Joan. "You and Sam have been my oldest and dearest friends in Westbury. You've been there for me every step of the way. I didn't have anything borrowed to wear. I'd be so honored to borrow your stole. The fact that Sam gave it to you for your anniversary makes it even more special."

Joan hugged Maggie hard. "I love the thought of that." She leaned back and looked into Maggie's eyes. "Can I tell you something? You can't ever tell Sam." Maggie nodded. "I've never liked that stole. I thought it was incredibly sweet of Sam, and I've worn it to make him happy. But I always felt it was a little too old-fashioned for me. After this wedding, I think I'll have a whole new appreciation for it."

Maggie laughed. "I hope so. And your secret is safe with me."

Joan placed the creamy mink around Maggie's shoulders and secured the clasp. She stepped back and brought her hands to her heart. "I've never seen a more beautiful bride. You're glowing."

Maggie turned to one side and then the other, studying her reflection in the full-length mirror. Her eyes moved over the creamy organza gown adorned with champagne-colored lace and seed pearls, the off-the-shoulder top hugged her body all the way to the dropped waistline, where it flared into a full skirt with a modest train. "You don't think I look ridiculous in this gown? At my age?"

"Absolutely not! Why would you say such a thing? You're going to knock John Allen's socks off, and every woman in town will be talking about it for weeks. It's perfect."

Maggie closed her eyes and drew a deep breath, savoring the moment.

Both women turned at the light knock on the door. "Mom," Mike called softly. "Are you ready? Can I come in?"

"She certainly is," Joan called. "Don't you look handsome?" she said as Mike stepped into the room. "I'm going to collect my husband and make sure we get a seat in the front row." She took Maggie's face in her hands. "Many blessings, my dear. You're marrying the second-best man I know."

Joan closed the door quietly behind her. Maggie and Mike stood at arm's length, smiling at each other. "Gosh, Mom, you look beautiful."

"Thank you, sweetheart. And Joan's right. You look like you stepped out of a magazine. You should wear a tuxedo more often."

Mike approached the full-length mirror. "I do feel pretty dapper." Maggie laughed. "But *you* look positively radiant." He turned to her. "You're very happy here, aren't you?"

Maggie nodded. "I've never felt so at home, so connected, or so vibrant in my whole life. Meeting John Allen and marrying him today is the best thing that's ever happened to me—except for you and your sister. And the girls."

Mike paused. "John is a very fine man. Susan and I both think the world of him. I'm relieved to know that you're marrying someone who'll take care of you. I was concerned, having you so far away from us." He held her gaze. "You and Dad weren't very happy at the end, were you?"

"No, we weren't. But today's not the day to think about all that," she said. "And don't worry about me. With or without John, I can take care of myself." A piano prelude emanated from the floor below. "Is that coming from the conservatory?"

"Yes," Mike replied. "I was supposed to tell you. The grass is too wet for Marc to play his keyboard outside. They tried to dry things off and make it work, but couldn't manage it. They've opened the doors of the conservatory, and Marc will play the piano for the service. He says it'll be plenty loud enough to be heard."

Maggie smiled. "Why didn't we think of that in the first place? Much better."

Mike stepped to the window and pulled the drape back an inch. "Most of the snow has melted and Sam and Tim have dried off every chair. Sam also borrowed a carpet runner from the high school for the aisle. You get to walk down an actual red carpet. Once you get to that point, you won't have to worry about slipping," he turned to Maggie. "It's a full house." He motioned to the window with his head. "Take a look."

Maggie ducked under his arm to survey the scene below and drew a deep breath. "I feel like I'm living a dream," she whispered.

Mike checked his watch. "Susan and the girls are waiting downstairs. It's time we joined them and got this wedding started."

The sun shone brightly over the happy scene on Rosemont's back lawn as Marc struck the first chords of the processional. The girls held hands to steady each other on the slippery grass until they found solid footing on the carpeted aisle. They floated along in a sea of pink organza until they reached the rose-draped trellis. Susan followed, stately and tall, looking like a runway model in her gown and mink.

Mike squeezed Maggie's hand. "This is it, Mom."

Maggie swallowed the lump in her throat as the piano surged with Pachelbel's Canon in D Major. The wedding guests rose and turned to follow Maggie as she and Mike walked slowly down the aisle. George Holmes towered over the crowd and caught Maggie's eye. He winked and made a thumbs-up gesture. She smiled and swept her eyes back to the center aisle, passing over Frank Haynes along the way. He stood with the others, but his attention was not on the bride. Frank Haynes was staring up at Rosemont. An involuntary chill ran down Maggie's spine. Her gaze then fell on the beaming face of John Allen and all else melted away.

Mike shook John's hand, then kissed his mother on the cheek and stepped to the side. Maggie put her hand on John's arm. His eyes sparkled and he leaned toward her and whispered, "You look stunning."

The pastor raised his hands and motioned for the crowd to be seated as the piano fell silent. "Dearly beloved," he intoned the familiar words of the traditional ceremony, and the couple embarked on this most profound of human commitments. Both of them repeated their vows in strong, sure voices. When the pastor turned them to the crowd and proclaimed them husband and wife, everyone leapt to their feet and clapped as John and Maggie made their way back down the aisle.

The wedding party followed closely on their heels. Maggie clutched John's arm as they approached the slippery uphill climb to the area designated for the receiving line. She turned as Amy called her name.

"Here." Amy thrust a pair of plastic rain boots at Maggie. "Aaron and I went out and bought these this morning. We got them for Susan and the girls, too," she said proudly as Aaron produced the other sets of boots. "Slip your shoes off, and put these on. You can't navigate this lawn in rain-soaked satin shoes." Her tone indicated that she would brook no opposition.

"I can't," Maggie began and turned to Susan, who had already slipped off her shoes and donned one boot.

"Come on, Mom," Susan said. "They're right. You don't want to spend your honeymoon in a cast."

Maggie looked between Amy and Susan, and slipped off her shoes. With John's help, she tugged on the practical footwear and concealed them under the layers of hem.

"See," Amy said, "you hardly even notice them."

Maggie took a tentative step. "You're right. Much better. Thank you for thinking of this." She kissed her daughter-in-law on the cheek.

The wedding party formed a receiving line, and Maggie and John introduced Maggie's children and grandchildren and hugged and kissed their friends for the next forty-five minutes. Even Frank Haynes shook Maggie's hand warmly. "Thank you for coming, Frank," Maggie said. "I'm looking forward to meeting your friend. Your RSVP said that you were bringing a guest?"

Haynes recoiled slightly and cleared his throat. "She was called out of town on a family emergency," he said. He'd been sure that Loretta would find the prospect of spending the day at Rosemont irresistible and would change her mind, but she had not.

"I'm sorry to hear that." They stared at each other awkwardly. "I look forward to meeting her another time. Glad you're here, Frank," she said as she turned to the next person in line.

At twelve thirty, Pete positioned himself at the head of the receiving line and announced that lunch was being served. "I'm stealing the bridal party to take them to their table. Everyone else—please find your table, and we'll let you know when you can visit the buffet." Groans emanated from those left in the receiving line. "Don't worry. You'll have a chance to visit with the bride and groom after lunch."

Pete motioned to the wedding party to follow him. "We plated your lunches," he said. "We decided the wedding party shouldn't go through the buffet line. I want the two of you to relax and eat." He eyed them sternly. "I'm going to stand at the end of your table to make sure you have everything you need and to chase people away."

"I'm starved," John said.

Maggie smiled. "I was too nervous to eat breakfast, so I'm hungry, too. Good idea, Pete."

Pete beamed and ushered them to their seats.

Maggie enjoyed everything on her plate; though reflecting on the meal later, she couldn't remember what she ate. What she did remember was looking out at the sea of their friends talking and laughing, sitting in groups enjoying lunch or milling about the lawn that sparkled in the midday sun.

She turned to look at the rear façade of Rosemont, the sun glinting off the windows. Susan followed her mother's gaze. "Look at how the sun hits the windows. If I didn't know better," she said, "I'd swear the house was winking at us." Maggie smiled at her daughter and nodded.

Pete approached the table at one fifteen. "I think it's time to cut the cake."

The five-tiered masterpiece of cream-colored fondant decorated with white roses had been wheeled to a spot in the center of the tables. Waiters were busily passing out glasses of champagne, and an expectant hush settled on the crowd.

Pete handed the couple two Waterford champagne flutes Maggie recognized from the collection at Rosemont. Mike picked up his glass, cleared his throat, and began. "Thank you all for joining us today for this very happy occasion. When our mother moved here, my sister and I had misgivings. What would happen to her so far from us? Well, what's happened to her is that she's made a new life in a town filled with the most charming and hospitable people we've ever met, and she's married a man that my sister and I have come to love very deeply—a man of sterling character and deep integrity. John— welcome—we are honored to be one family." Mike turned to the crowd and raised his glass. "To Maggie and John. May God bless them with a long and happy marriage!"

Maggie and John entwined their arms and sipped champagne as the crowd raised their glasses and clapped. All except Frank Haynes, who quietly made his way to the exit.

Maggie carefully cut a small slice of cake from the bottom layer, and placed it on the plate Pete handed to her. John ate the small bite she held up to his mouth on a fork, then he smiled mischievously and grabbed a large chunk of cake. *Don't you dare,* Maggie mouthed to her new husband. He laughed and broke off a tiny piece and fed it daintily to her. The photographer, who had been busy all day snapping candid shots, took their photo and leaned in. "Can we get some formal pictures? The light is perfect right now."

They finished the wedding portraits in front of the soaring staircase of Rosemont. "This is such a magnificent setting," the photographer said. "My camera loves it. I could take pictures here all day. But I'm sure you'd like to get back to your reception. I've got more than enough photos." Maggie sighed and turned to John. "We should go back to mingle with our guests. I know we haven't spoken to everyone."

Susan stepped in front of them. "That is impossible, Mom. You'll never get out of here if you don't leave now."

"We can't do that," Maggie gasped.

"Sure you can," Aaron said. "That's the beauty of being the newlyweds. You get to leave when you want to."

"John?" Maggie turned to him.

"I have to agree with these two," he said. "And I'm exhausted from it all. I'm not used to this."

"I'll need to get my suitcase," Maggie said. "And say goodbye to Mike and Amy and the girls."

Susan shook her head. "I packed your bag for you, and it's already in the car." Her eyes sparkled at John. "You're going to love the fabulous honeymoon John's planned. And you don't need to say goodbye. We were all in agreement on that." She put her arms around both of them. "I love you both to pieces. Take good care of each other. And have fun! We'll get Rosemont cleaned up before we leave on Monday morning."

"But I should stay for the rest of my wedding reception," Maggie stated feebly, knowing she'd been defeated.

"We'll take pictures and send them to you," Susan assured her.

"We've got it all set up," Aaron said. "Let's go back to the lawn, and I'll signal Marc. He's going to play 'How Sweet It Is (to Be Loved by You).' We'll start clapping and cheering, and you'll take her hand." He turned to John. "Run along the side of the house to the Town Car waiting out front. It'll take you to the airport hotel where you'll spend the night before you fly out in the morning."

Maggie looked at John and nodded. They walked onto the lawn, the music began, he took her hand, and they were off.

Maggie sat back in her seat at the gate the next morning and watched her handsome husband—what wonderful words those were—approach with two steaming cups of coffee. They'd arrived at the airport for their trip to Cornwall the recommended two hours ahead of their scheduled departure, sailed through check-in, and now had plenty of time before they boarded their flight.

"Cornwall!" Maggie said as John handed her the paper cup. "I've always wanted to go there. Ever since I read *The Shell Seekers* years ago. The hotel you picked in Penzance looks charming. We can do everything at our own pace."

"And the Internet connections are limited," John said. "So you'll be forced to unplug and pay attention to your new husband."

"Nothing I'd rather do. Which reminds me," she said, setting down her cup. "Let's see if the kids sent us those photos." She removed her tablet from her carry on and opened her email. "Here they are. They've sent us pictures from the reception and from the week before."

They leaned over the tablet together and were scrolling through the photos when Maggie froze. "Who are those people?" John asked. "It looks like they're in a hospital." He turned to her. "Maggie. You look like you've seen a ghost."

Maggie stared at the photo for a full minute, holding her breath. She slowly exhaled and turned to John. "This is Sophie and Sarah's friend who came for the sleepover last week," she said pointing to Marissa. "Her little sister was in the hospital, and Susan stopped by to deliver presents they'd picked out for her and her mother. I'm assuming that's her little sister with the doll and matching dress. And this must be their mother." She tapped the screen.

John nodded. "So? Why is this upsetting you?"

Maggie struggled to draw a breath. "Because that woman is Loretta Nash." She turned to John. "*Paul's* Loretta Nash. The woman he had the long-standing affair with—the one in Scottsdale he supported like a second family. And this little girl," she said, moving her finger back to Nicole, "the one that is so sick. She must be Loretta's daughter. She would have been born around the time of Paul's death, so she's the right age to be Paul's child." Maggie leaned close to the screen. "Her eyes are Paul's eyes." Maggie turned to John, wide-eyed, fighting down her rising panic. "Susan and Mike may have a half-sister, right here in Westbury."

The End

Thank you for reading!

If you enjoyed *Uncovering Secrets*, I'd be grateful if you wrote a review.

Just a few lines would be great. Reviews are the best gift an author can receive. They encourage us when they're good, help us improve our next book when they're not, and help other readers make informed choices when purchasing books. Reviews keep the Amazon algorithms humming and are the most helpful aide in selling books! Thank you.

To post a review on Amazon or for Kindle:

1. Go to the product detail page for *Uncovering Secrets* on Amazon.com.
2. Click "Write a customer review" in the Customer Reviews section.
3. Write your review and click Submit.

In gratitude,
Barbara Hinske

Acknowledgements

I'm grateful for the wisdom and support of many gracious and generous people:

To my wise medical consultant, A. D. Jacobson, M.D.

To my cadre of attorney friends (who never dodged a phone call from me): Michael Scheurich, William Novotny, Mark Herriot, Jason Castle, and Howard Meyers.

To knowledgeable accountants: Robert Hinske (my incomparable older brother), Lela Lawless, and Linda Blessing.

To the professional "dream team" of Linden Gross, Jesika St Clair, Mat Boggs, Suzie Welker, Mitch Gandy, and Jesse Doubek.

To Matt Hinrichs for my beautiful cover.

To my beta readers, Helen Curl and Deb Vesey.

To the Tooms family for generously allowing me to use their Texie as my Eve.

To the best friends and supporters in the entire world: Jeffrie, Georgia, Donna, Charla, and Norma.

To my loyal and encouraging children: Kate, Edward, and Adam.

Book Club Questions

1. Have you ever abruptly changed your mind about a major life decision, and were you happy you did?
2. Have you ever trusted someone that betrayed your trust?
3. Have you ever found or inherited a valuable collection or treasure? What did you do with it?
4. If you got married at your current age, what would you plan for your wedding?
5. What new trends or traditions have you seen at a recent wedding you attended or heard about?
6. What traditions would you like to see revived?
7. If you were to go on a honeymoon now, where would you go?
8. Have you ever travelled to a place (or wanted to) because it was a setting in a novel?
9. Have you participated in agility trials or hospital pet therapy visits with your dog?
10. What is the most unexpected weather "surprise" that you've experienced and how did you handle it?

About the Author

BARBARA HINSKE is an attorney by day, bestselling novelist by night. She inherited the writing gene from her father who wrote mysteries when he retired and told her a story every night of her childhood. She and her husband share their own Rosemont with two adorable and spoiled dogs. The old house keeps her husband busy with repair projects and her happily decorating, entertaining, cooking, and gardening. Together they have four grown children and live in Phoenix, Arizona.

Other books in the *Rosemont* series
Coming to Rosemont

Weaving the Strands

Also by BARBARA HINSKE

The Night Train

Available at Amazon and for Kindle

I'd love to hear from you! Connect with me online:

Visit **www.barbarahinske.com** to
sign up for my **newsletter** to receive your Free Gift,
plus Inside Scoops, Amazing Offers,
Bedtime Stories & Inspirations from Home.

Facebook.com/BHinske
Twitter.com/BarbaraHinske
Email me at **bhinske@gmail.com**

Search for **Barbara Hinske on YouTube**
for tours inside my own historic
home plus tips and tricks for busy women!

Find photos of fictional *Rosemont*, Westbury,
and things related to the *Rosemont*
series at **Pinterest.com/BarbaraHinske**.

Made in the USA
Lexington, KY
07 April 2017